MIXED SIGNALS

Alyssa Cole

Also by Alyssa Cole

Radio Silence (Off the Grid book 1)

Signal Boost (Off the Grid book 2)

Eagle's Heart

Agnes Moor's Wild Knight

Be Not Afraid

Let It Shine

MIXED SIGNALS

Edited by Rhonda Stapleton

ISBN-13: 978-1539712565

ISBN-10: 1539712567

To my sister, Evan, who is off to college even though she was just toddling around my dorm room. Or at least it feels that way. You're going to knock their socks off.

1

The mirror needed to be cleaned. I was trying to gaze soulfully at my reflection, like people were supposed to do when facing a life-changing event, but I kept getting distracted by toothpaste spittle and random smears. It didn't matter, really. If after twenty years on this planet I still needed to remind myself what my nose was shaped like and what color my eyes were, I should probably be checked for some kind of neurological issue. I looked like your average Korean girl—at least I assumed I did. It'd been almost four years since I'd seen one besides the frowning girl staring back at me through the smudged glass. Not since before the Flare.

I ignored the sound of my family bustling past the bathroom door, carrying the life I'd shoved haphazardly into garbage bags down to the front porch. I wasn't taking much with me—if you learned anything during an apocalypse, it was how to get by with the basics. Still, it was hard to pretend that everything was just fine when your family was literally putting your belongings out like the trash. Thinking of what was about to happen made me feel ill.

Just do it, already.

No more stalling. I grabbed a handful of my hair, held it away from my head and snipped.

The scissors moved through the strands with a quiet shushing noise, like the sound of the wind in the trees that I'd grown used to since society had fallen apart and my family had fled to this remote cabin. The sound was usually calming, but this time it made me feel queasy. I examined my handiwork; my ear was usually covered by a curtain of hair that hung to my waist, but now it sat exposed in the gap between black strands. It looked silly, all pink and curved. I'd never paid attention to how it folded a bit at the tip, like I was some kind of elven creature in one of the games John liked to play. Oh well, too late to go back now. I dropped the hunk of hair to the ground, kicking at it when it landed in a ticklish heap atop my bare foot, and grabbed another handful.

You think I need a change? My mouth twisted into a frown as I remembered the family powwow I'd walked in on four months ago, the day after I'd come home with my high school equivalency degree. I'd been homeschooled by my family, but the post-Flare GED program had actually been fun. It'd been designed as a bridge for young adults who hadn't been able to graduate since our planet had almost bit the big one and half of humanity had either died or come close to it. I'd been so proud of that little piece of paper and the ease with which I'd obtained it—barely needing to study, practicing guitar riffs and writing songs instead—but it hadn't been enough to please *some people*. My family kept emphasizing that I was an adult now and should make my own decisions, but that rationale ended when I'd told them I wanted to stay close to home.

"Maggie, I found an ecosystem growing in some Tupperware under your bed," my brother John called out from down the hall. "If I'm patient zero of some postapocalyptic plague, I'm eating your brains first."

I ignored him, like he'd ignored me when I pleaded to stay at the cabin with our parents. It was as if my family had forgotten all the things that could happen to a woman out in the world, or maybe they just didn't care. Perhaps if I'd told them of the memories that plagued me, they would've let me stay. Grappling with a camo gear–clad man before being bound and tossed in the snow. Blindly clutching for a door handle to escape a grasping hand and wondering if I'd be able to jump from a moving car without breaking anything. Danger was always lurking just around the bend in this world, but according to my family, going down my own path would be a great learning experience. It never occurred to them that I wasn't interested in all of the lessons that awaited me.

I hacked at another hunk of hair, and then repeated the motion. Sweat ran down my neck and popped up on my brow, despite the fact that I was getting rid of the heavy mass that usually weighed me down. The silky locks were stronger than they looked—my deep conditioning routine had apparently worked *too* well—and what I thought would be a quick and liberating experience was turning into a nightmare. Years of my life pooled at my feet in a mound of split ends and loneliness, yet another reminder of the lack of forethought that often led me down the road to "Why the hell did I do that?"–ville. I didn't feel any better and, even worse, I still had so much left to cut. If I stopped now, I'd be mistaken for a deranged mole person who'd wandered onto campus. And who knew what Edwin would think when he came to pick me up? He was already wary of me; if I showed up looking like I might drag him to my underground lair, I'd have to walk to Oswego.

I groaned in embarrassment and tried to block out the memory of our awkward encounter, but of course it's the things you want to forget that your brain preserves for the ages. *Maggie, I can't do this. Your family trusts me.*

My calm and deliberate cutting turned into a panicked weed-whacking that only came to a halt because the scissors got hopelessly tangled in a knot of hair. I felt the hot pressure of impending tears spread through my sinuses as I reached up and tugged helplessly at the scissors hanging from my strands like a sad Christmas ornament.

What had I done? I was about to travel far from home for the first time ever, and I'd chosen now to go full Edward Scissorhands? This had been a mistake. If this was an omen of things to come, it was probably best if I returned to my room and hid under my quilt.

"Maggie—ohmysweetjesus!" John's hand flew to his chest as he stepped in through the door he'd pushed open. His head snapped back, like the sight of me had sucker punched him, but he almost succeeded at pulling his features into something resembling a smile of encouragement. "Pre-college makeover, I see? How...feisty of you."

I felt foolish standing there with an asymmetrical nightmare on my head, like a little girl who'd done something just to be spiteful and ended up hurting only herself. I nodded miserably, unable to talk around the sudden lump in my throat.

John held up his other hand and waved the tablet, our family's latest return to the technological age. His job in the communications department at Burnell University definitely came with perks. "Someone wanted to talk to you before you left."

"What the hell is going on over there?" a familiar voice called out from the wide, slim device, and I was torn between deepening embarrassment and elation. "What is all that stuff on the floor? Is Maggie shedding?"

He turned the screen, and I saw my sister-in-law Arden's face, much too close to her phone's camera, as if she were trying to jump through the screen to get a better look at what was going on. She wouldn't want to miss out on anything, even from three thousand miles away. I was still mad at her, too, but I missed her too much to waste time and a good internet connection by rejecting her call. She and my brother Gabriel had left to visit her parents in California two months ago, after the trip across the country had finally been cleared as moderately safe enough by the government. It hadn't been easy, but they'd gotten there in one piece.

I took the phone and held it in front of me. Her smile was bright and her curly mane was glorious, but her eyes were tired. Although her parents were survivors, her mother had hepatitis and trying to get her health back to where it had been before the Flare required a lot of work. Gabriel being a doctor helped immensely, but Arden had spent years harboring guilt about not being with her mother when the Flare had occurred. She'd been avoiding her mother's illness then, and now that her family was reunited she was running herself ragged trying to make up for it.

"So what's up with this?" she asked. "Did you get gum stuck in your hair or something? I hate to tell you this now, but a little peanut butter would have gotten that right out."

"I wanted a new look before leaving for school," I said. "I thought a haircut—"

"Would be a great way of telling everyone in the family to fuck off? That was stupid." Arden's tinny voice echoed off the bathroom tile, amplifying the last word. Stupid, indeed. I almost let the tears come, but then she continued. "Because once John helps you even that out, you're gonna look fucking fantastic. If you were trying to scare people away, you totally failed. Have you always had those cheekbones?"

Her words released the pressure valve on the fear that had been building up inside me as I'd frantically cut, leaving my face open to judgment. Looks weren't everything, but my hair had always been my most complimented feature. Even if Arden was the only one who thought I was pretty without all the hair, her opinion meant a lot. I sucked in my cheeks and prodded at my face. "They are pretty nice."

John opened the medicine cabinet and plucked a fine-tooth comb from behind a stack of Tiger Balm. Pain flared in my scalp and then receded as he tugged the scissors from my hair and took up a position behind me. "I hope you didn't volunteer me because you think all gay men have some hairdressing gene, Arden."

"I volunteered you because Gabriel is here with me, so you have to handle all older sibling duties, including 'crazy haircut prevention task force.' Besides, you've been cutting that mop on Mykhail's head for years now, so this shouldn't be a hardship for you." Arden looked at me for a long time, and even the pixelated video image couldn't hide the way her eyes went soft and shiny. I was tempted to stroke my finger across the screen, but realized I'd probably end the call if I did. I missed everyone being together so much, even if it was childish to think that we could continue the way of life we'd started in those first months and then years after the Flare. Everyone had interests outside of the cabin, but this house and the people in it had been my entire world for years. Would things ever be the same?

The connection froze, and I clutched the tablet harder, willing the tetchy Internet connection—which was better than nothing, of course—not to crap out, just this once. My pleas were answered by the internet gods, and when the video unfroze, Arden was shaking her head. "Well, this little stunt of yours makes what I have to say even more important. Let's get down to it." She leaned her phone against something to free up both of her hands and reached for something off screen. When her hands came back into view, I cringed and my cheeks flamed. Maybe the internet spirits had been trying to warn me of what was to come.

I shook my head. "No. No, you don't have to—"

She wiggled the banana in her left hand toward the screen. "Someone has to teach you these things! Sex is about more than sticking tab A into slot B. First, this is how you put on a condom." She was holding a square aluminum packet toward the screen when a pale hand shot into the frame and snatched the banana away so hard that it squeezed out of its skin.

"Here we go," John muttered behind me.

"Arden! What the hell?" Gabriel growled. My oldest brother's stern face suddenly crowded Arden out of the screen, his amber eyes narrowed. "Do you need me to list off all the sexually transmitted diseases out there? Trust me, I've had to treat plenty of cases at the clinic. Ever hear of the clap? There's been an uptick since the Flare because people haven't been as cautious. Penises are disease vectors and should be avoided at all costs. End of lesson."

"Get out of here with that abstinence-only stuff, Gabe." Arden pushed her way back into the picture. "I'm too young to be an aunt. After Morris, I don't want to see another diaper for at least ten years. Wrap it up, Maggie."

She tried to shove the banana into the condom she'd opened, but it broke in half and fell on the floor with a loud *splat*. That summed up my previous forays into sexual liberation pretty well, actually.

"Gabriel, Arden is right," John said from behind me. His confident snipping gave me hope that perhaps I wouldn't have to shave all my hair off and start from scratch. "We can't send our sister out into the world unprotected. Hernandez will be around to watch out for her, but he's ex-military, not some kind of virginity bodyguard."

Edwin. If only John knew how wrong he was. As if my siblings casually discussing my virginity wasn't bad enough, they had to remind me of my failed attempt to rid myself of it. Edwin Hernandez had made it clear that guarding my virginity was the only interest he had in it.

"Guys, I'm an adult now. I don't need your advice here. And Mom and Dad already had this talk with me." That silenced them. "Except Mom pulled a giant zucchini from the garden and used that instead of a banana. Dad got all freaked and suddenly remembered he had to go build some plant boxes, and I escaped with him. But I get the gist. I mean, I hate to break it to you, but I've seen a penis before. Not a big deal."

The penis belonged to a creepy dude who'd flashed me during a history class at my program, but that was none of their business. The sad facts were that I had recently turned twenty and the only relationship I'd had with a guy had taken place four years ago and played out completely online.

The Flare had put an abrupt end to that courtship, and Devon probably hadn't survived its aftermath. I tried not to think about him too much anymore, but I vividly remembered how excited he'd been about college and the possibilities that lay ahead of us. He'd likely have jumped at the opportunity I was sulking over.

"I'm sad that the penis you saw was no big deal, but point taken," Arden said, interrupting my thoughts. She put her props down out of frame.

Gabriel sighed in resignation and grumbled, "Just be careful, okay? Make sure you practice the self-defense moves Dad taught you every day. Five eye gouges, five ball busters, five hold wiggles, then repeat."

"Oh, and don't accept drinks from strangers," Arden contributed.

John grabbed my head and turned it to the side. He stuck the comb between his lips as he snipped close to my ear, so his words were muffled. "Or just don't drink at all and save us all the worry."

I rolled my eyes. I wasn't very keen on drinking and they all knew it—Arden and John shared the title of family lush. "You guys are the ones who said I had to go out and experience the world. There are dangerous things out there, and you have to deal with the fact that if I encounter them, I'll handle them as best I can." Part of me thrilled at getting to guilt trip them, but most of me was scared because I was right. I wouldn't have my family for backup anymore.

Gabriel and Arden wouldn't come save the day if some sicko kidnapped me again. John wouldn't be around to say just the right thing to help me get through the day. My mom and dad wouldn't be there to shower me with love, even when I was being an asshole.

"Well, if in all this time with us you haven't learned enough to get by, there's no hope for you, child." John tried to play his words off as world-weary, but there was a tremble in his voice that made my throat tighten all over again.

"I was scared shitless when I first left for college," Arden said, leaning into Gabriel. I repositioned the tablet to keep them in sight as John turned my head this way and that. "I really did sleep with my baseball bat in bed next to me. I once burst into tears in the dining hall because I missed my parents' cooking so much."

Gabriel cleared his throat. "I may or may not have cried during a bout of homesickness my first week. In the shower, no one can see your tears."

It was weird, and oddly reassuring, to imagine Gabriel, Mr. I'm-in-Control, having a crying fit in the shower.

"I was too busy drowning in peenish possibility to cry," John said, his voice dreamy. "I didn't actually do much, but the opportunity was there. It was glorious, those first few days of understanding what freedom was and how I could shape my own life."

I smiled. "So basically it's okay to cry, but if I don't want to I should distract myself with penises? Penii? Whatever. Sounds like a plan."

"The connection is starting to go," Arden said. Their image froze on the screen and then regained motion, backing up her words. "Love you! Message me when you get to Oswego!"

Gabriel nodded along with Arden's declaration of love. "They finally fixed up that stretch of railroad in Indiana that got taken out by the neo-Luddites, so we can get home in a week or so if necessary. If you need me to kick someone's ass, or surgically remove one of their vital organs, just let me know. Your hair looks really good, by the way."

I'd thought cutting my hair was shocking, but that paled in comparison to Gabriel complimenting it. Gabriel was a man of action more than words, despite Arden's influence. I wasn't used to getting any feedback from him beyond "good job" when I did something he approved of. My eyes flew up to the mirror to see what had prompted his words, and I completely forgot he and Arden were still on the line as I gazed at myself.

Holy shit. This time, I did inspect my features like an amnesiac coming out of a coma, which was excusable because I looked like an entirely different person.

My hair was short and choppily cut, a bit longer in the middle. I didn't quite know how to categorize it. Perhaps the spawn of a pixie cut and a fauxhawk. Whatever the name for it, it was perfect. *This* was the Maggie I imagined when I closed my eyes and let my fingers fly over the strings of my guitar. *This* was a woman who could go out into the world on her own and be just fine.

I'd always kept my hair long because I was tall and square-jawed—exactly the opposite of everything people thought of when they rhapsodized about delicate Asian women. I'd told myself I didn't care, because fuck whatever expectations people had of me, but my hair had been a nod to the femininity that my height and bone structure had ruled out for me. Now I saw how ridiculous that had been. Yeah, my ears were kinda weird, but my nose was pert, my mouth was full and my jawline was perfectly made to balance out the rest of my face.

I was…kind of hot.

"Oh my God!" I turned back to the screen, but it was blank—the connection had been lost. A momentary sadness enveloped me when I saw the cute cat screen wallpaper instead of their faces, but I'd try to reach them again soon. At school, I'd hopefully have more reliable access to the internet. I turned to John and hugged him. "You are the best brother ever, you know that?"

"Nice try, but I heard you tell Gabriel the same thing before he left. And Mykhail, when he fixed your guitar for you." I grinned up at him; he looked pleased, despite my fickleness. "Besides, weren't you just cursing me for pulling strings to get you into the Oswego program? I believe I heard the term 'dictatorial tool of the patriarchy' once or twice."

I rolled my eyes. "Okay, fine. I may have been overreacting. I guess it *is* an honor to be enrolled in one of the first post-Flare college classes. Besides, it's only two years, right? It'll probably be fun, and if not then I'll run away and join a group of traveling Throwbacks." That part was definitely teasing. If people wanted to play at faux-Amish lifestyles while even the Mennonites were rebuilding their solar energy farms, that was on them. I enjoyed the perks of modern life, like sewage treatment plants. "Thank you, John."

"You're welcome, dear sister. Lord, as if you being a little rock star in the making wasn't bad enough." He looked at me the same way he looked at the couture blazer I'd stolen from his closet earlier that day, so I knew his words were meant as a compliment. "This haircut just guaranteed you'll have half of the coed student body sniffing after you. I know you're smart, and that this world really just operates on luck, but please promise me you'll be as careful as you can. The new satellites they launched aren't online yet, so the GPS tracker I had implanted in you when you turned thirteen is nonfunctional. I'll need you to give me your word instead."

"I promise to be careful," I said. I went to pull my fingers through my hair, like I always did when I was nervous, but my hand passed through air. I'd always wanted to break the habit, and now I didn't have a choice. I'd also have to work a little harder at controlling my facial expressions since I couldn't sweep my long bangs in front of my face.

The crunch of tires on dirt outside grabbed my attention and set off a panicked hammering in my chest.

"Maggie, your ride is here!" Dad's voice boomed from the bottom of the stairs.

Get a grip. It's only Edwin.

The whole thing was ridiculous, a stupid unrequited crush on a stupid guy and his stupid morals. If Edwin still wanted to see me as the seventeen-year-old who'd mooned after him when he first came to visit with John and Mykhail, then it was no skin off my back. I glanced at myself in the mirror, then spotted the red lipstick that had fallen out of the morass of expired cosmetics when John had grabbed the comb. I swiped it on and stared at myself.

Oswego, here I come.

2

After cleaning and taking a quick shower to get rid of the itchy post-haircut feeling, I squeezed into my lucky skinny jeans, plus a camisole topped with a hoodie, and marched down the stairs. I took a deep breath and steeled myself against the fear and sadness at leaving my family, only to discover that the apprehension had mostly disappeared along with the hair I'd been using as a shield. I'd always laughed at the makeover scene in romantic comedies, thinking it silly that something as inane as a new look could change a person's mindset. I'd add that to the list of things I'd been mistaken about, right behind *A guy will never turn down an opportunity for no-strings-attached sex.*

I walked past a family portrait that hung on the wall and checked myself out again. John had gifted me with some expensive hair gel he'd been hoarding for the last few years, so my hair had a cool spiky look to it now and smelled fab to boot. With my guitar case strapped to my back, and my eyes smudged in smoky black in addition to the bright rouge on my lips, I felt like a rock goddess descending to meet a throng of her groupies. There was only one person I wanted to impress, though, even if it was just to prove to myself that I was capable of it.

I searched my mental repository of music, scanned down the "Feeling Sexy" playlist, and chose Fiona Apple's "Criminal," an oldie Arden had passed down to me. I'd practiced the song enough that I didn't struggle to recall the dramatic, sensuous melody vibrating down the strings as I strummed, or the way the lyrics rasping out of my mouth made me feel like sex on a stick. *I've been a bad, bad girl...* With my mental theme music in place, I clunked down the last two steps in my high-heeled booties, ready to take on the world. If I didn't trip and fall on my face.

John, Mykhail and my parents were clustered near the bed of Edwin's beat-up truck talking animatedly. From a distance, it looked like they were being attacked by a cloud of insects with the way their hands were swinging to and fro, but that was a normal level of conversational liveliness for them. Edwin was bent over in the driver's side door, conveniently displaying how well his jeans hugged his ass. That same feeling I always got when I saw him, a weird mix of elation and nausea, surged in my belly. Puking would kind of ruin the "I'm sexy and I know it" effect I was going for, so I gulped a calming breath down deep into my belly, forcing myself to relax.

I was so focused on making sure I looked cool during my approach that I'd forgotten no one had seen the new Maggie besides John. My mother's serene expression changed so quickly that it would have been comical if not for the high-pitched wail she emitted when she saw me.

"Maggie! All your beautiful hair! Gone!" It was as if my appearance had shocked the ability to form complete sentences right out of her.

My dad hid his surprise better, giving me a jovial, "Hey now! Who's this beautiful stranger?"

John must have told Mykhail what to expect because he pushed his glasses up his nose and nodded in exaggerated appreciation, like the weird guy in the corner of a techno club.

In my peripheral vision, I saw Edwin turn to check out the commotion. I hadn't been able to fully meet his gaze since the whole *Hey, can you devirginize me?* incident. When we spoke, I was usually looking at an eyebrow or some point just above his ear. But that was before I felt this unfamiliar self-assuredness nudging at me from behind, pushing me toward the road that lay ahead whether I was ready for it or not.

I lifted one corner of my mouth, the look my high school friends and I had deemed "the coquettish smile" during our selfie sessions, and peeked up at him from under my lashes. "Hey." A simple greeting, but I hoped it transmitted the essence of a line from one of the movies that played on the classics channel all the time before the Flare. *Big mistake. Huge.*

I didn't know why it mattered. I was going to college, where I'd meet people I liked and who actually wanted to "give me the D," to quote Arden, sex ed teacher extraordinaire. It would be beyond uncool if one of these hypothetical futuristic suitors decided to keep pestering me after I'd said no thanks. I didn't want to be that creep, fawning over someone with the hopes that one day I'd beat them into submission and they'd settle for me. What kind of love song would that make? *It only took ten years, of you living in fear, but finally you're mine, baby, please stop crying...*

Although I filed away those lyrics for later, I didn't want to make them a reality. I needed something, though. Recognition? Validation? And the ridiculous part of my brain still hung up on a teenage crush needed it from Edwin.

"Hey, Mags. You look—different. Great, I mean." Edwin flashed me the same dimpled smile he always did. His voice was the same baritone that always made warmth pool in my stomach. His bronze skin was darker from a summer spent doing construction work, but not by much, since Gabriel had hectored him about the importance of sunblock and wide-brimmed hats. Only one thing was different, really, and it wasn't anything that would be noticeable to someone who hadn't analyzed his every move for years—he didn't touch me. Usually, he pulled each of us into a big hug, this new family of his who had replaced those who'd been lost to him. But instead of giving me the usual hug and kiss on the cheek, a routine he'd kept up even after my awkward request, he took a step away from me. And then another. And then slid his hands into his pockets.

Interesting.

I should have been chagrined, but I'd seen him retreat from me in awkwardness and discomfort before—this wasn't that. When he looked at me again, there was something in his gaze that I knew had never been there before. A flash of interest that was deeper than "Did you have a good day at school?" or "Do you have a five of hearts?"—the polite but distant questions that had made up most of our conversations. This was interest of a more personal nature.

"Thanks." I closed the space between us. I didn't look away, and he didn't either; I felt a little surge of power at that small exertion of my control because I didn't think he *could* look away. When I'd walked right up to him, I stretched my arms up over my head, feeling the cool breeze brush against the exposed skin of my belly and wondering if his eyes traced the same path. After wriggling out of the guitar case's strap and pulling it over my head, I turned and shoved it in the backseat.

He was still looking at me a little warily, like I was playing some kind of joke on him and he wasn't sure whether it was funny or not yet. "You ready to go?" he asked. "We should get on the road so we have plenty of time to get there before dark, in case there are delays."

The delays he was talking about were of the sinister variety, like modern-day highwaymen and the inevitable detours caused by roads that weren't safe enough to pass, but my mind immediately jumped to the more enjoyable ways we could bide our time. I thought of Edwin reaching across the car for me with longing in his eyes and my fantasy soured immediately—I'd been in that situation before, and it hadn't been sexy, in the least. I didn't want to associate Edwin with that particular moment in time, so I suppressed the thought. It could go back in that mental trunk where women hid the memories that reminded them of how unsafe the world could be, lest they never leave the house.

"Thanks for offering to drive me to school, by the way. I really appreciate it," I said. "Let me say see you later to the family and I'll be ready to go."

He nodded his assent, and I turned to face the now-standard "Seong, So Long" hug assembly line. We were as efficient as Ford at this point—there were only so many long, drawn-out goodbyes a family could take. With John and Mykhail living full-time at Burnell, Arden and Gabriel across the country, and Darlene completing her emergency services training in a nearby town and moving out with Morris, this was par for the course, even if I felt a little like my chest was being kicked in.

"You did this to spite me, didn't you?" my mother asked as she hugged me so hard that my back cracked. She reached up and tugged at the short hair behind my ear.

"Yup," I responded. "And because I wanted a change. But mostly to spite you. I'm going to knit you a sweater with the hair I cut so that every winter you're reminded of my act of defiance."

She laughed and gave me an extra squeeze. "You remind me of myself at your age."

"Don't say that, Kit," my dad interrupted, tugging me into his own quick hug. "I'd just convinced myself not to worry about her, but if she's anything like you were..."

"Then some man or woman will be very lucky to have her one day, yes?" My mom smiled at my dad, and it was a bit too close to seductive for my liking, continuing the trend of "the Seongs get their groove back." They'd taken a shot at reopening the small grocery store they'd had in town, but the new normal made procuring items at a reasonable cost and in a timely manner way too annoying. They'd finally settled on early retirement since they'd grown used to living off the land and bartering anyway. I did *not* want to think about what they were going to get up to now that they had an empty nest and all that free time.

My dad winked at my mom and his mustache twitched flirtatiously.

"Gross, you guys," I said as I pulled away and stepped into John's embrace. "See you later, big brother. I would have a saccharine moment with you, but I shouldn't keep Edwin waiting."

"Oh God. I'm sure your version of saccharine involves sadly strumming some late-nineties power ballad. I can live without that, thanks."

"Don't think twice about calling us if you need anything," Mykhail said, giving my shoulder a squeeze. He ruffled a hand through his shaggy blond locks and stared at me for a moment, his blue eyes focusing on me as he processed whatever thoughts were bouncing around in that beautiful astrophysicist brain of his. "The adjustment to college can be rough. Really rough. You can go from feeling like you know everything to thinking you're a moron overnight. I know you can handle this, but remember that it's okay if a program isn't for you. If things suck out there, classes will be starting at Burnell in another year or two, once the government agencies move to their new location. Whatever happens, you won't be a failure, okay?"

Mykhail had a pretty stressful life in academia, but I wondered if he'd somehow read my deepest fears as he'd studied me because his words were so exactly what I needed to hear in that moment. I knew my family believed in me, but hearing him say it eased some of my burden. I pulled him into a long hug, messing up our assembly line. "Thanks." It was nice to be reminded that fucking up wouldn't be the end of the world.

"Don't listen to him," my mother said, slapping at his arm. "My wishes take precedence since I was the one in labor with you for thirty hours. I want good grades, lots of activities and no dropping out. Oh, and a list of people you think could have marriage potential by midterms. You have to make up for lost time!"

John slipped his arm through mine and walked with me to the car. "I'll probably be at Oswego at some point to follow up on business with the mesh network and internet systems in the region. The school is serving as the local hub, and there's the power plant and all that…" He waved his hand around. "I won't bore you with the details. When I visit, you can take me to the dining hall so I can relive the glory of my college days. Well, the disgusting food portion of my glory days." He looked at Mykhail with a level of adoration that ruled out any future peenish possibility.

"Okay. We can meet up if I'm not drowning in peen, I guess. I'll keep you updated." I turned to catch Edwin looking at me with a slightly horrified expression. It wasn't as if I'd never joked around with my family in front of him before, and sex jokes with John were a given.

"Ready to ride?" I asked flirtatiously, just to see if his eyebrows could lift any higher. They drew together instead. He slipped on his mirrored aviators, shielding his eyes from me. Instead, I saw a warped reflection of how I must look to him—tight jeans, high heels and hair that spiked out as if trying to gather attention from the atmosphere around it. Was this me? Really? For some strange reason, I almost asked Edwin. I stopped myself right before he shook his head, laughing to himself.

"Let's roll, Mags. Wouldn't want to keep your fans waiting."

"I don't have any fans," I said, my voice neutral. I didn't know whether to be snarky or smiley since his tone was unreadable.

"Not yet, you don't. Let's go." It should have been a compliment, but it left me feeling exposed instead. I reached for the hair I used to be able to pull across my face, but the old Maggie was gone. I climbed into the rumbling truck and watched my family recede in the side-view mirror as we pulled off.

3

Edwin's truck was old, like most cars that were still up and running. It was the high-tech ones, operated by key cards and running on electricity, that had borne the brunt of the Flare, their systems combusting as the burst of energy flooded their circuits. Like my parents' old-school van, the engine in Edwin's aging monster growled steadily and ran without a hitch. It would've been a smooth ride if not for the cracked and pocked roads that had gone three harsh winters without upkeep.

There simply weren't enough government workers to do everything. The rebuilding effort had become the biggest supplier of jobs in the new economy, with the president enacting a kind of postapocalyptic New Deal. Most of the contractors who'd been recruited to work on the massive repair jobs were funneled to the larger cities first, where the population was still relatively high despite the number of casualties. Others, like Edwin, did what they could in the areas that had been deemed lower priority. Unfortunately for everyone, roads weren't prioritized over repairs to the power grid, infrastructure reinforcement and making homes and buildings places where people could live and work again.

Living in a less populated area had one perk, in addition to the relative insulation from the calamities people trapped in major city centers had experienced— parts of upstate New York were serving as a testing ground for the first new electrical grids, as well as the mesh networking that was taking the place of fiber optics and cell towers. While many of the more populated areas still had patchy access to power sources, with rolling blackouts becoming the norm, we were doing well. Strange that it took an apocalypse to make me appreciate living in the middle of nowhere. The horror stories that had come out of places like New York City...

I glanced at Edwin, and his gaze shifted from the road to me and back again. He was a hard guy to sneak a peek at. One of the things I'd noticed the first time John had brought him home, apart from his attractiveness, was how closely he paid attention to everything. Not in a scary way, like Gabriel had when we'd first ventured out of the house to interact with other people, but as a kind of default. He'd been the only one to notice Stump, who'd just become mobile, almost tumble off of the couch. He'd brushed past me, carefully, and tugged him back by the diaper. At dinner he caught a cup of water that John had knocked off the table with his elbow while talking too animatedly.

John had chalked it up to Edwin's military training, but I'd done JROTC for two weeks, eventually giving it up due to my ill-fitting uniform and an embarrassing experience with what happened when you locked your knees while standing at attention—and I knew being in the service didn't necessarily make a person so aware. It was something that was just part of him.

I pulled my gaze away from him as he ran a hand over the close-cropped hair that converged into a smooth vee at the back of his neck. He wore his hair shaved down and edged perfectly now that barbershops were back in business, but when I'd first met him it'd been longer, thick and tightly curled. I'd wanted to run my fingers through his hair, to feel the soft part of a man who was hard everywhere else under my palm, but Arden had trained me well enough to resist that impulse. Touching someone's hair was an intimate act, she'd said as she'd brushed through my tangles one day. A pang of longing I thought I'd gotten under control throbbed through me as I imagined what it would be like for Edwin to run his fingers through my newly shorn locks, how the tips of his callused hands would feel caressing over my scalp.

Outside my window, a group of kids marched through the overgrown grass alongside the road, heading in the direction of the town we'd just passed through. It'd looked better than the abandoned places with boarded-up stores and houses marked with spray painted crosses to show where bodies had been found, but for some places, "better" was an inconsequential term. One of the kids had a rifle tucked under his arm, and the other carried a brace of limp rabbits. I'd had a pet rabbit when I was that young, but things were different now. Those kids might be the only ones putting food on the table. Meanwhile, I'd been complaining about going away to school, where other people would be taking care of most of my needs.

"Are you excited?" Edwin asked, finally breaking the silence. "I heard you weren't that into leaving your family, but that'll change once you get to school. You're gonna love it." Was he always this chipper? I couldn't remember the last one-on-one conversation we'd had since my spontaneous v-card offering. "Independence, making new friends, learning mind-blowing shit. It's gonna be great. Learning mind-blowing *stuff*. Sorry."

I dropped my head back onto the headrest and groaned in annoyance. "You know you're driving me to college and not preschool, right?" I took a deep breath and sang in a cartoonish falsetto. "Shiiiiiiiiiit!" I filled my lungs and belted out again, this time in a deep alto, "Fuuuuck!"

He ducked his head in embarrassment. "Okay, I get it, Maggie. It's just a little hard to remember you're not a kid anymore."

Wonderful.

I tilted my chin up in the air. I certainly wasn't behaving like an adult, but he'd hit a sore spot. *When you're older, you'll be glad I said no.*

I leaned back in my seat and crossed my arms against my chest. "Since the tender age of sixteen, I've been living with someone who uses the term 'fuck-fuckity-fuck-fuck' at least three times a day. Cursing won't scar a kid for life. And, again, I'm *not* a kid anymore."

Edwin was now wearing the uncomfortable smile he sported when we usually interacted. "I didn't mean to offend you. I'm not used to being around younger people, okay? Maybe it's because I skipped a grade," he mused playfully, but he'd opened himself up to interrogation now.

I turned in my seat so I was leaning a bit over the invisible driver/passenger divide. "You're only six years older than me, Old Man River. Or is it five? Tell me again about this huge gulf between us." I cocked my head to the side and watched him, not leaning back in my seat until he'd squirmed enough for my taste. I was being overdramatic, but the residual humiliation I was feeling spurred me to make him feel awkward too.

"Maggie, there are certain points in your life when one year is like...a dog year, or something. Life changed so much and so quickly when I went away to college. You'll see soon, and then maybe you'll cut me some slack." His voice wasn't angry. It was placating.

I wasn't the only one thinking about our previous encounter. He was referencing how I always had just a little bit more edge in my voice when joking around with him at family dinners. How I went for the jugular when we played board games and badgered him until he folded during poker. Ever since that night he'd turned me down.

Edwin, I'm old enough to know what I want. I don't need flowers and a soft bed. I need my virginity gone and with the person I choose. Is that really so hard to understand?

I cringed in my soul at the fact that I'd actually said those words aloud. I had wanted it over with, and still did—that passage to adulthood that had become less and less likely as the years passed at the cabin, surrounded by my family. I couldn't explain to him why it was so important to me to be rid of it; he hadn't believed me when I'd told him I was being practical and not romantic. Why wait for an inevitable disappointment, or worse, when you could get it out of the way and continue on with your life knowing it'd happened on your terms? Unfortunately for me, I'd chosen a dude who'd almost made a career out of following strict codes of conduct, so my plan had been foiled.

I turned my embarrassment outward, onto him. "So, in your mind, I'm like forty-two years younger than you? That doesn't even make sense. How did you skip a grade with that shoddy grasp of mathematics? And how did you manage to get along with the older kids if age difference is such a big deal?" I was annoyed with him, but also a bit intrigued. Keeping my distance from him over these past years, first because of my inability to speak in front of him and then because I was too angry and ashamed to try, had also meant that much of what I'd learned about him had been secondhand. When he came to the house, I'd go up to my room and blast one of the eclectic CDs John had gifted to me or run chord riffs until my fingers bled. So I didn't know he'd gone to school young, or even how he'd ended up at military school.

"I skipped two grades, actually—fifth and sixth. I guess the math wasn't so hard at that point," he said. His hands were tight on the wheel and he glanced over at me. "Besides, I'm talking theoretical mathematics, and it doesn't come into play at that age, really. There are plenty of differences between a fifth grader and a seventh grader, but they're basically still in the same time zone. But—and maybe we can ask Mykhail about this—I think there has to be some kind of space-time rift that happens when people who are twenty-six talk to people who are twenty. It garbles the communication and makes everything weird."

"Well, I wasn't exactly interested in talking back then, so that wouldn't have been a problem." I hadn't meant for those words to leave my brain, but there was no taking them back now.

His head swiveled in my direction, and I was surprised to see his dimples emerge instead of a scowl. "I can't argue with that logic. Doesn't mean I'm wrong."

It was obvious that we were both talking about what had happened between us, even if we wouldn't admit that out loud. He was trying to make me smile, but I hated the way he could so calmly dismiss what I'd wanted. I reminded myself that he couldn't have known why his refusal was such a blow to me; to him I had just been a silly girl acting on a whim. "Look, I'm only saying that you don't magically get some special skills once you turn twenty. The adulthood fairy doesn't drop down and sprinkle you with responsibility dust. There have always been teenagers with full-time jobs, living on their own or supporting their families, hell, even raising children. There's no reason to act like they aren't as capable of making decisions as adults."

Edwin sighed, and I couldn't stop my eyes from straying to the rise and fall of his chest and the patch of skin exposed by the unbuttoned collar of his shirt. I'd seen him without his shirt as he hammered and sawed and built a home for Darlene from the ground up; I didn't have to imagine the musculature beneath the fabric. His deep voice drew my gaze to his mouth, but I looked away before I got to his eyes. I didn't want to know if he'd seen me blatantly eye-fucking him in the middle of asserting my maturity.

"Everything you said is true, Mags. But there are also people who've spent their teenage years in an isolated environment and who've only recently started venturing into the outside world. Someone has to look out for them, right?"

He wasn't trying to be cruel. In fact, his voice was warm and supportive. But his implication, that I was an inexperienced baby lamb, still stung.

I reached over and turned on the radio, only to be met with static. I hit the seek button, and eventually the tuner picked up a working station. The familiar, jangly guitar of a Beatles song filled the car.

I sat back in my seat and crossed my arms again, but the sulk that made my bottom lip poke out began to diminish as the interplay of rhythm and melody seeped into me, lifting my spirit even as I tried to keep it tethered to the ground. John, Paul and George were strumming, Ringo was banging away and despite the sometimes depressing views outside my window, my life was pretty good. I could sit and sulk, like the kid I was trying to prove I wasn't, or I could take this opportunity for a fresh start with Edwin. Now that we'd cleared the air between us, at least a little, I could appreciate why he hadn't slept with me, even if it had ruined my plan.

My foot began jumping of its own accord and my fingers tapped against my elbows, hitting notes on invisible guitar strings.

"I tried to learn this song once, and I just couldn't get it right, no matter how many variations I tried." I hope he recognized my music talk for the olive branch that it was. "Arden walked in on me one day and laughed because I hadn't realized that this part—" I paused and bounced in my seat as a complicated arpeggio trilled through the car "—was actually a recording being played backward."

My seat dancing came to an abrupt halt when Edwin jammed his finger into the search button, filling the car with static. When I looked at him, his hands gripped the wheel hard. His mouth was a grim line and little crow's-feet at the corners of his eyes showed the footprints of some deep-seated pain.

"Are you not a fan of the *White Album*?" I asked, trying to lighten the mood.

His hands squeezed the cracked plastic of the steering

wheel. "That was one of Claudio's favorite songs. I just...I can't."

The white noise emanating from the radio station seemed to pick up the broadcast of his despair, transmitting the emotion so that it filled the cab of the truck. I felt nearly suffocated by it; I wanted to hold my breath like I used to do as a child when we drove past the local cemetery, to keep the bad luck out.

Unlike Arden, Edwin had always been positive that his family had survived the Flare. Unlike Arden, he'd been wrong. New York City hadn't fared well during the blackout. Even though they'd had a larger law enforcement presence and more resources, the population was too large and the resources too few and far between. Millions had survived, but thousands had also died in the panic and food shortages that had followed the Flare. Edwin's mother and brother had been in the latter group.

"I'm sorry."

"No worries. You couldn't have known. It's just...some days are better than others. All of this back-to-school stuff is making me think of him a lot, so hearing that particular song really—" He stopped and took a deep breath. "Claudio never went to college, but he worked his ass off to make sure I could without my mom having to pay for it. That sounds like an after-school special, right?"

"After-school special? What's that, some kind of weird sex act?"

Edwin gave a rueful shake of his head. "See, and you

just tried to argue that age differences don't matter. That isn't helping your case."

God, I was rude. He was sharing something about his dead brother, and I was bringing up weird fetishes. "I'm sorry. I didn't mean to interrupt, especially with that."

I'd covered my mouth with my hand, as if I could keep any additional childish outbursts contained, and now my palm was covered in red lipstick gunk. I sighed and accepted the grease-stained rag Edwin pulled from under his seat and handed to me.

"Thanks," I said, feeling every inch the ridiculous girl he thought I was. I thought of the Flare, of all the possibilities for learning and growth that had been stripped away from me. If I had been out navigating the world and not stuck in a house with my family, I wouldn't be acting like a fool right now.

He chuckled. "It's okay. My brother was a fan of saying inappropriate things, so he wouldn't have minded." His smile faded a bit. "He wasn't happy when I decided to go to military school, but he was still proud. It fucking sucks knowing that he never got to see a return on his investment, that I'll never get to tell him about anything I accomplish ever again. I used to get so annoyed when he pushed me to fill out applications, to do my homework, to stop complaining about how hard life is. And now..." He made a frustrated motion with his hand, splaying his fingers as if to say, "That's that."

I didn't know what to do. Death was a specter that had hovered over my family since those first uncertain months after the Flare—I still sometimes dreamed about Gabriel carrying a bloodied John to our doorstep, still had nightmares about Arden ripping Gabriel's jacket open after what should have been a fatal shot to the chest. But although it stalked outside our cabin like the Big Bad Wolf, death had never gained entry. My family was safe and whole. In fact, we'd even gotten some awesome new additions, namely Arden, Mykhail, Darlene and Stump. I imagined anything I could say to Edwin would seem mocking, maybe because if my family had died and his had survived, I'd resent the fuck out of him. So I changed the subject, like a coward.

"Is Claudio the one who taught you how to do all this construction stuff, or did you learn in the past few years?" I asked. I probably should have been asking about his feelings or how he was handling their loss, but he looked relieved to be able to talk about something other than his pain.

"Yeah. He worked construction with one of my uncles. I was always scared the other guys would try to mess with him because he was gay, but considering that he could bench-press most of the dudes he worked with, they were sure to treat him with respect. He used to call himself my vocational school, giving me something to fall back on in case college wasn't for me."

"That was cool of him," I said. "I wish my family understood that there were alternate paths besides school."

Edwin laughed. "Don't get it twisted. He believed in alternate paths, but I would've had to travel down them with his size-fourteen boot up my ass."

I joined him in his laughter, and it felt nice. Natural. The tension in the car dissipated, and we drove on in silence. Still, as I looked at the row of houses we passed—beautiful but empty because the Flare had snatched their owners away—I knew it would take more than laughter to fix so many of us. For the first time, I really thought about what the program I was attending would mean to people who'd suffered misfortunes I couldn't imagine.

Perhaps John had been right all those times he called me spoiled. I didn't like thinking of myself that way—weren't spoiled girls supposed to be rich and beautiful? I wasn't either of those things, but I sure as hell wasn't as grateful as I should be. I began to feel a new excitement for the trip I was taking. Not because I looked cool or because I'd get to hook up and stuff like that, but because I was about to learn something important. Who I was, and who I could be.

4

"Shit, there's a roadblock up ahead."

I'd dozed in my seat and had no idea where we were in our route, but I jumped awake and grabbed the road atlas that sat on my lap as if I'd been fulfilling my role as navigator. Up ahead, I could see an older-model police cruiser and a couple of men in beige uniforms standing in the road. Their boxy car was like something out of an old TV show. It would have been cool if it wasn't so creepy. With the empty stretch of road ahead and behind, it felt a bit like we were rolling into a scene from a Stephen King book.

"Well, is there anything you have to tell me? Like you're carrying forty pounds of uncut cocaine in the cab of the truck?"

He shot me an exasperated look. "If you're going to

accuse the one Puerto Rican guy you know of being a drug dealer, you should at least have your regions down. This is meth country."

Oh God. I cringed at what my words could have been construed as. "Edwin, I was—"

"Joking. Yeah, so was I. Don't worry, I won't tell everyone at Oswego that you're prejudiced." He almost smiled, but then his eyes narrowed on the road ahead of us again. "Our actual problem is twofold. First, some people who set up these checkpoints aren't really cops. They're people looking to rob you blind and maybe leave you dead in a ditch. Second, if they are cops, some of them are power-tripping assholes who are even worse than the first option. It's not like municipalities are selecting officers from the cream of the crop. Half the crop is dead."

As the two men and their cruiser drew closer, I felt fear start to edge its way into my space. I grabbed for my hair, hoping to hide behind it as I always did, but that built-in security blanket was gone. I scratched my ear instead, running a finger over the ruby teardrop earrings I'd borrowed from my mom. I remembered her wearing them all the time when I was a kid, during that magical time when I thought she was the strongest woman in the world.

Edwin's hand brushed my knee, gave it a quick squeeze. "It's probably fine. If it's not, I won't let anything happen to you." His voice was reassuring, but as we pulled close to the police officers his expression went blank and hard. It projected an air of authority, one that said he wasn't looking for a fight but he could sure as shit handle it if one popped up. His face going all badass like that stopped the "I can take care of myself" that was on its way out of my mouth. Sometimes I forgot Edwin had been in the military, but watching his demeanor gave me a quick reminder of the kind of man he'd been before he came into my life. I shouldn't have been turned on by it, especially since we were approaching a possibly dangerous situation, but I squirmed in my seat a little. His strength had been apparent in that touch on my knee and even if I didn't need him to protect me, that strength felt damn good.

Still, I readjusted the baseball bat Arden had bequeathed me long ago, positioning it so I could grab it and jab it into the face of anyone who got too close to the truck. I wasn't going to give up my autonomy just because Edwin could bench-press me.

The car rolled to a stop, and one of the officers approached.

"Good afternoon, Officer," Edwin said. "Is there a problem?"

The man looked wary, but Edwin's conciliatory behavior seemed to loosen some of the stiffness in his shoulders. He approached the window, but stayed far enough away that he wasn't a threat—or that he could get out of the way if Edwin was. "Sorry, sir. Miss. We received a tip that there's some neo-Luddite activity in the area. Given the proximity to the power plant and the new electrical grid setup, we're trying to be careful."

"I work for the Department of Infrastructure Repair, so I'm definitely not trying to take everyone back to the Dark Ages," Edwin said. "I'm going to reach for my ID now."

He slowly retrieved the plastic rectangle from his wallet, then held it up but didn't pass it over. The officer seemed to understand his reticence. Edwin turned the ID back and forth to display the holographic insignia that was supposed to prove its veracity.

"Thank you, sir." The officer gave a respectful nod, then turned to his partner. "They're cool. Let 'em through."

As we drove away, I checked out the two men in my side-view mirror. They leaned back against their cop car and chatted, waiting for the next car to come through.

"Do you think they're legit?" I asked. Only now that we'd passed them did the goose bumps raise on my arms. There had obviously been crime before, but society had operated on an unspoken system of trust, and that trust had been backed up by decades of social norms and, eventually, the ability to look someone up online to see whether they were lying or not. The Flare had interrupted all that. It was horrifying to think that in its aftermath, anyone could claim to be anything and the only way to know whether you were being conned was to have a good gut instinct and, failing that, quick reflexes.

Edwin shrugged, glanced in the rearview. "Yeah. I've been getting update texts from the department all week. Apparently, they caught some assholes trying to break into one of the recently opened electrical plants. Their plan was to burn the place."

"And they were serious?" Doubt was the first emotion my mind would allow entry to, although fear pushed at the floodgates. I didn't want to believe such a thing was true. "Are you sure this wasn't one of those situations like the last time, when it turned out the guy was some weirdo who said he wanted to blow up a power plant but didn't have the means to do it?"

A random guy with destructive thoughts was better than a coordinated plan of attack.

"No, this was the real deal," Edwin replied, dashing my hopes. "Government intelligence agencies have been picking up a lot of buzz on the wires. These groups are scattered around the country, but they've started interacting with each other, making plans."

"I can't imagine," I said. Fear had finally gotten through, crawling over my skin like the ants that invaded the house every spring. "If they'd succeeded—"

"It would have been a huge setback. Really huge." Edwin's jaw was a tense line. "We're just eking by with the equipment needed to rebuild, even with people working around the clock. They had to beg and scrape and improvise like motherfuckers to get that place up and running."

I knew from John that the hardest part of the rebuilding was getting the right parts for the electrical grids. Electricity was needed for large-scale manufacturing—there weren't any artisanal electrical transformer markets around—creating a postapocalyptic catch-22.

"I don't get it," I said, shaking my head. My seat belt felt like it had tightened, holding me in my seat, and I wanted nothing more than to make Edwin turn the car back around and take me home. "Do they not remember that we need electricity for clean water? Do they want to go back to shitting in the woods? Maybe they should do a poll before acting on everyone's behalf. Who wants to keep the internet?"

I raised my hand and waved it around.

"Some people think the Flare was a judgment from God, or that we need to go back to basics so the next natural disaster won't wipe us out again," Edwin said. "And that's understandable. People need something to believe in, and a random burst of solar energy is something that you can't fight with guns or fists. For the zealots among us, this is a way of controlling things."

I knew all about the Throwbacks, neo-Luddites and various other groups that had formed in the shadow of ruined cities and destroyed towns, but in a way they'd been boogeymen. In the relative safety of my home and the surrounding area, they didn't seem very threatening—not compared to the scavengers. Hadn't the world always been full of people trying to impose their lifestyles on others? But knowing they were organizing attacks and trying to change things in earnest out here in the real world was the first time I'd felt that paralyzing fear, one rooted in complete impotence, since the lights had first blinked out and not come back on. I wasn't afraid of the dark, but of all the horrible things that had come after it.

I hooked a thumb under my seat belt and pulled it away from me. "If people want to live like that, it's fine. Why do they care what everyone else does? There are plenty of places that won't be on the grid for years, decades even. They can move there."

Edwin lifted a shoulder as if he didn't know, but he still spoke. "I guess I get it in a way. Think about all the stuff that was going on before the Flare—global warming, wars, cyberbullying, governmental abuse of power. To them, this is our chance to start over and to do things right."

"Why do they get to decide what's right for everyone else?"

"Why not?" He said the words easily, like he wasn't advocating for a bunch of people who wanted to finish off what the Flare had started.

I flipped the chest strap of the seat belt behind my back so I could lean closer to him. "Because I don't want to live like that."

"And they don't want to live like us. Can you put your seat belt back on? Flying through the window if we're in an accident won't make your argument stronger."

I slipped back through the strap and dropped into my seat in a huff. "I don't understand why you're defending them. Please don't tell me you're one of those guys who thinks he has to play devil's advocate in every conversation, because that's an unattractive trait."

He sighed, something he'd done a lot over the last

few hours. I seemed to have that effect on people. "I'm not saying they're right. I'm saying that people do things they'd never imagine in the name of trying to survive. I've done things I'm not proud of. But if you asked me back then, I could justify my actions in a heartbeat. I thought I was doing what was best for everyone, but really I was doing what was best for myself."

Although they'd never told me exactly what had gone down at Burnell, I'd pieced things together over the years. Edwin's comrades had done some horrible things to the students left behind at the school. Edwin had never joined in, and had helped John save the day, but he'd also done nothing to stop the abuse before then. I couldn't imagine all the ways something like that could twist a person up inside. I glanced at his profile, and the strained expression on his face. Could the Edwin I knew really have been a bad guy? I could ask. He would answer honestly, I knew that. What I didn't know was how I'd think of him after; I wasn't ready to let him step down from his pedestal quite yet.

I drummed my fingers on my legs. "I guess everything can't be so clear-cut. I just don't want to be kidnapped and forced to churn butter."

He made a sound close to a laugh, but we were probably thinking the same thing: a woman who got kidnapped should hope churning butter was the worst that would happen to her.

"What are you most looking forward to at school?" he asked. I was grateful for the subject change.

I thought about replying with "wieners" just to mess with him, but I answered truthfully. "Making friends who aren't my family members or their significant others. Getting to experience something like the life I could have had before the Flare changed everything." I took a deep breath. "I thought that when I got to the GED program I'd see all of my friends from high school. We'd catch up and it'd be just like old times, right? But so many of them weren't there. My best friend, Marisa...her family was found during one of the sweeps of our town. Their bodies. None of them made it."

A memory of Marisa's fingers sweeping through my hair rocked through me then, almost stealing the breath from me. *You have the best hair. One day I'm going to cut it off and steal it for myself.* The crushing, heart-compacting feeling I thought I'd mastered started up in my chest. *Marisa. Lacey, Jaden and Jaden number two.* We'd never sit at a lunch table and complain about smushy peas, or make fun of the athletic director who lingered a bit too close to the girls' locker room. So much lost, and that didn't even include Devon.

He moved his hand from the wheel and rested it on my knee for a moment. The motion should have made me jump out of my skin, but it was an act of comfort. Besides, this was Edwin. He wouldn't hurt me. "Trust me, I know what that's like. Even after everything I saw and did with my fellow cadets, I was so optimistic. I thought my family would be waiting for me, that I'd get home and find my mom cooking *arroz y gandules* and my brother sitting at the table with a crossword puzzle."

That wasn't what had happened.

I glanced at Edwin and realized my hands were flat across my chest, as if holding in the emotions that tumbled there. I raised a hand hesitantly and then brushed my fingers over his forearm a few times. I could feel the flex of muscle underneath the warm skin, and the light dusting of hair tickled the undersides of my fingers. "Do you have extended family?" I asked.

"Only in PR," he said. "I don't know them, though. I've never been. I thought one day we could take a family trip, and I'd finally get to see the place that was supposed to be such a big part of who I am. Meet my *abuela* and cousins." He lifted his shoulders in a tight movement. "I have your family, though. I don't know how I would have gotten through this without John and Mykhail, and all of you." He glanced at me out of the corner of his eye, then sighed deeply. "You can't replace the friends you've lost, but you'll meet good people at school."

"I know. It'll be different, though. There were so many little things I took for granted. Like calling each other and giggling over TV shows. Messaging each other online until all hours, or waking up at three a.m. with my cell phone next to my ear and hearing Marisa sleeping too. That sounds creepy now—I'm too old for all that—but I miss it at the same time."

"Um, you lived with the two creepiest best friends of all time. I once heard Arden call for John to come to the bathroom and bang her knees because she was blocked up. Any weird high jinks you want to get up to with new friends can't surpass that."

I laughed, but I was also a little surprised that he'd unknowingly cut through to the heart of the matter. I wanted what Arden and John had with each other. I wanted what they had with their significant others, what my parents had. I'd spent the last few years watching everyone have someone to depend on, someone who'd do anything for them, and although I usually just made faces when they were all lovey-dovey, I'd felt so alone.

I knew part of it had been teenage angst, but there was regular old angst mixed in there too. I wasn't hoping college would bring me love, but that it would provide the sense of camaraderie that had been missing from my life. My family couldn't provide that particular brand; I mean, they were obligated to love me. I hadn't even made it to school yet and already I felt a sense of the kinship I'd been missing, and with the person I least expected it from. I'd thought I couldn't be friends with Edwin because of the wedge of humiliation between us, but talking to him was nice. I wouldn't see him all the time, but maybe something could be salvaged between us and created anew, like the art made from the steel of buildings that had burned when the gas mains went.

"Whoa," Edwin said, hunching forward over the wheel. I leaned forward too, although I didn't have to search hard to see what had grabbed his attention.

Along one side of the road there were clusters of military vehicles that looked like something out of a movie about a viral outbreak. Men in military uniforms marched with guns. In the background, a huge facility loomed: Falling Leaf, the nuclear power plant none of us had paid much mind to until it had been almost too late. The stories of the brave men and women who'd stayed behind to make sure the generators kept going and the reactor didn't go were among the first universal tales that had spread across the country as everyone strove for national heroes. The first post-Flare book to be published had been a fictional account of the lives of the engineers who'd stayed to work on failing reactors, knowing they were being irradiated in the process. I'd started the copy Arden had brought back from Burnell, but stopped at the introduction. It was too gut-wrenching to read.

"I guess they're taking those threats seriously," I said. "Or maybe it's just a front."

"That isn't for show," Edwin said. "Trust me."

I glanced over my shoulder as we passed, a chill running down my spine. I'd heard about the few locations across the country where the nuclear plants had blown because the workers hadn't been able to prevent a meltdown like the Fallen Leaf Five. I lowered my head for a moment in silent acknowledgment.

When I turned back around, the roadside sign announced Oswego 15 Miles.

I took a deep breath and focused on my future—the one that was possible because of people like the engineers at the power plant. I couldn't worry about the scary possibilities ahead of me; I'd go crazy if I did. For now, I'd have to start small.

5

"Hey, you got a single. Every freshman's dream! Although I guess there aren't that many of you guys, so it probably doesn't have the same cachet it used to." Edwin dropped my bag onto the floor of the dorm room.

Cachet? Was he seeing the same thing I was? My room was completely sterile. The walls were *cinder block*. I sat on the edge of my the extra-long twin bed and hopped back up, hoping the lumps that had poked into me weren't living creatures, or deceased ones for that matter. Papers spilled out of one of the bags he'd placed near my feet as I scurried away, but the room was going to be a mess sooner or later anyway. My laziness made an executive decision to leave the pile for later.

"I'm kind of sad I don't have a roommate," I said,

giving the mattress a vicious kick and waiting to hear any telltale rustling. "Who will help me ferment wine using garbage bags and dirty socks? Who will let me know which gangs to look out for?"

"It's not that bad," Edwin scoffed.

I pulled aside vertical blinds that weren't doing such a great job at keeping the sun out and pointed at the bars crisscrossing the window.

Edwin walked over and gave the bars a shake. "Well, they have to keep you safe. You're on the first floor, and anyone could get in."

"I've visited John at Burnell. I know what a nice dorm room looks like," I said.

His smile faltered, only for a moment, but so suddenly that I knew I'd touched on something that hurt him. Again. One thing I'd discovered while trying to make friends at my GED program and talking to the odd stranger here and there was that we humans were a sensitive bunch. In the aftermath of such a widespread catastrophe, there was barely anyone left unscathed. One minute you could be discussing sandwiches and the next thing you knew you'd walked into a minefield because someone's dead dad made great chicken parm.

"Is everything okay?" I asked him. It was the only question that mattered once that look crossed someone's face. Usually, some selfish and scared part of me hoped they kept whatever sad story they had to themselves. I was full up on things that made me want to scream at the unfairness. But I'd enjoyed the way he opened up to me in the car, like I was someone he could trust with the memories of his brother, so I was a little sad when he nodded his head and pasted on a smile.

"Of course." He stepped closer to me and pulled the shades down. For a moment, it was too close to one of the fantasies I'd slipped into during a nap in the car. Heat stomped an ungainly path from my neck down to the area where my jeans chafed against my thighs. Then he ruffled my hair, like my brothers did, and the millisecond of hope I'd entertained disappeared. "You'll get used to it. This is bigger than the room they assigned to me. I won't complain, though. I should just be happy that I have a place to stay."

My autonomic nervous system chose that moment to misfire and when I swallowed, my spit went down the wrong pipe. I coughed violently, the burn in my throat almost distracting me from the information he'd just dropped at my feet. Edwin rushed over and brought his warm hand down on my back again and again, sending me into another spasm of coughs.

"Are you okay?" he asked.

I nodded. I looked up at him, sure that my perfectly smudged smoky eye was now raccooned and my bright red lipstick was even more out of place. "You live on campus?" I croaked when I was able to talk.

His eyebrows knit in confusion. "Yeah. I work here and take classes...where did you think I lived? In a van down by the lake?"

My face heated as I realized two things: one, when giving people the silent treatment, you should still listen to what they say to other people so information like this doesn't bite you in the ass. Two, Edwin's hand was still on my back, the heat of it intense even through the layers of clothing.

"You don't live in this dorm, do you?" I tried to keep the hopefulness out of my voice, but I did too good a job of it because he moved away from me.

"Don't worry, I'm not going to cramp your style."

I had to fight hard not to roll my eyes at him. Did he think that was what I was worried about? I thought being at school would get Edwin out of my head, but now I was going to be in even closer proximity.

"Hello, neighbor!" A high-pitched voice sent shock waves of cute through the room, shattering any lingering annoyance. A girl poked her head in, and the heart-shaped face, kewpie lips and fantastically well-done eye makeup that made her look like an anime character matched her voice perfectly. For a moment, I thought some fuzzy creature rested on the young woman's sleek brown hair, then I realized it was a panda bear head. Not a real one, but one of those silly stuffed animal roadkill hats that had been popular back before the Flare. Hers had obviously seen better days, but the rest of her matching black and white outfit, a schoolgirl-esque ensemble complete with knee-highs, was flawless, so I let it slide. Then she started talking, and I reconsidered. The hat would make a wonderful gag if shoved down her throat.

"Oh! How wonderful! *Nihao!*" She clapped her hands in front of her and bowed deeply, and I allowed myself the satisfaction of a long, luxurious eye roll.

"I'm not Japanese." I didn't sneer because my tone did it for me.

She suddenly stood ramrod straight, hands still clasped, eyes squinting as she examined my features. "Oh! Pardon my rudeness. *Anyoung haseyo.* Sometimes it's so difficult to tell the difference between Japanese and Korean. I've watched like fifty K-dramas, so I should be an expert by now."

In that moment, I wished I was in one of the shows she was referencing, the comic ones I used to watch with my mother. If that was the case, I could suddenly develop martial arts skills that would allow me to slo-mo kick her across the hall into her room, which I could already see was half wallpapered with manga posters. Like in the television shows, she wouldn't suffer any injuries, Edwin would suddenly think I was super cool and I'd score a point for annoyed Korean girls everywhere. But this was reality.

I threaded my hands together and spoke very slowly to her. "Okay. Am I supposed to ask you for the mayonnaise-based recipes of your people now? Is there anything you would be comfortable with me assuming just from looking at you? I'm gonna guess no."

Her lower lip began to tremble and her eyes seemed to get even larger, shine even brighter. Her cuteness was like some kind of kryptonite to my righteous indignation, and I was already regretting getting on my soapbox. I should have just pretended not to speak English, like my mom did when people asked her stupid questions, but with my luck this girl would speak better Korean than I did. "I'm sorry," she said. "I just got excited because I thought I'd finally be able to talk about— I've never had anyone to talk about stuff with—"

Her voice was getting higher and higher as she spoke, and she wrung her hands in front of her, obviously distraught for having offended me. I sighed. Now was the moment when I had to be the bigger person, because otherwise I'd scar this fragile young woman forever. "It's okay. But just because I'm Korean doesn't mean I've got hand-painted mecha figurines in my bag. Cool it with the assumptions."

Her eyes lit up again. "You know what mecha are?"

I considered just turning around and ignoring her, but she was staring at me so hopefully that I held out my hand instead.

"Maggie," I said.

"Danielle." She kept her grip on my hand and leaned forward conspiratorially. "Is that your *real* name? Like, what's on your birth certificate? Because I read that sometimes people have two names—"

I strengthened my hold and gave her what John liked to call my "murderous innkeeper" grin. "If I *did* have another name, I wouldn't tell you. Ever."

"Everything cool here? If it is, I have some pre-req

reading to do for my Mythology class." Edwin drew my attention back to him. One good thing about Danielle was that she made it hard to focus all my attention on a certain tall, hot, bemuscled dude standing in my room, the one who was suddenly part of the student body I'd intended to trawl for my harem.

"I'm taking Mythology too!" she squeed, then whirled back to me. "Is he your boyfriend?" She twirled one finger around a frayed string that hung from the hat as she regarded him. "Hi, Maggie's boyfriend!"

Oh God.

"We're just old friends." Edwin recovered smoothly while I felt suddenly stuck in a quagmire of unhelpful thoughts. *No, but I did ask him to bang me once.*

"So *he's* your boyfriend?" Danielle made a face as she picked up a paper under the sole of her loafer, one that had fallen out of the bag I'd kicked over earlier. It was a picture of Devon I'd printed out, and seeing it was like a boot to the clavicle. She frowned. "He doesn't seem like your type, but different strokes I guess."

"Old flame," I said with feigned sophistication as I snatched the paper out of her hand and turned it over. A familiar pang of sadness throbbed in my chest.

She lifted her head toward the ceiling in relief. "An ex? Good, so you won't mind if I call him a jerk." I stared at her a long time, not comprehending what she meant. She placed a hand on her hip. "All I did was introduce myself, and he acted like I was a ration scammer and kicked me out of his room. I hate when people are mean just because they can be."

"What are you talking about?" Edwin asked helpfully. I'd been trying to ask the same thing, but my lips had sealed themselves shut.

She twirled the string of her hat again. "He was complaining about not getting a lake view so loudly this morning that I had to go see what the hubbub was about. He was just as rude to his parents as he was to me. No wonder they ran out of there so quickly."

The room spun around me, and even though it would be a totally uncool move, I briefly thought I would faint. My voice sounded distant when I finally spoke. "No, you don't understand. It can't be him. You just confused me for a Japanese person, so maybe you think all white people look the same too."

She tilted her head, and both her and her panda hat seemed confused by my behavior. "If you don't believe me, we can go to Devon's room and you can check for yourself."

I dropped down onto the edge of the bed. "Devon?"

The annoyance faded from her face. "You didn't know? Darn…maybe it's another Devon? Did he have a twin?"

"Why would his twin be named Devon too?" Edwin asked, entirely confused by what we were talking about.

Their conversation flowed past me as I perched on my bed, fighting numbness. Devon was supposed to be in Tampa. He was supposed to be dead. Everything he'd told me about himself—not very well-off, neglectful parents, limited resources—had spelled out certain demise for him. What was he doing all the way up here, and how had he made it into this program, one that I'd only snuck into with John pulling strings?

Even though I hoped Danielle was tripping on shrooms or some other substance that was supposed to be a hallmark of the college experience, I knew there was only one way to stop the quaking in my knees. I stood.

"Take me to his room."

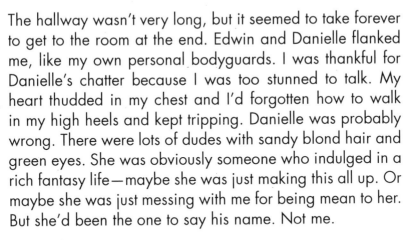

The hallway wasn't very long, but it seemed to take forever to get to the room at the end. Edwin and Danielle flanked me, like my own personal bodyguards. I was thankful for Danielle's chatter because I was too stunned to talk. My heart thudded in my chest and I'd forgotten how to walk in my high heels and kept tripping. Danielle was probably wrong. There were lots of dudes with sandy blond hair and green eyes. She was obviously someone who indulged in a rich fantasy life—maybe she was just making this all up. Or maybe she was just messing with me for being mean to her. But she'd been the one to say his name. Not me.

Devon.

I teetered into Edwin, and he placed a steadying hand on my shoulder. "You okay?"

No. I wanted to shout. *The only boy I've ever shared all my secrets with might be in that room five feet ahead of us. The boy I thought about every night, until you showed up, might still be alive, and you think it's possible that I'm okay?*

A shadow stretched out of the room and into the hallway, and I thought I was going to puke up the deer jerky I'd snacked on during the ride. I closed my eyes for a moment and took a deep breath. I remembered how I used to center myself during the archery competitions I'd competed in, when shaking hands and a scattered mind were absolutely not an option.

When I opened my eyes, the nausea had receded. I leaned away from the warmth of Edwin's body and faced the shadow moving like Nosferatu against the hallway floor. The prospect of seeing Devon was scarier than any pointy-eared vampire—I preferred mine sparkling, thank you—but I was ready.

"I got this." I strode extra wide those last few steps and struck a power pose in the doorway. I probably looked like I thought I was cool, with my hands on my waist and my head angled back, but I was hanging on by a thread.

Devon.

Anguish and hope leaped up in my throat at the sight of him. He stood on his radiator hanging a pennant in the window, and the light streaming in around him made him look like an angel. An angel who regularly worked his trapezius and glute muscles at the gym, that is. That was one explanation for his presence here.

74

"Devon? Is that you?" His name left my mouth high-pitched and off-tune, like when a guitar string broke during the best part of a song. Something inside me did seem to snap when I saw him standing there. He was alive and unharmed, and emotion slammed into me powered by a nostalgia-fueled engine.

He glanced over his shoulder and his eyes slid over me without registering anything other than annoyance. The same green eyes I'd stared at night after night as we'd video-chatted, as we'd laughed and revealed our hopes and fears, fixed on me with disinterest. "If you're another emissary from the anime fan club, I already said I'm not interested in hearing about your favorite *Naruto* episode."

Every bit of hope I'd had was suddenly pulled out of my body and exchanged for the particles of humiliation that lingered in every college dorm room, an act of existential osmosis.

He didn't know who I was.

His voice was deeper, his face leaner, more masculine and scruffy where it had been baby smooth before, but it was Devon. I'd thought of him so many times over the last four years, even after I'd given him up for dead. I could recall every feature of his face just by closing my eyes, but he'd looked at me like some kind of louse that had crawled out of his mattress.

My mouth opened and closed, and the muscles in my body contracted quickly, as if I'd been Tasered.

"Hey, asshole. You have a guest." Edwin's voice was the furthest from friendly I'd ever heard it, and even in my cocoon of embarrassment I was aware that it was pretty hot. What was wrong with me?

"An uninvited guest," Devon said without turning around. What the hell? *This was the same person I'd once thought was the sweetest boy in the world?*

Edwin took a step toward Devon, then shook his head. "Maggie, you can try to talk to this dude if you want, but he's not worth your time. Actually, he's exhibit A of the type of entitled douche you should stay away from."

Devon flinched at my name. His hands dropped to his side, and when his head turned over his shoulder, his attitude was gone and he looked almost frightened. He stared at me for a long time, his eyes growing wider and wider. "Maggie?" It was his turn for the guitar string to break. "Holy hell. Holy shit. Holy fuck."

He scrambled down from the radiator after his strange litany, nearly falling but still unable to look ungainly, given his well-built frame. He ran, scooped me up into his arms and crushed me to him and, just like that, my humiliation was forgotten. For months and months, we'd spent almost every night virtually connected at the hip—or screen—but we'd never touched. Sometimes I'd wanted to feel his hand against mine so much that it had been a physical pain. The distance between us had hurt, and once I thought he'd died it had been insurmountable. But he was here now and he gave even better hugs than I'd thought possible. His whole body was warm and hard, and he smelled like something citrusy. It was appropriate. He'd once described the orange groves near his house, and every time the tart, sweet smell hit my nose I thought of him. Every time. And now he was here, hugging me.

"BodkinBabe?" he whispered.

I groaned. My all-purpose user name had been created when I was still way into archery and young enough to want something punny with a hint of sexual innuendo as I traversed the interwebs.

"Yes, ThrashBandicute, it's me," I mumbled against the fabric of his white T-shirt, which most definitely had whatever was left of my lipstick imprinted on it. I wrapped my arms around him and held him as tightly as he held me.

He laughed, and then loosened his grip so he could hold me away from him. We studied each other and the way the years had changed us. His face was so angular now, and I wondered if that was because he'd gone without food for long stretches of time.

"You cut your hair," he said, and as he ran his fingers through the short strands, I sighed. It should have been weird, but it was comfortable instead. Devon was alive. I could feel the weight of his presence instead of just the weight of my laptop.

"I'm kind of a rebel now," I said with a smirk.

"I always knew you were." His eyes were intense as his gaze swept my face. "I still can't believe you're here. That I get to do this."

"Wha—"

His mouth came down on mine, and I didn't have time to think, only to react. My dad and brothers had taught me all the best ways to repel unwanted advances—jabs, kicks and twisting of joints—but when I slid my hands up to his ears, it wasn't to disable him with a cuff that sent a painful rush of air straight to his eardrum. It was to grab him and pull him toward me, to bring his lips, his body, closer to mine.

I'd been so fixated on all the stuff that came after my first kiss that I'd never given much thought to the actual event. It didn't matter, because I certainly would never have come up with anything close to this. His mouth was firm against mine, his lips warm, his tongue slick. There was a feeling I got when I could play a song through correctly without error and without looking at the tablature, a pleasant kind of warmth as my fingers and breath and brain combined to make something beautiful. Kissing Devon was kind of like that, but turned up to eleven. The hazy pleasure enveloped me as different parts of my body began to work in harmony—the ache between my legs playing a thrilling harmony with my hammering heartbeat.

"Oh my God, this is just like in a drama I watched where two childhood friends reunited as restaurant workers in Taiwan and fell in love!" Danielle's voice reminded me that I had an audience. Her. And Edwin. Fuck.

I pulled my mouth away and disentangled myself from Devon's limbs. When I looked at Edwin, his face was blank, as it had been when we'd encountered the roadblock. Embarrassment tried to dull the bright, happy feeling Devon's kiss had instilled in me, but I reminded myself firmly that Edwin was just a friend. Getting hot and heavy in front of friends wasn't a life goal, but it wasn't every day you ran into your internet beau. He could deal.

"Sorry." I glanced at myself in the room's standard full-length mirror. My hair stuck up every which way, and my mouth looked like something out of a horror movie starring killer clowns. Devon's wasn't much better.

"Why are you apologizing? This is amazing! You have the best first-day-of-college story ever!" Danielle clasped her hands and looked excitedly at Edwin, whose enthusiasm level wasn't quite as high.

"Do you want us to leave you here?" Edwin asked. His tone indicated he thought that was a less-than-optimal idea, and something about that irked me. I fought against my urge to go into brat mode.

"Yes. Devon and I have a lot of catching up to do. Thanks for asking, though."

Edwin gave a nod and turned to go. "Let me know if you need anything."

"Don't worry, Maggie's not-boyfriend. If you come to my room, I'll show you my chibis. They always make me feel better," Danielle said, slipping her arm through Edwin's. His eyebrows raised, but he didn't look as put off by the suggestion as I would have thought.

"She's talking about cute little anime figurines," I called after them.

Danielle dragged him out of the room, and Devon immediately leaned in to resume where we'd left off. I placed a hand against his chest to stay him and extricated myself from his embrace. I was still excited to see him, but our brief pause had enabled the million questions his kiss had distracted me from to take precedent.

"That was a nice greeting, but maybe we should catch up first. I mean, it's been years. I thought you were dead!"

"I thought you were too," he said. "I never thought I'd talk to you again."

There was such genuine longing in the way that he looked at me and how his fingers grazed over my skin. He touched me softly, the way an archaeologist would brush the dust away from an ancient treasure they'd unearthed. I'd never wanted for attention, but this kind of reverence made my breath catch and my brain scramble.

"Well, I'm here now. Let's talk." I sat down on his bed and patted a space a reasonable distance away from me. With room to think and process my feelings provided by the space between us, the immediate comfort I'd felt with him started to wane. We were essentially strangers, despite our shared past. A lot had happened in four years, and whatever he'd gone through had turned him into a guy who bit strangers' heads off without a second thought. My hands started to sweat and I inched away from him a bit. "Well, first of all, the obvious. What are you doing in New York? I didn't think there would be too many people from out of state, and I can't imagine the trip from Tampa was an easy one."

It wasn't impossible, but the more I thought about it, the more unbelievable it was. Arden and Gabriel had just traveled across the country, but the trip had been grueling. Devon ending up here of all places? Impossible. I knew the world worked in weird ways—I'd seen it myself any number of times since the Flare—but this was pushing it.

He shifted uncomfortably, and the last bit of the openness we'd shared fizzled into nothing. He'd been gazing into my eyes as if he couldn't look away before I'd asked the question, but now his shoulders were hunched and his gaze had moved to my shoes. He took a bracing breath. "Actually—"

I jumped to my feet, my instincts already way ahead of whatever he was about to say. That word, said in that tone, never boded well. He grabbed my hand, which made me that much surer he was about to say something shitty— he already expected me to run away.

"When we first started talking in the forum, I didn't know how things would develop. You were just an avatar of a cat holding a bow and arrow. I didn't know how important you would become. I couldn't have."

Oh fuck.

Dread was already seeping through me, and I wanted this over with already. "Spit it out, Devon."

He glanced up, apparently surprised at the harshness of my tone. I chalked it up to the fact that we hadn't argued before, but then remembered that wasn't true. We had once, when I'd told him my church was organizing a mission trip down to Florida, to help rebuild houses after a hurricane. I'd thought maybe there was some way we could meet, but he'd blown me off with a weak excuse. I'd been so mad at him that I hadn't talked to him for days, but I'd missed him enough to make a million excuses for why I should overlook his behavior. *It's not like we'll never see each other,* he'd said when we started talking again. *We have time.*

My memory prepped me for the blow of his next words, but not by much. "I'm here because—" he took a deep breath "—I live in New York, and I have for a long time. For most of the time we were together, actually."

I pulled my hand away and drew myself up to my full height to stare down at him. "What? Why would you lie like that to someone you cared about?"

He looked away from me, too cowardly to even explain himself after dropping that bombshell. He'd just given me an emotional donkey punch and now he was going to make me beg for an explanation?

"You know what? I don't care," I said. He looked up at me, distress in his eyes like he was the one who had been wronged. I shook my head. "We're stuck living in this building together, but don't you ever fucking talk to me again. You've been dead to me all these years, and now you really are."

I marched out of his room, ignoring him when he called after me. Chin up, back straight and blinking away tears at the realization that I'd barely lived away from home for a few hours and had already managed to have my heart broken. They weren't kidding when they said this program was fast-paced.

7

My phone buzzed later that night, a message from my mom. I read the text and responded to her queries. Yes, I'm okay, Amma. No, I haven't accepted drinks from a stranger. No, I don't know where the fuzzy handcuffs Arden left behind are. Please traumatize her and Gabriel with that question. I hit Send, and the phone buzzed in my hand before I could shove it under my pillow. Her message read, It's okay if you're partying, just be careful!

Ha. If only she knew.

After running from Devon, I'd hermited myself away in my room, alternating between unpacking and repacking my things and ignoring Danielle's through-the-door pleas to grab dinner at the dining hall together. People wandered past my door, but there were no wild parties or even loud talkers. It seemed the bulk of the student body would be arriving the following day, if they showed at all. The welcome get-togethers were planned for later in the week anyway, and I could wait till then to be social—if I was even still around. I ate the last scraps of venison jerky and lay in my darkening room, feeling like shit. My thought patterns alternated between *I can't stay here* and *I'll show that fucker* and *Why can't things just work out for me?*

I wasn't used to being incapacitated by my emotions. I was easily annoyed, but I'd learned at the knee of Gabriel, Arden and John. Pesky feelings were usually dispatched by doing something useful, cutting a bitch or withering someone with a blast of sarcasm, respectively. None of those things felt right, though… I sat up in bed and grabbed my guitar. The dip and curve of it nestled against my body perfectly, and for a second a flash of how good Devon had felt against me popped into my head. Then how good Edwin had felt when I'd leaned against him in the hall.

Enough!

I wondered how soundproof the cinder-block walls were and opted to play quietly since it was late. I didn't want to be the asshole of the floor—Devon already had dibs on that position.

I didn't play any song in particular, just let my fingers skip across the strings as they wished. I'd played for long enough that I could zone out and still put together combinations of notes that complemented one another. Out of the random sequence of notes, something began to take shape. I pressed on, following the melody where it took me. The song was sad. The song was foolish. The song was…pretty fucking good.

Thoughts of Devon and his lies disappeared as the structure of the song overtook my consciousness. I had a groove going, something that was catchy with an undertone of melancholy. Once I could play that without making any mistakes, I began humming different melodies, trying to find one that was just the right mix of the emotions that had knocked me down for the count earlier. That was the funny thing about emotions—trying to capture the essence of them was the best way not to feel them at all. As I tried high notes and low, indie sprightliness and then folky melancholy, I was able to look at what I was feeling more clinically instead of curling up into a ball at the thought of what had happened.

Words began to emerge from my quiet humming. I avoided the phrase "you lied," which would be too cliché even if it was the truest thing I could say about Devon's actions, and opted for something poppy and peppy that clashed with the hint of sadness in the song. I frantically grabbed for a piece of paper and pencil with one hand while still thumbing the strings with the other.

The only sound was the scratch of my pencil, with the occasional strummed note as I made sure words and music matched. Finally, I put the pencil down and played the song through. By the time I got to the last verse, the power of the song was rolling through my body full strength, and I felt a vicious smile curve my lips as I belted out the words.

If I wanted a lost boy, I'd go read Peter Pan.

You think I'll forgive you, but you don't understand.

I've made my peace, you will not get a pass.

Ask me and I'll tell you: shove it up your ass.

There was a smile on my lips as the last note faded. Nothing had changed—Devon had still made a fool of me, and I'd still have to see him around the dorm, but damn if I didn't get a song out of it.

A light brush of knuckles against my door startled me, and I didn't ignore it as I had all night. Creating a song had purged enough emotion that I could interact with other humans without biting any heads off.

"Sorry for ignoring you earlier," I said as I opened the door and—yup. Not Danielle.

"No problem. Kinda hard to focus on other things when there's a tongue down your throat." Edwin had one arm against the door frame, but he took a step back so he wasn't crowding me. He nodded toward Danielle's door, which was now decorated with stickers of rainbow unicorns and dolphins. "I saw Pikachu at the dining hall earlier, and she said you wouldn't come out of your room. I told her it meant things went really good with you and that dude after we left, but then I thought maybe it meant things went really bad." He held up his hands, and there was a sandwich in one and a glass bottle of soda in the other.

Oh God. Why is he here? Why is he being nice to

me? I ignored the way my heart bumped in my chest and the dimples that formed in his cheeks as I stepped away from the door to let him in.

"Your family would kill me if I let you starve," he explained, but even that caveat couldn't douse the warm happiness that his gifts had brought me. He thought enough of me to make sure I was okay and had something in my belly, late as it was. Even if he only ever thought of me as a friend, having a friend like Edwin wasn't something to snub your nose at.

"Soda? I thought I was supposed to be doing keg stands and taking shots."

"You are, but the best part of college is coming up with inventive ways to find booze. I'm not gonna make it easy for you." He cleared a spot on my already messy desk for the food and then sat down on the edge of my bed. Only as I approached the sandwich did I realize how hungry I was. I unwrapped it and took a bite just as he said, "So, do I have to kill this guy?"

I took my time chewing, swallowing the morbid desire to say, "Yes! Finish him!" along with the chicken and lettuce. "No. If he's going to be throttled, I prefer to do it myself."

He nodded. "You can talk about it if you want. I know you're fully capable, but I might have to kill him without your consent if he did anything too unforgivable."

I considered not telling him, but then I remembered that Edwin already knew the first most embarrassing thing that'd happened to me; he'd participated in it. What difference would it make if he knew the second?

I opened the soda and took a huge gulp that left a sweet, fizzy burn at the back of my throat. "So, we dated for six months. But...online. We never met in real life because he was in Florida. Or he said he was in Florida. Turns out that was a bit of a fib. He was here in New York the whole time." I bumped a fist against the burp forming in my chest. No need to rest on formality with Edwin.

"Damn." He drew the vowel out long and high, and his face scrunched up like he'd just been kicked in the nuts. That was the look of someone who not only listened to you, but actively felt embarrassed on your behalf. There was a German word for it, but I was too lazy to see if the basic online search engines would pull it up. "You got catfished. I'm sorry, Maggie. I thought that only happened to people I didn't know."

I laughed around a bite of sandwich. "Hey, at least I never sent him my Social Security number." A memory came back to me then. "After we first talked, he sent me a letter, and it was postmarked from Florida. I don't get why he'd go through all that trouble. Maybe he's some kind of sociopath."

"Did he say why he did it?" Edwin asked, and when I just kept chewing he shook his head. "Maggie, I'm the last one to go to bat for this guy, but let me guess what happened. He told you he'd lied, and you whupped his ass and left the room."

I shot him a disgusted look. "I didn't lay a finger on

him. I'm not trying to get kicked out of school for battery before the semester even starts."

"Look, I'm not a fan of a guy whose first instinct is to make out with you instead of asking you how you survived and whether you're okay, but maybe that's just my superior intellect and years of experience talking." Edwin took a piece of candy out of his pocket and unwrapped it. The scent of butterscotch wafted over, and I wondered what it would've tasted like on his tongue if Edwin had kissed me instead of Devon.

"I don't know about the last part, but I hadn't even thought of that." I started to get mad all over again. Devon likely would have pulled me toward his crappy dorm bed if I hadn't stopped and made small talk. And given how caught up in the moment I'd been, I might have let him. I sent out a thank-you to the universe for not letting that happen. I wanted to get rid of my v-card, but not at the expense of my dignity. That would have been just as bad as what I was trying to avoid.

"Yeah, he seems like a little shit, but maybe he has a good explanation." Edwin stretched, displaying how the muscles of his chest and abs worked beneath his shirt, and heat tingled at the back of my neck. I looked away. Maybe there was something in the venison that was making me so aware of every move he made, which might explain my parents' sudden amorousness. Edwin kept talking, and I made sure to keep my gaze on his face. "Maybe, you could, you know, give him a chance to explain. If he was just a dick for no reason, then we kill him. If he has a good excuse, then maybe you can still be friends. Either way, talking to him is better than ducking and dodging him all year because you feel ashamed every time you see him."

I stared at him, overwhelmed by a feeling of solidarity that surpassed the crush I'd nursed on him. He wasn't just comforting me. He was sharing something of himself, something unpleasant.

"Have you ever lied to a woman you cared about?" I asked. "Is that why you think he deserves a chance?"

"No." His mouth twitched, its corners tugged down by an unhappy memory. "I wish lying was the worst thing I'd done. I didn't protect her. Because I thought that some stupid oath of fraternity I'd taken was more important than my own conscience. I told you, I've done things I'm not proud of." He hopped to his feet in one fluid, undulating motion. "Anyway, it's not about giving him a chance. It's about giving yourself one, to not have a cloud hovering over your head from day one here."

He ruffled my hair again and walked toward the door. His hand lingered a bit longer than it had before, and his index finger slid over the exposed shell of my ear. Something in me tightened; no one had ever touched me there before, not like that. I had no idea it could feel so good, could send a battalion of tingles charging toward every outpost of my body.

I reminded myself that he didn't feel any tingles. Not for me. "Did she forgive you?" I asked.

"No. And I don't want her to."

With that, he swung the door open and slipped out.

For so long, I'd been angry with Edwin for not thinking of me as more than the littlest Seong. But as I picked up my guitar and began strumming the song I'd just written, I realized that he'd been little more than a hot cardboard cutout to me. The real Edwin Hernandez had a story and now that I was learning it, I wondered if I knew anything about him at all.

8

The next morning I was awoken at an ungodly hour by the sounds of people banging around and yelling back and forth like the hallways weren't echo chambers funneling sound into each dorm room. Well, by that cacophony and my screaming bladder. I hadn't gone to the bathroom since the day before, and thanks to the soda I'd chugged before bed, I was dangerously close to reliving my short but humiliating bed-wetting period.

I stumbled out of bed and fumbled with the unfamiliar lock on my door, dodging a guy carrying a stack of boxes and jumping over a milk crate filled with books. I was still half asleep and probably looked like a horror show, but my only thought was finding the familiar white ceramic bowl before I became known as "that girl who peed in the hallway." No one wanted to be that girl.

I pushed my way into the bathroom and into an open stall, painfully aware I wasn't wearing shoes and hoping it was early enough in the semester that I wouldn't catch some kind of infectious disease. I'd just begun the most transcendent piss of my life—I couldn't imagine sex being better than that sweet relief—when the door swung open and I remembered I'd be sharing the bathroom with complete strangers. Whoever was out there probably thought a racehorse had broken into the building, and there was no end to my stream in sight.

Why are they being so quiet? Am I trapped in here with some weirdo who gets off on hearing people go to the bathroom?

"Maggie?"

Devon? No. Why?!

"I recognize those Dora the Explorer pajama bottoms from our video chats." He spoke calmly and casually, as if he hadn't introduced chaos into my emotional life yesterday.

"Number one, these are Dora *and Friends* pajama bottoms. Number two, we are not on good enough terms for you to be speaking to me while I'm using the bathroom. What is wrong with you?"

The door opened and closed as I finally finished my record-setting pee, and then I cracked the stall door and peered around. There was no Devon in sight, so it was safe to step out. I was not excited to spend the rest of the year like this. Maybe Edwin had been right.

I washed my hands, then wet one of the small cloth towels stacked by the sink and scrubbed my face. Washable cloths seemed fancy, but at this point, they were easier to deal with than paper towels, which still weren't being produced on a large scale. Toilet paper trumped paper towels in the grand bathroom hierarchy.

The door opened again and Devon strolled back in, dropping a pair of much-too-large flip-flops at my feet. Seeing him raised all kinds of thoughts—the kiss in his room, and how the night before our last video chat years before he'd told me he was learning to play a song called "I Think I Love You." I'd had to look up the song, and the tune had been stuck in my head the entire next day. All that day, I'd looked forward to asking him if he'd meant anything special by that. I'd fantasized all of the different ways he would explain, "Yes, it means I love you," and how I would reply, "I love you too." But I'd never had that opportunity. That night, I'd video called him. He'd picked up and said "Maggie" in a way no one had ever said my name before. And then everything had gone dark.

And now, here he was, bending over to slip my feet into his flip-flops as I stood staring at him. He looked up and smiled. "Can't have you getting some mutant strain of athlete's foot."

"Why?" The word came out hard, probably a reaction to the weird sensations his hand cupping my foot was creating in me. Warmth raced up from where my sole connected with his palm, arrowed straight up between my thighs and throbbed there, perhaps hoping his hand would follow like a homing beacon.

"You *want* athlete's foot?" He was still smiling, and it was still tugging at the memories, pulling them to the forefront. I considered kneeling him in the face to make it stop, but instead I slipped my feet into the too-large sandals and gave him my best withering stare.

"Why did you lie to me? I don't want an apology, because I'm not going to forgive you. I just need to know how sociopaths operate so I can avoid them in the future." I bit my lip because it served two tasks: it made me look angry and stopped it from trembling.

He stood and crossed his arms across his chest. "Not exactly what I wanted to hear, but I'll take that opening. I'd love a chance to explain. Doing it in the bathroom? Not so much."

Not so much. My throat tightened at that. It was funny, the things that hit you below the belt. The three words comprised one of those throwaway lines he'd said all the time, probably as much as I'd once said "duh," but suddenly they seemed like something painfully intimate, even more than his hands on me had been. I hadn't felt homesick for my family yet, but that phrase made me wish for my life all those years ago, before I knew Devon had been deceiving me.

The door swung open, and two women a bit younger than me, at least in appearance, walked in. One wore her hair in multicolored braids that hung down to her waist, and the other had frizzy strawberry-blond hair. Their gazes slid from me and then to Devon before connecting with each other. Both smiled as they scented the drama in the air.

"All right. You can walk me to my room." I wanted to be "the girl having an emotional moment in the bathroom" even less than I wanted the title of hallway pisser.

He caught the door with the tips of his fingers and ushered me out. "Thank you," he said as we dodged more incoming students. "I know you don't have to give me a chance to explain, and I appreciate it."

He followed me into my room, and I closed the door after him, leaving it cracked so he didn't think anything too exciting would happen after he spilled the beans. I sat on my bed and he sat beside me.

Less than twenty-four hours at school, and I've already had two dudes on my bed. Arden would be proud.

I thought of how Edwin had sprawled comfortably last night, legs spread, body relaxed. Devon was tight, pulled in on himself, and I was surprised to find myself feeling a little bad for him just below the anger. It wasn't even exactly anger anymore, just a kind of numbness that stole through my body and kept all the other feelings away. I hummed a few bars from my song, the fact that he didn't know what the cutesy tune represented making it like a secret weapon I was wielding against him.

His leg jumped up and down, transmitting his nervousness through the bed, and I was forced to bounce along with him. "I *was* living in Florida when I first talked to you on that music forum," he began. "I was spending the summer with my aunt and uncle because my parents were traveling outside of the country for my dad's job. Diplomat stuff."

Well, that explained who'd pulled his strings for him. "Why weren't you with them?"

"I was tired of traveling. Tired of not having any friends. My aunt and uncle said I could come stay with them for high school, so I'd have a steady life. A normal life. That summer was supposed to be a test run. I get along great with my parents, but I just wanted to be normal." He scratched his elbow nervously and stopped when something on the ground near his foot caught his eye. I'd crumpled the picture of him up, but not well enough. I reached down, picked it up and tossed it in the plastic trash can across the room, all while holding his gaze.

"That doesn't explain the whole living-in-New-York thing," I said tartly.

"Oh. My dad got cancer, so he was pulled from his assignment and came back to New York for treatment."

I winced. "Sorry."

"No need. He's fine. He's lucky, even. If they'd found it any later, he wouldn't have completed his chemo before the Flare." He paused then, and not in a reflecting-on-my-parents'-mortality kind of way. Whatever he had to say next was going to piss me off.

"So...?"

"So, my dad was receiving treatments at SUNY Upstate—"

"That's where my brother was doing his residency. You were that close and you never said a word. You let me prattle on like an idiot about visiting you in Florida." Shame heated my face and, again, I missed the built-in coverage my long hair had provided. "You didn't even tell me your dad had cancer. I told you *everything*."

He looked down at the ground, shoulders humped like a dog waiting to be kicked. "I was scared, Maggie. Everything in my life was changing. I'd just lost my chance at a typical teenage life. My dad was fighting something that kills lots of people and my mom was beyond stressed."

"And you didn't think enough of me to share any of that?"

He straightened and almost reached a hand toward me, but thought better of it. "You were my safe harbor. You have to believe me, I wanted to say something, but what we had online together, it was so perfect. I just kept thinking about what would happen if we met in real life. Maybe you'd think the way I chewed was weird, or that I smelled funny. Maybe I'd do something to piss you off and you'd dump me. Our video chats were the only stable thing I had in my life. I didn't want to lose that."

"Well, shit." I jumped off the bed. "How am I supposed to be mad at you when you phrase it like that?"

"I was still wrong. But it wasn't because I was trying to deceive you or because I thought you were unimportant. You don't have to forgive me, just know what we had was real to me." His face was so damn earnest.

"You have to go. Now." I pointed at the door but dropped my hand when I saw how it shook. I was too close to crying or, worse, hugging him and telling him it was okay when it was definitely *not* okay. I needed some space to process everything he'd told me, but I didn't think I could explain all that without my voice breaking. I flicked my head in the direction of the door to urge him along.

His hands flexed on his knees before he nodded and rose. "Thanks for letting me tell my side." He took a few steps. "I still talked to you, you know. Even after the Flare. We got taken to some government facility, but I had a picture of you taped to the wall. I talked to you every night because I hoped it meant you were still alive. Even if we're not friends, or anything else, I'm glad you survived."

And then he was gone, leaving me to sort through the mountain of emotions—more like a trash heap of emotions, as there were years and years of layers there. I could understand, in a way, but lying was lying. I thought back to how much being separated from him had affected me, back to that terrible night I'd drunk too much and hurt Arden more than I'd ever hurt anyone, in part because I missed him so much. And he'd been lying to me the whole time.

I decided then and there to never talk to him again. Then again, Arden had forgiven me for the ugly things I'd said to her. More than forgiven me—she'd showered me with love. Did this mean I should forgive Devon, that the past was the past? I didn't know. The only thing I was sure of at this point was that I needed to brush my teeth and get some coffee in me.

I was still standing in the middle of my room a few minutes later when Danielle pushed the door open. She wore faded black jeans and a black turtleneck topped with her panda bear hat. On her feet were white spats that were miraculously clean and shiny. Her makeup was still perfect, but much more understated. "Hey! Did you go get your work study assignment yet?"

"I haven't even showered," I said. I noticed she hadn't knocked and wondered if she'd done so to avoid being ignored again.

"Good. I was hoping we could have breakfast and then walk over together. If you want."

I was tempted to brush her off, but that would have been petty. She'd been nothing but nice to me, even when I'd bitten her head off. There was no reason not to give her a chance. Wasn't that what we all wanted out of this new experience? For people to look at us and see not a dumb kid, but someone who might be worth caring about?

I remembered how when John was feeling down, before Mykhail and Burnell had come around, he'd sometimes push my hair aside and ask me to smile. He said I was selective enough in bestowing it that it could make the difference between a good day and a bad day for him. The way Danielle was looking at me, like she was already bracing for dismissal... I took a deep breath and smiled.

"Give me ten minutes? Is that cool?"

She let out a low sigh of relief and nodded. "Of course. I'll wait in my room."

I dug into a pile of clothes for my towel and grabbed the small plastic caddy filled with my toiletries.

It seemed I had two friends. Three if I could ever forgive Devon.

Not a bad start to coed life.

9

The dining hall food was good. I'd had doubts, wondering if it would be like the disgusting unidentifiable meals we'd had back in high school, but in this brave new world, mass production of processed food wasn't king. Most of our meal was locally sourced—a lot of it came from the huge convert-ed greenhouse on the agricultural campus, where student workers grew what they'd later eat for dinner.

"Maybe I can work at the farm. I did a lot of garden-ing work with my family," I said to Danielle as we walked toward the Registrar's Office, which also served as a work allocation center. One side effect of the Flare was that mon-ey, which had after all mostly been an idea, didn't have a stabilized value yet. While the remaining economists figured out the best way to start from scratch—and my dad and brothers argued over the ideas of dudes named Keynes and

Picketty as if the government advisers were listening in— many people and places had fallen back on an older institution. Bartering.

At universities, the idea was particularly easy to implement. Academic and other non-teaching staff both received housing, food and protection as payment. For students, the work study program had been retooled so students worked more hours per week and in jobs that had often been handled by professionals before, but their entire education was paid for. Things would change as the world regained more and more technology and the information that had been lost with it, but the Oswego program was big enough to have plenty of student laborers and small enough for the bartering system to work. In theory, at least.

"That sounds fun! I'm terrible with plants, though. They always end up...you know." Danielle gave a sad little laugh, and I understood. "Dead" was Voldemortian now, a word people didn't like saying anymore, as if uttering it could give it power. Or perhaps it just raised the specter of memories that many people couldn't bear. I wondered about Danielle and what memories the word raised for her, but we weren't quite friendly enough for me to ask yet. One thing I'd learned at my GED program was that what one person thought was a simple inquiry or conversation starter could be hugely triggering to someone else. When most of the world's population was struggling with PTSD and assorted other mental trauma, curiosity took a backseat. If she ever trusted me enough, she would share her past with me.

We entered the building, which was much nicer than

the dorms but still rinky-dink compared to the marble columns I'd seen when I'd visited my older sibs at Burnell. There were two middle-aged women at the door greeting students. They clutched clipboards and flashed us the brief smiles of those who prioritized efficiency over small talk.

One of them, who wore glasses that needed a visit from the scratchproof–coating fairy, hurried over to us. "Hi, ladies! Are you here for your job assignment?" She knew the answer, since she was already pulling forms from her clipboard and handing them over. "Fill these out, and we'll take them to be processed. You'll be notified of your job placement in one to two days." She said the words with relish, as if she'd waited a really long time to feel like she was doing something worthwhile again. Or maybe that was just me projecting.

We took the forms and I jogged to slide onto a bench just as two guys got up to turn in their forms. Danielle followed close behind me. She was staring at the paper in dismay.

"Skills? None. Aptitude? Reading manga." She sighed. "My uncle told me I should be more serious."

"Oh, come on." I stopped scribbling "badass guitar player" under the skills column and looked at her. "You're not shy, you like engaging with people and you're completely nosy." I glanced at the list of job positions, from which we were supposed to choose four top possibilities. "Here. Student health center receptionist. Check that. Umm…student activity center welcome desk attendant. Gymnasium monitor…"

"And library assistant! Don't you want to work in the library, Maggie?"

I scrunched my face up. "Uh, no. Why would I want to do that?"

Her delicate brows furrowed. "Because you're smart. You would get to read books all day. And maybe meet a boy who loves them as much as you do."

I rolled my eyes. "Reading is cool and everything, but I just spent years of my life cooped up in one place reading a bunch of books. The thought of being stuck in a quiet library for hours at a time…" I shuddered. "Plus, I can't even listen to music there. I'm not allowed to just start belting a song if the mood strikes, because I might disturb someone with their face stuck in a book. No thanks!"

I crossed out the option on my form, just in case they assumed someone with the name Margaret Seong would prefer a library position.

When I looked up, Danielle was staring at me. "But intelligent women enjoy reading books and other academic endeavors." She said the words like someone had ground them into her. I thought about her room covered in manga posters that certainly didn't fall into any high-brow reading categories.

"Some do. Others prefer reading music. And others want to get their hands messy. No one fits into a neat little box, Danielle." I scanned the form and checked off the last of the things I thought could work for me. "Okay. So I chose farm assistant, dining hall worker, student security guard and maintenance crew. I'm hoping for dining hall because that means I get prime food access."

I turned in my form and glanced over at Danielle, who was scribbling much more than seemed necessary. In the "Additional comments/concerns" box at the bottom of the form, she was doing a quick sketch of an anime-style cat, a scared one with the hair raised on its back and its tail straight up. Next to the cat, she'd written *I cannot work in tightly enclosed spaces. Thank you* in neatly blocked capital letters. She finished the drawing and looked up at me with a grin. "People listen better when you make them smile."

I gave her a nod and watched her skip off to one of the clipboard women. Danielle said something and tittered behind her hand, and then the woman nodded goodnaturedly and gave her a pat on the shoulder.

"What should we do now?" she asked as she approached me.

"Go eat again?" I ventured. I'd botched my first attempt at using the waffle maker that morning and wanted another go at it.

"No, Maggie. Let's go explore the campus. I want to go see the lake." She skipped ahead and then turned to look at me. The day was just warm enough to pass for late summer, although autumn seemed eager to move in. Soon it would be cold enough that just walking to class would be a danger to all of my extremities.

"Smart. With the way weather works up here, it might be frozen over soon," I said.

The college area along Lake Ontario had once been beautiful, with walkways and metal benches and manicured shrubbery. A few years of neglect, and the lake had scrapped all of that. We found a wooden bench that was so new it hadn't been painted yet and took a seat.

"It feels weird being here," Danielle said. "But good weird. I thought I'd be stuck with my uncle forever."

"Was he an asshole or something?" My family often annoyed me, but even being stuck with them hadn't felt like a bad thing. It was the leaving that'd felt weird for me.

"He's a brilliant man," she said. "Everything I did was wrong to him, though. Now I can be myself without getting a lecture every five minutes."

I thought about how I'd immediately shut her down when she'd walked into my room, and how Devon had treated her. I made a mental note that perhaps I could use a less abrasive approach if she did things that annoyed me. Not everyone communicated the way my family did.

"Was living with your uncle something that happened after the Flare?" I asked, trying to be tactful.

She nodded. "I think in a weird way he was sad I left. He thought he could make me into the same person my mom was. I got a special scholarship here because he has a little bit of post-Flare celebrity. Well, that and some stuff with my parents. I don't feel like talking about it. " She shifted around on the bench and crossed her legs beneath her. She gave a nervous laugh, one that almost covered the sadness of her words. Almost. "What about you?"

"I lived with my parents and brothers," I said, feeling that strange guilt that always wormed through me when I talked to those who'd suffered more than me. "I didn't want to leave them, but I'm glad to be here too."

It was true. Despite the Devon drama and being in an unfamiliar place, I was starting to feel like I was exactly where I was supposed to be. I thought of all the things I was supposed to have experienced by now in the normal timeline of things. I always came back to the idea that I'd been cheated somehow. But so many others would never get this opportunity. They were stuck in terrible situations or, worse, dead.

"I'd forgotten how beautiful the lake is," I said. I didn't want to focus on the bad things in the world right now. Not when the sunlight was skipping off the waves and hitting the prism of optimism in my soul.

"It's so big! I can't believe Canada is over there," Danielle squealed. "Do you think we could row a boat across?"

"With these string beans?" I poked her arm, and she glanced down at herself judgmentally. "I'm joking, Danielle. Your arms are lovely. And, yeah, we could totally row across. You'd do the work, and I'd recline in the back of the boat with a parasol, because I'm a lady."

She sat upright on the edge of the bench and mimicked rowing for a moment before leaning back and staring at the waves rolling into shore. "Sitting right here, you can pretend it's the ocean," she said. "You can just stare out there and imagine that whatever you want most is waiting in the distance. I figure that's what it's like to look out at the ocean, at least. I've never had the chance."

"I've seen the ocean once," I said. "I grew up not too far from here, but we went to visit a family friend in New York when I was about five, and someone decided it was a great idea to go to Coney Island."

"You're lucky." Danielle turned on the bench to face me. "My parents said I had to wait until I was eighteen to travel the city alone, and I had a whole trip planned out. I'd go to the big comic book convention they have every year, and before I came home I'd take the subway to Coney Island. I turned eighteen this summer, but the boardwalk burned to the ground years ago, apparently."

Despite her impressive makeup skills, Danielle was two years younger than me. The Flare would have happened during her first year of high school or last year of junior high. And now she was here with all of us, expected to behave like someone who hadn't been a child when the world had gone dark. I felt a sudden tenderness for her then, a desire to shield her from people's curious looks and rudeness, even my own.

"Did you go on the roller coaster?" she asked. "Or check out the sideshow acts? I wanted to see the sword swallower. I watched a video of her once, and she had tattoos and cool hair and would have made the perfect superheroine."

"That, I would have remembered, but unfortunately the only thing I can recall is the beach. It was dirty and super-crowded, and a seagull stole my last French fry. Garbage was blowing everywhere, and I'm pretty sure one dude was swimming naked. I prefer the placid shores of the lake. You're not missing out."

There was the sound of grass crushing beneath boots behind me, followed by a deep voice. "Maybe my ears are ringing from using a power drill all morning, but did I just hear you talking shit about Coney Island? I know that couldn't have been what I heard."

"Hi, Not-Maggie's-Boyfriend," Danielle chirped.

I leaned my head back over the edge of the bench and discovered that Edwin was gorgeous upside down as well as right-side up. He stood over me, a fake scowl on his face, and I hoped my nose was clean. I pulled my head up so I was facing away from him again, unsure if my head was spinning from the change in blood flow or his presence.

"Oh, it's the city boy," I said. "I was just explaining how that beach was a filthy trash pile. Nothing to be offended about."

The next moment seemed to be picked up by my senses in snippets. More crunching grass. The heaviness of Edwin's presence was a tangible disturbance in the air behind me. His hands gripped my shoulders, but not too tightly.

The spicy smell of his gum as he leaned over me, and the way his eyes met mine when my head snapped up. His expression was serious, but not like it had been when we'd stopped at the checkpoint. Something flared in his eyes. Anger? No, but whatever it was made his gaze go warm.

"Danielle, say goodbye to your friend." With that, his grip on my shoulders slid to my arms and tightened, and he lifted me out of my seat as easily as if I were a munchkin like Arden. He clutched me to his chest and stomped toward the lake. The freezing lake. "This is what happens to suckers who blaspheme my hometown," he growled as he stopped short at the edge and his arms kept going. I screamed and clutched at his neck before realizing he hadn't thrown me into the water. It was simply a ruse.

I peeked up from the crease of his neck and shoulder where I'd planted my head as I held on for dear life. He was giving me one of those white-teethed, big-dimpled grins and, fuck, he smelled good. His mouth was so close I could kiss him, just once, to see if it was the same as when Devon had kissed me. My whole body went tight and hot because he was holding me way too close for someone who'd turned down my advances. And then I realized something mortifying—he could hold me like this because he didn't see me as anything more than a friend. Meanwhile, I was getting all lathered up about it.

I pinched his neck, a ridiculous reflex as my libido's personal fight-or-flight response kicked in, and he dropped me.

"Ow! What the hell?" He rubbed at the spot I'd

pinched. "What was that for?"

I looked up at him from where I'd landed on my ass. "You scared me." My calm voice didn't sell that line, but what was I supposed to tell him? The truth?

He gave me that weird look again, and then shook his head. "You'd better not pull any stuff like that when we're working together. I have a reputation to uphold. And if this develops into a bruise, I'm telling the rest of the crew you gave me a hickey."

I was starting to get back up but flopped down at his words. "Excuse me?"

He walked over and held out a slip of paper, staying as far away from me as possible like he thought I'd reach out and pinch him again.

I snatched it from his hand.

"Apparently, you were easy to place. I guess a couple of positions for a surly, needlessly violent agent of annoyance opened up."

The sheet of paper almost got snatched away by the wind, but not before I saw the words *Job 1: farm (Agriculture) Job 2: maintenance (construction crew)*. I'd thought maintenance would be, I don't know, going down to the basement and banging on the boiler with a monkey wrench. Instead...

"Looks like we're going to be co-workers," Edwin said. I couldn't tell if he thought that was good or bad, or what I thought of it either.

10

The day of my first maintenance shift, it took me entirely too long to find the facilities building, a feat that seemed impossible on such a small campus. I was still groggy from the unplanned nap I'd taken in my first period class, Resilient Hearts: Disaster and Recovery in American Literature. Given the wide variety in age range and educational experience among the students, and the limitations of the staff, there weren't many 101 courses. I thought the idea behind this class in particular was good, but forcing a group of people who undoubtedly had some level of PTSD to talk about disasters probably wasn't the greatest idea.

I had no idea what the class had been like, though. After staying up late working on another song, this one a ballad about a modern highwayman posing as a cop to provide for his family, I'd taken my seat at the back of the class.

I'd nodded along to the soothing-voiced female teacher's discussion of literature as therapy and had promptly fallen into the most delicious nap of all—the forbidden classroom nap. My notes had started out as intelligible, then became chicken scratch, then simply a squiggly line that ran off the edge of the page. I'd jumped awake as my fellow students stood and started filing out.

Professor Grafton, a woman in her later forties with a shock of pink hair, had given me a disappointed look as I slunk past her.

I showed up at the facilities building well rested and hoping my first shift would go better than my first class had.

"Margaret Seong?" A man who looked like a rock creature that had been transformed into a human hurried over to me. His voice was gravelly to match, but his eyes had a kind light that immediately warmed me to him. His hair was graying, and as he held my work assignment sheet, I could see that the middle and ring fingers were missing from his left hand.

"You can call me Maggie," I said. My two older brothers had Korean names on their official documents that made each bureaucratic encounter bothersome. Each such situation required them to explain that, yes, they went by Gabriel and John, but also to judiciously avoid that it was because people inevitably treated them like they couldn't speak English if they used their Korean names. By the time my parents had to name me, they'd decided on a fully American name. I never told them how it made me feel left out because I knew they'd done it to save me, their only daughter, trouble.

"Okay, Maggie." He made a note in a notepad that appeared out of the pocket of his quilted flannel jacket. "I'm Joe. I thought you were gonna be a little slip of a thing, but you look solid. You might actually be useful."

He said the words in such a friendly way that I couldn't even be offended.

"It says here that you have basic carpentry skills, can use a circular saw and a drill and have helped build houses. How much of this is bullshit? I'm not asking 'cause you're a girl, but because I don't want to put you in a situation where you could get hurt as a result of you overstating your experience. Don't worry, your job is safe. I just want you to be safe too."

"Why would I lie?" I asked, drawing my shoulders back. I'd done way too much backbreaking work over the years to have this guy question my cred.

He glanced around, and when he spoke his voice was lower, like he was sharing a secret. "Listen, hon, I've already got three guys with broken thumbs and another who nailed his foot to the bench I had him building. Guys see maintenance and assume because they have something swinging between their legs this is the job for them. It's not just you—I'm asking *everyone* to give me the real deal on their experience. I don't want to file another report with Human Resources. They scare me."

I'd never known my grandparents, but Joe hit some sweet spot that had been hardwired in me from a lifetime of commercials and sitcoms. He was the perfect blend of gruff but sweet, and I had to fight my desire to hug him.

"Everything I listed there is true. I've worked with my dad over the last few years, maintaining our house, renovating the family store after it was ransacked and doing odd jobs for neighbors. I'm not an expert and I don't have any kind of licensing, but I can hold my own."

Joe gave me a craggy smile. "We're going to start you off with inventory first. I'll walk down with you and go over all the different tools the contractors will need and where they're stored. We have a project coming up that we might be able to use you for, but it doesn't start until next week."

We walked down a set of steps to a level that was belowground. The hallway managed to be dark despite the fluorescent lights lining the ceiling. In the few doors that were open I could see that there were no windows. I briefly thought of Danielle's scrawled note about enclosed spaces and felt a millisecond of panic on her behalf. I didn't know what had compelled her to sketch that scared cat, but I hoped the library, where she'd been assigned, didn't require her to go into any sub-basements.

Joe pulled a jangling set of keys from his pocket when we reached a thick metal door. Just as he moved to push the key into the lock, it opened, and Edwin and another man walked out. The other guy was shorter, his skin slightly fairer than Edwin's but still darker than my deepest tan.

"Hey now, what do we have here?" The guy was talking to Joe, but his eyes were running over my body as if he could see through my hoodie and jeans. I pulled my hands up into the too-long sleeves as if they were what he was ogling.

I ran through the first options that ran through my mind: break his nose, flip him off, quit this job if he was an example of the other workers. I was a grown-up now, so I decided to use my words. I snapped, and when he looked at my fingers, I pointed at my eyes. "We have your co-worker, who knows every single painful pressure point on your body and can skewer you with a bow and arrow from a hundred feet away."

His eyes narrowed. "She a carpet-muncher?" he asked Joe, still not addressing me, and my anger spiked. I tried not to be afraid, but everywhere I went there were men waiting who thought my body was theirs for the taking, whether I was interested or not. The guy who'd whipped his dick out during my economics class, Brad, was a prime example. I didn't allow myself to think of Kenny, who'd offered me a ride home when the engine on my parents' van had stalled. I'd been trusting enough to accept.

Before I could say anything else, Edwin turned and began speaking in Spanish. He was calm and smiling, but he underscored certain words with a slap of the crowbar he was holding in one hand against the palm of the other. I had no idea what he was saying—I'd taken Mandarin in high school—but he had an air of command that was magnetic. The other guy's mouth pulled down a bit at the corners, but he nodded as if he were listening. "*Comprendes*, Felix?" Edwin asked, and even I could understand that.

"*Si.* Yeah." He turned to me. "Sorry. That was inappropriate and probably made you feel uncomfortable. It was an asshole move, and I won't do it again."

I was speechless. I'd been prepared for him to protest and continue being slimy, which was what usually happened when I explained to a guy how fucked up his behavior was. But I guess having a penis had added some power to whatever it was Edwin had said. I didn't like that his words had more impact than mine, and I didn't like the grin I had to fight to keep off my face. Edwin had schooled someone for me, and I enjoyed it way too much.

"No problem," I said. I heard my voice come out deep, like I was trying to imitate their manly tones. I cleared my throat and adjusted to my natural alto. "I'm going to be handling inventory for a little while, so hopefully we're cool now."

"I was going to show her around," Joe said. "Make sure she knows what's what so guys don't get sniffy with her when she's working." He glowered in Felix's direction, but then someone shouted, "Joe! We got more fresh meat!" and he ended his staring contest before it had begun.

"Maggie knows her shit," Edwin said. "But I can show her around if you want to handle the incoming student workers."

"You guys know each other?" Joe asked. There was no insinuation in his voice, and I was glad for that. I gave a sharp nod. "Good. Yeah, you do that. I have a feeling that not everyone who shows up today is going to know their shit, as you put it."

He hurried down the hallway, and Felix followed behind, strolling casually as if whatever weirdness had passed between him and Edwin had been no big deal.

"What did you say to him?" I asked as I followed him into the room. There was a beat-up desk at the entrance, which would probably be mine for the few hours of my shift this week.

Edwin pointed out the labels on the top left corner of each wooden shelf and cabinet, not condescending to explain what the tools were used for. "Felix has two sisters. I asked him to imagine if they walked into their first day of work and some *pendejo* walked up and started messing with them. How would he like that, if his sisters felt unsafe in a place they had to go every day? And then I asked him if having sisters was the only reason he understood why it was wrong to harass a woman, to imagine that the guy messing with his sister is an only child." He opened a cabinet and began rooting around for something.

"Whoa." Again, I kicked myself for seeing Hernandez as set of cute dimples and washboard abs. Now that I was actually talking to him, those dimples and abs had lots of good stuff to say. As fun as each discovery of a new facet of his personality was, it set me back miles in my goal of getting over my crush on him. "I mean, thanks. I'm so tired of guys thinking they can treat women however they want. It sucks always having to be on guard because men think they can treat women like shit for the hell of it." Images of Brad and Kenny and Devon flashed in my mind. Their behaviors were totally different, but each of them had seen me as an object instead of someone deserving of the same respect they'd want.

When he leaned back to look at me, his brows were raised in a way that wasn't whimsical at all. "You spoke to Dude Down the Hall, I take it?"

He handed me the strappy leather thing he was holding, which freaked me out for a minute before I realized it was a tool belt. I wrapped it around my waist and fiddled with the buckle as I tried to adjust it. Edwin's hands pushed mine out of the way and began resizing it for me. His fingertips brushed my waist, and I knew he was just helping me to be efficient, but his touch felt good. I steeled myself against the sensations he drew from me. If I took advantage of him helping me, I'd be no better than Felix.

He looked up at me, a question in his hazel eyes. My inner perv hoped the question was "Do you need help out of those skinny jeans?" but that wasn't going to happen. I remembered what he had asked me before I was distracted by his touch. "Yeah, I talked to him. He said he moved back up here because his dad needed cancer treatment, but he never told me because he didn't want to mess up what we had."

"Sounds legit," Edwin said in a tone that implied quite the opposite. I felt the belt pull snugly around my waist, and then he stood back and surveyed his handiwork. I thought his gaze lingered a bit long on the journey from belt to eye level, but it was probably just a remnant of my inappropriate fantasy. "Now you have his excuse. You gonna forgive him?"

I wiggled my hips, enjoying the weight there and the way the hammer bumped against my thigh. I felt a bit of the same security that came from having my guitar at my back, like I was suited up and prepared for battle. "Since you're dead-set on acting like my wise elder, why don't you give me some advice? Would you?"

His lips twisted in annoyance, but his dimples still showed, so I guess that meant he was somewhat amused. "I can't tell you how to proceed. Sometimes people do things that seem like the best idea at a certain point in time, but in hindsight, they turn out to be the worst choices they could've made." He raised a hand to his chin. "Do you think he's worth a second chance? You should keep in mind he's not the only guy on campus. Sometimes it's best to move on to greener, less complicated pastures."

I mulled over his advice. "'Less complicated' sounds good, but 'pasture' implies that I'll always have to watch where I step. If not, I'll end up ankle-deep in cow shit."

Edwin laughed. "Welcome to the world of dating."

I chuckled and then realized that this was an opportunity to find out some relevant information. "So how have you found dating on campus?" His gaze flew to mine, and I raised my hands defensively. "I'm not trying to be nosy." *Lie.* "I just thought you might have some advice. It's hard on these Oswego streets, Edwin."

His laugh was rueful this time. "That it is. I've seen a couple of women here and there. Nothing serious, which works for me. I don't think I have the right equipment for that."

"Ummm, not to be weird, but I'm going to have to dis-agree. I mean, I've seen you in gym shorts before." My brain short-circuited for a moment as it conjured a mental image of the time Edwin was working on building plant boxes for my dad and got caught in a sudden downpour. His shorts had clung to his body, and noticing said *equipment* had been difficult to avoid. Arden had placed a hand over my eyes to stop me from staring.

"Maggie!" He gave me that weird look again, but this time I swore that I could see the slightest touch of pink on the apples of his cheeks. "Thanks for the support, I think, but I wasn't being literal." Great. I'd just revealed that I was thinking about his penis while we were in an enclosed space. This had to be some kind of violation of workplace rules. His next words helped shut off the perv valve in my imagination. "I wasn't talking about the plumbing. The head and the heart are where things start getting wonky. Blown fuses, lost parts that are impossible to replace these days. You know how it goes."

But I didn't. I was one of the few people who couldn't empathize with loss and how it could change you. I'd known fear and pain, but nothing that held me away from others. In fact, my last harrowing moment had sent me barreling straight for Edwin, seeking comfort I thought only he could give me.

"Well, I guess we can be on the prowl together," I said, hoping my voice didn't sound as forced as my words were. "I can be your wing woman. Maybe help you find someone who replaces those missing pieces." I didn't know why I was saying these things. Maybe if I was cool enough to help him get a date, he wouldn't know that my breath caught every time he got too close, like he was right now. Then I would be in control, even if only of his disinterest in me as more than a friend.

Edwin shook his head, and I felt actual relief. "If there's one thing the last couple of years has taught me, it's that we can make do, we can innovate and we can push forward, but we can never replace." I didn't know what my face showed then, but after looking at me, he tacked on an amendment. "But stranger things have happened, I'm sure."

"Like my internet ex living in my dorm?" I asked.

"Exactly like that." He grinned at me. "I was starting to feel a little sorry for myself, but my love life isn't weird-internet-ex bad. Thanks for the perspective, wing woman."

"Glad my romantic disasters can keep you entertained," I said. For the first time, I didn't immediately cringe when I thought of our shared less-than-romantic past.

11

The first two weeks of school went by in a blur. Danielle and I fell into a rhythm of breakfast together every morning, and if it was a day when I had to work a maintenance shift, Edwin joined us. He and Danielle had Mythology together, and they'd regale me with stories about their teacher and the strange vocal tic he had; it sounded uncomfortably like a gobbling turkey.

Text messages and emails kept me connected to my family. Arden was helping to sell the produce from her parents' garden, and Gabriel had taken a temporary position at one of the clinics there. John was busier than ever, traveling all over the state as they prepared for larger-scale implementation of the microgrid system and upgrades to the current phone and internet services. Mykhail had delegated his work to some students at the lab and now served as his driver; he wasn't codependent, but having experienced unthinkable loss once made it very hard for him to let John travel alone without going crazy with worry. My parents had finally sold off their store and our place in town, or bartered for them rather. Among their new possessions—five baby goats that they hoped would be the beginning of a cheese business. Mom was happy to report that the goats were just as good company as her children had been and better at cleaning up after themselves than I was.

Everyone seemed to be getting it together, but college life wasn't as easy as I'd expected it to be. My first shifts at the farm hadn't gone as well as at maintenance, and not just because there was no Edwin. I'd walked in just as a man in coveralls and stinking to high heaven rushed out past me in an angry huff; it appeared a position had just opened up. I'd imagined I'd be reaping and sowing, but I'd been assigned to the bottom rung—compost sifting. I had to go through trash from the dining hall and make sure all biodegradable, nutrient-rich matter was collected for the compost pile. I had a mask, and gloves that went up to my shoulders, but as I worked I heard my mom's voice echo in my head. *One day you're going to get your sweet reward for being such a bratty teenager. Please let me know when that happens—it's the least you can do.* She'd cackled with loving malice when I'd told her and Dad my work assignment because I'd been such a jerk about composting at home.

I missed my family, but to be honest I was so busy I

hardly had time to feel it. My days at home had been spent searching for things to keep me occupied. My chores had increased exponentially, given that we were basically living Laura Ingalls Wilder–style, but even after our household had shrunk to just me and my parents, they enjoyed doing work so the onus hadn't been on me.

Now I was responsible for keeping up with my coursework. I'd had to read a short story about Pompeii and write a thousand words on it, which was just about as long as the text itself. I went with the title "Isn't It Ironic?: Preservation through Destruction in Dana Tarp's Tale of Pompeii." Professor Grafton had loved the paper, forgiving me for my snoozy participation in her first class. She admitted to being an Alanis Morrisette fan, which had led to an in-depth discussion of *Jagged Little Pill*. I hadn't had anyone to talk music with since Arden had gone, and I'd never had anyone to discuss Alanis with since Arden thought she sounded like a strangled cat.

At my maintenance job, I'd made friends with just about everyone on the small staff, including Bulldog Rosie, who'd earned her nickname for biting a co-worker's hand and not letting go after he'd grabbed her ass. My kind of woman, obviously. Felix had taken Edwin's harassment talk to heart and occasionally stood sentinel when deliverymen lingered a little too long at my desk. "Be respectful, man," he'd say. Like any new convert, he was a bit overbearing, but it was kind of sweet.

Between my two jobs, my classes and school social functions, I hadn't even picked up my guitar in a week. My fingers were itchy, but my body was exhausted. I remembered a time when I'd multitasked with the best of them, balancing school activities with archery competitions and swim team. Now I wondered where that younger Maggie had gotten the energy. She must have been mainlining Red Bull and sugar straws, because it was all I could do to even manage to brush my teeth.

Being so busy also meant the few times Devon had stopped by my room, I'd been gone. He'd left a couple of messages on the whiteboard attached to my door, some nonsense about going to a meeting for an environmental club with him. I guess he figured I'd be into it since he knew I was working at the farm, but 4-H had never been my style, even back in my overachieving days. He waved in the dining hall during mealtimes but never tried to join me, either out of shyness or because Edwin was often with me. I'd considered it luck that our schedules were so different.

I was slogging through one of my farm shifts, looking sexy in coveralls, goggles and rubber gloves, when my luck ran out.

I was separating piles of foul-smelling cabbage into the compost heap, each loud *plop* making me fight against a gag, when my manager's voice rang out behind me. I hadn't seen Sheila since the day she'd taken me to the compost room, and I hadn't had many generous thoughts to spare for her since that day. When I turned around, the number of them dropped into the negatives.

Devon stood behind her, and even though he was

wearing a mask that covered his mouth and nose, I knew he wore that sheepish grin of his by the tilt of his head and the hunch of his shoulders. Sheila's eyes were tight above her mask, like she could only stand being in the room for a few moments. "Margaret, this is Devon. He's just been transferred over from the Student Center. You're great at this job, so I'll let you show him the ropes."

Then she scurried out of the room, leaving me in the company of the last person I wanted to be alone with. I regretted not pelting her with a handful of rotting cabbage as she fled; instead, I turned to the pile in front of me and went back to my job.

"It's simple. Step one, open one of the bags of trash. Step two, separate all the things that can go into a compost heap—egg shells, vegetable matter, what have you—into a pile and throw it in the compost bin." I jerked a thumb to my right. "Should be pretty simple to figure out, even if you can't tell Florida from New York on a map."

Damn it. That last bit slipped out without my permission. I was trying to project an air of detachment, not lash out like someone who was still hurt over the fact that the guy I liked had lied to me.

"The bags are over there," I said quickly, not giving him a chance to launch into another apologia.

He nodded and set to work. I wasn't a completely evil person—after he dug through the first bag without complaint, I broke and let him know where the rubber gloves were kept.

After a while, the silence of another person trying not to annoy me was heavy enough that I finally cracked. "You must have really pissed someone off to get stuck with this job," I said, pretending it wasn't a big deal that I'd initiated conversation.

This doesn't mean I forgive him.

He chuckled. "Let's just say I had a difference of opinion with my supervisor at the Student Activity Center."

"How so?"

"She thought I should work at the SAC, and I thought my talents could be better used elsewhere."

I laughed, but then something occurred to me. "So, you asked to be moved to the farm and they did it? I thought it was tough to get out of a job once you'd been assigned for a semester." Because the whole work-for-credits program was new, the school administration was trying to be strict about reallocating people after they'd been assigned. Once you gave people the idea they had a choice in a situation like this one, it was all downhill. People would be begging to be assigned with their friends or boyfriends, to be moved to cushier positions, to jobs where they had to do less physical labor. I'd read a history of the Soviet Union I'd found at my parents' house; Oswego wasn't a gulag by any stretch of the imagination, but it seemed strange to just give a freshman whatever he wanted.

He flashed me a grin that I didn't understand. "Let's

just say I'm the son of diplomats. My dean says I'm not supposed to talk about it anyway. They got their revenge by
sticking me here, in the worst job on campus besides the
weekend bathroom cleaners."

"Yeah, worst job on campus. The job I was assigned
two weeks ago and didn't even think about getting out of." I
untied a new garbage bag and wondered just how dumb I'd
been when I'd thought Devon hung the moon. I'd been great
at multitasking but had shit taste in guys apparently.

He made a sound of agitation. "My supervisor didn't
like me, okay? She didn't like me, so she pulled some strings
so I could be moved. It's special treatment, but not in the
way you think." There was silence, except for the sound of
squelching garbage and rustling plastic. "I'm having a hard
time making friends, to be honest."

I rolled my eyes, even though he couldn't see me.
"You're not some special snowflake. Making friends is hard.
Making friends as shell-shocked adults who've spent the last
few years scraping to survive is even harder."

He didn't push back against that. "I know. The thing
is, I used to be good at this. I had to transfer schools all
the time because of my dad's job, and breaking into the
established cliques wasn't easy. Along the way, I learned
how to be cool, funny and interesting in five languages.
But here, I'm trying to just be me, and it seems that *me* isn't
very likable."

This guy and his guilt trips. I was kind of glad we
weren't actually dating. That would mean he'd meet my

mom, and they'd combine to form some kind of unstoppable guilt-fueled robot.

I stopped sorting and turned to look at him. "I see you eating with a group of people every day at the dining hall. You have friends."

All the muscles in his neck tensed, just for a moment, and then he shook his head. "Those aren't friends. They're cool, but they're people I know from the environmental club. We talk about club stuff all the time. It's nice to have them, but it's not like they know anything about me."

I didn't even think he was trying to guilt-trip me this time, but it happened anyway. I was still mad at him, but the fact of the matter was that we'd been close once. Closer than anything, even though we'd never been in the same room before that first dorm room encounter. I didn't like feeling all schmaltzy, but it kind of hurt to see him so lonely when I was standing in the same room. Because I knew him, obviously not as well as I thought I had, but enough to understand that he couldn't have faked everything between us. I thought again about Arden's expression when I'd hurled angry words at her—the one clear thing from that angry, drunken night—and the relief in her face when she'd found me in the woods, still alive. She was no one's pushover, and she'd forgiven me without hesitation.

"Do you still play guitar?" I asked, searching my brain to see if I recalled seeing one in his room in the brief moment after he'd been a dick and before he'd kissed me.

"No. I didn't bring it with me when we evacuated to the shelter, and I haven't replaced it yet." He tied up a bag that had borne no compost and tossed it aside.

That little detail was what did it. He'd loved playing, and it was yet another thing gone from his life. In the grand scheme of post-Flare losses, it wasn't much. But when I thought about how much of my anger and desperation I'd channeled into my music, and how I'd discovered my love of music because of him, I realized I owed him one.

"Well, I still play and I'm really fucking good now." Modesty wasn't a strong point of mine, I was discovering. "Maybe...maybe you can come to my room and we can have a little jam session?"

"With one guitar?" he asked carefully, as if he thought I was trying to play a trick on him.

"Well, you can sing along," I said. I wouldn't offer him the use of my guitar just yet. That was an advanced friendship–level favor. "It'll be fun, like when we used to video-chat. For a little while I thought you had the most beautiful voice in the world, you know." I didn't tell him that to make him feel better—it was true.

"Remember that song we sang every night for a week straight?" He was working too slowly as he talked, but I'd harped on him enough for one day.

He sang out the first lyrics to a Katy Perry song I'd shunned in the last few years. When Arden had asked me to play, I'd pretended I was too cool for some dumb song about fireworks, but really it had hurt to sing it without him. His voice had been higher the last time we sang, in a register closer to mine; now it was deep and resonant and did something strange to my insides. My heart kicked up, I took a deep breath, and then launched into the next line with him. We didn't look at each other as we sang, as if that would kill the magic arcing across the room between us as we pushed our voices to join in a way our bodies had never been allowed to. We picked through our trash, the smells and textures anchoring us as our voices soared. His sifting increased to match mine as the music progressed, as if the song were connecting us even on this most mundane level.

When we got to the last word, clapping sounded from outside the door.

"Do another one!" an unknown co-worker yelled. My face flushed—not because I'd been caught singing, but because singing with Devon had felt so intimate, even though we hadn't taken one step closer to each other.

"Should we give them what they want?" he asked.

I didn't care what they wanted. It was what I wanted that mattered.

I turned to look at him. His eyes flashed happily above his mask, and in that moment he could have passed for the boy I used to know. There was a twisting sensation somewhere inside of me as I looked at him, and I couldn't tell if the feeling was good or bad.

"Let's do that Justin Bieber song you liked," I said. "He was a shit, but he has a good repertoire."

We were elbows-deep in refuse and our masks muffled our voices, but as I said, modesty wasn't my thing. We sounded good. Just like that, the band was back together.

12

Although it was frustrating being relegated to desk duty at the maintenance job, it allowed me to get a lot of my reading done. I'd pretended like reading was no big deal to me when Danielle had suggested I work in the library, but that had been to prove a point. In reality, Professor Grafton's disaster lit class was my favorite by far. It wasn't just that the reading selections were from fantastically well-written books, but also that none of them seemed to have been picked haphazardly. There was a unifying theme of growth through pain and unthinkable loss that was reinforced with each selection. Each work complemented or contrasted the others that had preceded it, and you were forced not only to think, but to feel. Our latest assignment was from a Murukami novel.

Memories warm you up from the inside. But they

also tear you apart. I read that line over and over, letting it absorb more deeply into my understanding of life. It seemed to represent everything I'd learned since venturing out into the real world over a year ago. It was the encapsulation of that wistful look people got right before sharing something very sad. It was the distilled form of what I felt when I pushed away thoughts of Dale and Kenny and blood in the snow.

"So, is there some part of 'organize the stockroom' that I was unclear about?" Joe asked as he walked into the room and dropped a pile of dusty hammers and screwdrivers for me to put away.

I slid the photocopied excerpt from Murakami's *Kafka on the Shore* under the logbook, and he pretended not to notice. If I seemed too eager to work, he'd know something was up, so I was sure to move slowly as I gathered the tools that had been left by a contractor two hours before. "Sorry the place is a mess. I'll make sure it's in order before Fred gets here for his shift." Fred, another student worker, had not been pleased about having to do his work and mine the week before, when I'd spent the entire shift reading a book we'd been assigned about a teenage girl who was the sole survivor of a nuclear apocalypse. The loneliness of her daily existence had been realistic and terrifying to me. Sometimes I forgot how lucky I'd been in the aftermath of the Flare. I'd had food and warmth, family and friends to trust and even a cute guy to crush on. When Fred had come in, he hadn't cared about my realization that I'd actually had a pretty normal teenage existence, despite the feeling of being denied something by the disaster. He'd just wanted to know why the drill bits hadn't been put away.

Joe sighed. "Yeah. I want you to do your job, but more importantly, I don't want Fred trailing after me listing the things he had to do because you didn't."

"Well, if you'd checked my references, my mom would have told you I can't clean for shit. I'm good at doing actual work, though. Maybe if you put me on one of the work crews, I could be more helpful." I gave him a toothy smile and blinked expectantly at him.

Joe scratched at his neck. "I'm sending Hernandez out to the lighthouse. We were doing some fortifications before it gets thrashed by another winter, and he's going to close it up. If you run, you can probably catch him before he goes."

Excitement thumped from my chest to my throat. I dropped the tools back onto the desk with a crash and booked it for the door. I crossed the threshold, then stopped and poked my head back in. "Who's going to put all this stuff away?"

"Fred can deal with one more day of double duty. I'll give him a candy bar to make up for it, and that should keep him from griping too much."

"Thanks, Joe!" I whirled and ran up the stairs. Edwin was just starting the ignition when I ran up to the passenger side of the truck and raised a hand to knock on the window, but he was already reaching over to open the door before my knuckle hit the glass. "Did you sneak out of your shift early? If you get in the back, I'll throw a blanket over you and haul you away before anyone notices."

"I would never shirk my duties, Edwin," I said. I climbed in and pulled the door shut, and turned to see him regarding me doubtfully. "Joe said I could come help you close up the lighthouse."

A strange expression shifted his features for a millisecond, almost so quick that I could have imagined it. I wondered if maybe he didn't want me tagging along with him, but then he smiled and shifted the car into Drive. "Cool. I don't have too much to do, and the view is awesome. People aren't usually allowed inside because of asbestos and structural issues, but since you're rolling with a VIP, you get the special tour." He plucked at the collar of his flannel jacket, the one that made him look like a sexy lumberjack.

"Is the VIP meeting us there?" I asked.

He replied with an annoyed *hmph* and we were quiet for the rest of the short drive. I liked the playful Edwin I'd gotten to know since we'd started spending more time together. Too much for my own good, actually; willpower alone wasn't proving to be an effective crush-repellent.

When we pulled up to the edge of the lake, I remembered a crucial point about the lighthouse. "We have to walk there," I said, looking out at the thin path that snaked out into the water toward the structure. White paint peeled off the square base building, revealing ominous streaks of red below. It was just brick, but from a distance it looked like blood. I hated that I knew that from real life and not a movie. The red roof and green trim were more inviting, so I focused on that.

"Yup," Edwin replied, climbing out of the truck.

"On that thin, crumbling rock pile that's supposed to be a bridge." Murky water lapped at the rock bridge, splashing up the sides and emphasizing how guardrail-less the thing was.

"Yessiree," he said. He popped open the trunk and handed me a sweatshirt. I had on a denim jacket and a warm scarf, but the wind off the lake was chilly, carrying early tidings of winter from the great North.

"Thanks," I said. I sniffed it surreptitiously as I slid it on and zipped it up. It smelled a little bit like the wash powder he used—that we all used—mixed with sweat.

He'd hauled a duffel bag out of the backseat and slung it over his shoulder. When he walked past me, he jerked his head in the direction of the lighthouse. "Come on. You won't fall in."

"I'm not scared," I said way too fast for it to be true. I annoyed myself with the defensive instinct that always led me to react first and then think about what I'd said. Of course I was scared. Dark water lapped at the edge of the stones, making the path nice and slick, which wasn't exactly what I was looking for in a bridge.

"This bridge is scary as hell," Edwin said with a shrug and began walking. "But think about it. Going to the lighthouse wouldn't be as fun if we could drive right up and walk in."

He *would* say something like that.

I followed closely behind him, watching where he placed his feet as he walked. He called back when there was a loose or particularly slippery rock, although he was never out of arm's reach.

The walk felt surreal. The waves of the lake frothed and churned on both sides of me, and from this vantage point the lighthouse seemed like the only place that existed in the expanse of dark sea. There was just me and Edwin and a darkly romantic lighthouse looming up out of the waves...

The thought was just the beginning of a fantasy, but it was enough to distract me at the wrong time. I made a little sound as I lost my footing, but Edwin was always paying attention, luckily for me. His head turned the slightest bit, and then he swung his arm back and scooped me toward him before I could fall. I didn't know if I would have hit the rocks or hit the water, but I much preferred being flush against Edwin's strong, muscled back, with his forearm pressing into me and keeping me upright. My arms were wrapped around him, hands splayed over his chest as I held him in a vise grip.

Turned out almost falling into a lake was kind of an adrenaline rush. That I was instead pressed up against a guy I had the hots for didn't help. I didn't know if the unsteadiness I felt was because of Edwin or my near miss.

"Fuck, dude. Are you okay?" He was standing rigidly,

like one small move could send me tumbling into the water.

"I am. Okay, that is. Yes." I wasn't making sense, but that was pretty much impossible given the position I was in. He was warm and his smell was pleasant and inviting, like pine needles and some other hard-to-pin-down manly stuff that wasn't old sweat. I inhaled deeply and then let go of him. "Death by small, slippery pebble would be a majorly embarrassing way to bite it after everything else I've been through."

"Let's take the necessary precautions then," he said. His hand clasped mine, and I pulled in a lungful of cold lake air at the shock of it.

Edwin is holding my hand. The words looped in my brain, driven by my racing pulse.

He didn't look back until we made it to the small island where the lighthouse sat sentinel, and I wished desperately I could see his expression. Was he annoyed at my clumsiness? Worried?

He let go of my hand slowly, and I slid both of mine into my pockets, just to give me something to do with my jangling nerves. Edwin hiked the duffel higher onto his shoulder and glanced at me. "Hm. The interior isn't entirely safe... maybe you should wait out here."

"A girl trips once and she's known as a klutz forever?"

"Look, there's a loose floorboard on the steps. I can't risk you tripping over your own feet and taking us both out."

"You're such a jerk, Edwin." I jogged in his direction with a fist raised in play, and he took off running. I followed after him, around the lighthouse and then pounding up the front steps and through the door he'd just fumbled open. I'd run a decent hundred-meter dash, but Edwin was fast. He was already on his way up the stairs as I jogged through the empty visitors' center on the first floor of the lighthouse. A cold breeze gusted into the room, and I pushed against it, up the short spiral staircase. The sky was blue outside the door at the top of the steps, except for a strip of be-flanneled arm.

"Did you think I was just going to keep running, like a lemming?" I said with an incredulous look when I reached him.

"This is called a widow's walk, Mags. I was just being careful. And yes, if you were focused enough on beating me to a pulp, you might just crash through the railing." He dropped his arm and we both turned to stare out at the amazing view. The lighthouse wasn't very tall, but from where we stood you could see the points where the Oswego River and Lake Ontario collided, as well as far out onto the lake. A few fishing boats bobbed against the horizon line. It was peaceful, and only in the silence of the waves did I realize how frenetic my mind had been since I'd arrived at school. At home, I was surrounded by nature and quiet. Oswego was no bustling metropolis, but school life was shuffling from a cinder-block dorm room to a fluorescently lit cafeteria to a stuffy classroom, and then back. Even working at the farm didn't provide much relief, because I was still stuck in the dank compost room.

"You stay here," he said. "I just have to do a window and door check so no meddling kids can get in and ruin the work we've spent the last month doing."

I doubted he knew how much I needed the moment alone, but he was observant enough that it wouldn't have been a big surprise.

As he clanked about downstairs, I circled the perimeter of the lighthouse, taking in a view of the area most people didn't have access to. Downtown fanned out from one street of densely packed buildings to the more rural areas. The cooling tower and containment structure of Falling Leaf loomed in the distance, feeding energy into the power lines that unfurled from it like the shoots of a plant. It looked bleak and ominous, so I circled back around to the seaside view again, where birds wheeled and clouds scudded overhead.

Boots clomped up the steps behind me. "Ready to go?" Edwin asked.

"Not really, but I have class."

He chuckled. "I appreciate that you'll cut work and not class. I like a woman who chooses her acts of rebellion wisely."

Even though a cold wind was blowing, I felt a sudden blast of warmth. *We're friends. He talks to all his friends this way,* I told myself. I repeated that mantra even as he held my hand all the way back across the bridge, like it was nothing for us to be touching in that way.

I had to believe my thoughts were true. Now that we

were getting to know each other, and not acquaintances forced into each other's proximity, it was even more imperative that I didn't get any crazy ideas about Edwin. Losing my heart and risking our newfound friendship were two risks I couldn't afford to take.

13

I was sitting at a table in the common area on my floor, trying to figure out a ridiculous word problem. I'd signed up for Math for the Liberal Arts on a whim, not realizing the subtitle for the class should have read Ridiculously Circuitous Word Problems Written by a Sadistic Lit PhD Student. I could take a tough equation and break it down easily, but the paragraphs-long word salad problems were driving me up the wall.

"Are you coming to the mixer tonight?"

I looked up to find one of the girls who'd witnessed Devon's down-on-bended-knee performance in the bathroom. She'd taped a paper with her name in glitter onto her door: Niesha. She twirled a braid around her finger as she waited for my response.

I slid my pencil into my sleeve to hide the bite marks I'd put there while puzzling over my assignment. "The meet-and-dance thing at the SAC? Yeah, I think I'll stop by."

"Cool." She bit her lip and gave me a hesitant look. "Is your friend coming, by any chance?"

"Danielle? Probably." I didn't know Danielle's sexual orientation, or rather whether she liked women as well as men, but Niesha was hot and if she was interested, I'd put in a good word for her.

Niesha laughed. "No, not her. The Spanish guy with the brown skin and the dimples and the nice ass." She grasped her hands to her chest and sighed dramatically as she looked heavenward. This was good, because if she'd seen the expression that crossed my face, I would've had a new nickname floating around—"chick who was possessed by a demon when asked to hook a sister up."

"Edwin?" *My Edwin?* Suddenly my joke about playing wing woman for him didn't seem so funny.

"I think so." Her eyes narrowed in contemplation. "It is okay, right? I mean, I assumed you and Devon were a thing after the bathroom kneeling and your little folk music parties."

I hadn't given much thought to what Devon coming to my room for a couple of hours every other night must've looked like to everyone else in the dorm. I was having fun, and maybe the sixteen-year-old in me was ready to take him back without hesitation, but in my mind we were just friends.

Friends who serenaded each other every night. If Niesha thought we were more, what was Devon thinking?

"Playing Beyoncé on guitar does not render it folk music, okay?" Going after the guy I was crushing on was one thing; dissing my musical taste was something else entirely.

"I like folk music. Why would you think I didn't?" She raised an eyebrow at me.

This was going downhill, fast.

"You seem more like an indie chick, but yes, we all contain multitudes. Devon isn't my boyfriend, by the way." I sighed and then conceded. "Neither is Edwin. He might show up tonight, but I'm not sure."

She clapped. "Oh, great! I hope he comes. It's slim pickings around here—well, everywhere now. He seems like a good guy, so I figured it wouldn't hurt to ask."

"Right." It wouldn't hurt *her*. I sized her up. She was attractive, self-assured, had curves where I didn't and a personality that seemed to be fun and laid-back, whereas mine toggled between aggressive and awkward. Plus, she'd been conscientious enough to ask before she made a move on Edwin. I kind of wanted to date her myself, so it would be no surprise if he took her up on her offer.

She lingered in front of the table, expecting me to dish more on Edwin, but I shot a glance at my homework and then sighed.

"Okay. I'll let you get to it. See you tonight!"

I stared at the worksheet in front of me after she left, but the words and numbers made even less sense. A chirping from the open door of my room let me know I had a message, which was also a convenient excuse to stop doing homework. I ran in and checked my phone.

Working at the farmer's market and my dad's rutabaga are killing it. Gabriel is doing a shift at the clinic. Want to video-chat about that weird, possible soul mate type situation tonight? -A

I responded quickly. I'm not sure about soul mates. Soul friends? I kind of like this other guy too. Why is this stuff so confusing? Can't chat tonight, there is a party. I hope they play the cha-cha slide so I can show them my moves.

I should have known what she was going to reply. Soul friends with benefits would be better. ;) 3:)Who is the other guy? And why do you have to choose? (Don't tell your bro I said that.)

I'm not even sure what to do with one penis, let alone two. I replied, and wished I hadn't. I'd already had a very vivid dream about skinny-dipping in the lake with Devon and Edwin. Both of their hands running over my body had felt way too real, lingering for a moment after I'd awoken; if I wasn't sure how to handle a threesome, my brain certainly had some suggestions.

Try some porn. It'll hold you over until you decide which D is right for you. I was still processing that when another message came through. Oh, and I didn't answer your question: this stuff is so hard because there has to be some way of finding the person who makes you feel at ease.

I laughed. Are you saying that things are easy with you and Gabe? I've seen your fights.

Not easy. Never easy. But so, so worth it. <3

I sent her dozens of hearts in return, wishing we could have this conversation in person. It kind of sucked that the period when we'd had unlimited time for girl talk was also when my love life had been nonexistent.

I put the phone down beside me and stared at the wall. Danielle was right—cinder-block was the worst. For the first time in weeks, I had nothing to do, besides the homework I was pretending didn't exist. I opened the web browser on my phone, typed PORN into the search engine and looked around the room guiltily, as if someone could tell what I was doing. The loading cursor paused, and I held my breath expectantly, but instead of sweaty bodies, a warning that I'd lost my internet connection popped up.

Great. Even the internet is messing with my emotions.

I flopped back onto my bed and stared at the ceiling, grappling with an unfamiliar boredom. I'd always had someone to talk to at home; there, I'd had to hide from company instead of seeking it out. Even though I was in a dorm full of people, they were all still relative strangers. All except one. Before I knew it, my feet were carrying me to Devon's room and I was knocking on his door. "It's Maggie," I announced.

There was a scrambling in the room, and when he opened the door his face lit up with pleased surprise. Seeing the way the smile changed his demeanor made me realize his default expression was usually a frown. "What's up? I thought I wasn't gonna see you until work tomorrow."

Oh. What *was* up? I hadn't thought about why I'd gone to see Devon. We'd spent plenty of time hanging out, but this was the first time I'd sought him out at his room instead of waiting for him to come to me.

"I was just passing by," I said. His gaze edged toward the hallway's dead end, which was right outside his door. Now I looked like a creep. "Passing by to see if you were going to the mixer, that is," I recovered. "I heard they might have a karaoke competition, and that could be fun."

He grinned at me. "It could be, but I'm kind of persona non grata at the Student Activity Center. Remember, the whole supervisor-hating-me thing?"

"Right. I guess that could get kind of awkward,"

I said. Unexpectedly, I was a little disappointed. Our hang-out sessions had been fun, and the sixteen-year-old in me had always harbored a fantasy of going to a party with Devon. Was he a good dancer? Would he bring me little sandwiches and cups of punch? I reminded myself I could have found out the answers back when we were dating if he hadn't lied about where he lived, but my anger wasn't as intense as it had been a couple of weeks ago. I hadn't forgiven him—I didn't know if I ever could—but the more time we spent together, at work and in the dorm, the more I felt like I was getting the old Devon back. I told myself that wasn't what I wanted or needed, but the lure of nostalgia was hard to resist.

"It would be like that time you had to share a ho-tel room at the archery competition with that girl whose super-expensive bow you stepped on and broke. I don't want to deal with death glares all night."

The distrust I was clinging to slipped a little further out of my grasp at his words. The broken bow. It was a silly story, something I wouldn't be embarrassed about now, but he was the only one who knew it. Marisa was the only other person I'd told, and she was gone. It was such an intimate thing, having him recall my story as if it was part of his life experience too. We were tied together, even if he was also a stranger. I managed a chuckle around the bittersweet angst his ease with me stirred up.

"I don't mind missing out, though," he continued. "I have some environmental club stuff to handle. The guy who organizes everything lives over in Minetto, so I'm going to swing by his place."

"Isn't that a no-go zone for students? We're supposed to stay within city limits." Some areas were unsafe for habitation because of structural issues, high crime stats or some combination of the two. North Syracuse was closer to Falling Leaf, and thus the risk of getting caught up in either military or anti-military activity was higher than on campus. The school didn't track our movements, but we were highly discouraged from going places that might require their intervention to get us out of.

"Greg isn't a student here. And he says all these rules and regulations are just a front for corporations trying to carve out their own interests. People got by fine without them, right?"

"He sounds delightful." He'd mentioned this guy before, and frankly, I wasn't a fan. There was something about the admiration in Devon's tone that irked me, bringing a welcome respite from the warmer feelings he'd just roused in me.

"What's the big deal?" he asked, a command to chill out underlying his words.

"My brother has to travel into those no-go zones all the time for work. He's had his life threatened by guys who think like your pal Greg, all because he's trying to get the infrastructure back in place."

"Your brother works for the government?" His eyes widened.

I rolled my eyes. "Yeah. So does your dad. So do

most people at this point. Why is that a surprise?"

Devon's brow scrunched up. "Did you come over here just to argue with me? Because we could have done that by video chat, and I wouldn't have had to put pants on for that." He gave me his endearing smile, and I took a deep breath and shook my head.

"Okay, sorry. I guess I'm just a little on edge." I couldn't tell him why. I couldn't even explain to myself why Niesha's request and Arden's words made me feel so jumpy.

"You could always ditch the mixer and come with me. I think you might like the group. I only went for the free pizza, but they have some good stuff to say." His smile was cute enough that I almost considered it, but then I thought about Danielle and her silly hat navigating the mixer alone. That and the fact that hanging out with a bunch of strange dudes far from campus wasn't exactly appealing. The more he talked about these guys, the more they sounded like the fedoras I'd avoided on internet forums. The kind of guys always trying to prove their superiority in the smuggest way possible, who thought they were so smart that they were incapable of believing otherwise, even when you proved them wrong. I wondered why of all the people on campus, Devon would connect with guys like that.

"No, I'll hang out here. I'd rather not end up shanked on the side of the road. Besides, I need to make some new friends, like you have."

An odd expression crossed his face and then he

shook his head and laughed. "Well, if you change your mind, let me know. Being with you makes me glad I came to this program. Seeing more of you wouldn't hurt."

My mouth formed a surprised circle and blood rushed to my cheeks. *Being with you?* What did that mean? "I've been having fun too," I said, leaning back as he held on to the door frame and leaned forward. Was he going to try to kiss me again? More important—did I want him to?

His lips landed on my cheek, close enough to my ear that it sent a small zing of something good through my body. I stood there, unsure whether I should turn and catch his mouth with mine, just to keep the trembly feeling in my stomach going, but he pulled away and stared at me. I often wondered what Edwin was thinking when I looked at him, but with Devon it was crystal clear. He wanted more than that chaste kiss. Having someone look at me like *that*—was that what made all the BS worth it? Or was this just another layer of confusion for me to wade through? The corner of his mouth tipped up, as if he enjoyed seeing the confusion and desire I was sure were plainly expressed in my features. "Have fun tonight. I'll be thinking of you."

"You too!" I zipped back down the hallway, wondering if there was dust flying up behind me. If I had stayed behind, I wasn't sure what my impulsive nature would get me into.

My phone chirped as I flopped onto my bed.

I expected to see another message from Arden. Instead, Edwin's name flashed on the screen. See you tonight!

I sighed, went into my room and picked through a pile of clothes. I needed to pick out my best wing woman costume.

14

The party was in full swing when I got there. The usually drab multipurpose room had undergone a makeover. Streamers hung everywhere, shaped into fun patterns that bordered on cheesy but weren't. Someone who had a deft hand with the scissors had made little paper-cut art that hung from the ceiling, held aloft by fishing string. Balloons swayed along the edges of the room like wallflowers who wanted to dance but were too scared to bust the moves they'd practiced in front of their mirrors. A song that was popular just before the Flare bumped through the loudspeakers, and I bounced along in time as I wound my way through the crowd.

Because there was only one class, us "freshmen," the staff was also invited. Even though there were lots of people I'd never seen before, the party space in the SAC was by no means crowded. There was a makeshift bar near the back where Larry, one of my co-workers on the maintenance crew, was bartending.

"Hey, Sing Seong!" He was the only person who called me this, and the only reason I allowed it was that I knew there was absolutely no ill will behind it. Larry was a nice guy, a real-life one; he was a little shorter than me, and a little rounder and way hairier. He always smiled at you like you were exactly the person he needed to see in that moment. Each encounter came with the little rush of happiness you got from making someone's day.

"Hey, Larry. How did you get stuck with bar duty?" I looked at the selection of drinks lined up, some alcoholic, some not.

"My wife, Nicole, is a manager here. I'm helping out since she was worried about people getting plastered and rowdy. You know how it is." In the aftermath of the Flare, a lot of people had turned to the bottle to help deal with their worlds crashing down around them. Gabriel once told me how Alcoholics Anonymous had become a mobilizing force in many post-Flare communities, as people searched for relief from their addiction and hope for the future. Sometimes surviving wasn't all it cracked up to be.

"Nicole is a lucky woman," I said, batting my lashes at Larry playfully. His cheeks went rosy, and I immediately dropped the flirty mode. I was having enough issues in the love department—I didn't need Nicole looking over and thinking I was trying to get a piece of her husband.

"What do you want to drink?" He waved his hand at the array of beverages in front of him. I gave a quick look around the room. Lots of people were drinking beers, even those who looked younger than me. Certain laws weren't being so strictly enforced. I wasn't a fan of beer, or drinking overall. I had wine or sake every now and then, but even small amounts left me with a headache and a raw stomach. The few times I'd gotten wasted after my blowout with Arden had left me feeling discombobulated for days.

"Maybe I'll just have a ginger ale for now," I said.

He raised his brows but didn't peer-pressure me. "If you want, and only if you want, you can try a nip of this moonshine. Nicole and I make it ourselves from her great-great-great-great-grandmother's speakeasy recipe."

"I'll have a little bit," I said, not because I felt forced but because who could turn down something that sounded as badass as speakeasy moonshine? He poured me the tiniest portion into a shot glass, just a taste, and pushed it over with a pleased look on his face. I drank it down and for a moment I was sure Larry had taken over the position at the bar because he was a serial killer hell-bent on poisoning everyone. Fire spread over my tongue and down my throat. My eyes watered and a cough was ripped out of me.

"Good, right?" He was nodding happily at my theatrics as if it was the reaction he was hoping for. Larry Romatowski, secret sadist.

A hand dropped into the space between my shoulder

blades, giving me a few light pats; I knew the warmth and the weight of it before I turned and coughed in Edwin's face. He waved a hand in front of his nose. "Hitting the hard stuff, Mags? The night's just begun."

"I tried a thimbleful of the Romatowski moonshine," I finally managed. "It's...potent."

"I can imagine," he said. His hand was still on my back. Every muscle in my body froze at the realization, and with the hope that if I didn't move, he would stay there. "I'll have a beer, Larry." He looked at me, his eyes crinkled at the corners from his smile. "It's brewed right here on campus. This last batch tastes way better than the first few. Or the time a rat fell into one of the vats and no one noticed."

"I'll take your word for it," I said, scrubbing at my tongue. "I'm hoping moonshine tastes stronger than it is."

"No. It's really strong," Larry said with pride.

"Aren't you supposed to be preventing people from getting plastered?" I asked.

He shrugged. "People who aren't my friends."

"Let's go take a walk around the room," Edwin said. His fingertips pressed into my lower back for a millisecond, and all the fire that had burned in my belly from the moonshine reignited.

It's going to be a long night.

"There's Danielle!" I hurried away from him and the

tactile pleasure he provided, taking a sip of my ginger ale before it could slosh over the edge. "You look amazing," I said as I got close enough to her that I wouldn't have to shout over the music. She wore a black scoop-neck dress with a flared skirt, cinched at the waist with a white belt. Her panda hat was still there and even though I was accepting of her quirk, I couldn't help but stare at it a bit longer than I should have.

"Thanks," she said. She gave Edwin a little wave with the hand that wasn't holding a beer, and smoothly segued in to meet his high five.

Edwin stood next to me and we all turned so we were facing the crowd. Some people had been there for a while, and Larry's moonshine—or just a desire to let loose—was driving them to the dance floor.

We spent much too long making fun of our teachers' dance moves, and then Danielle started making up background stories for people about what they'd done during the post-Flare years. "That woman lived in a cave with a bear," she said, pointing to Professor Grafton. "She didn't know the bear was there, but she needed to take shelter somewhere and he offered to let her stay, as long as she did his bidding. Eventually she killed the bear and made bear jerky out of him. When she finally emerged from the cave, she was strong from eating his flesh and warm from wearing his skin, and ready to start a new life."

My gaze immediately flew to her hat. When Edwin did the same, our eyes met, but Danielle was too busy smiling to herself.

A man and a woman jogged off the dance floor holding hands, both breathing heavily. "Are you guys having fun?" the woman asked, wiping the sweat from her temples. "I'm Candy, a manager here. This is our first big event, so if you can think of anything that can be done better, just let me know."

"The party is great!" I said. "I work at maintenance, and at the farm."

Candy and her dance partner exchanged a look, and he leaned closer to her. "I wonder if she's stuck working with that prick," he said. "Or maybe he already harassed them into changing his job again. Maybe he's a dean by now."

She rolled her eyes. "I wouldn't be surprised. Assholes always climb up the ladder faster than nice, normal people."

I wanted to ask if they were talking about Devon, but something stopped me. Maybe it was what I would do with the knowledge if they said yes. That would mean he'd bent the truth—lied—again. There was a sharp jolt in my stomach that had nothing to do with the liquid fire I'd swallowed earlier. My feet had carried me to Devon's room earlier, but they'd been acting under direct order from the part of my brain that still felt something for him, something that was in the gray area between love and betrayal.

Candy turned to Edwin, Danielle and me and made a shooing motion. "Go on and dance, guys!"

The hip-hop–infused pop song that we were all nodding to tapered off, and a faster-paced rhythm started, a salsa-inflected one backed by a booming bass line, maracas and the occasional blip of a police siren. Reggaeton, or the music that had taught me that my hips seemed to be missing a joint that allowed for pivoting in a certain way.

Edwin threw his head back and laughed as the first strains of the song pounded through the room. "I haven't heard this song in a *long* time." He lifted his beer in the air and began moving his waist in a way that shouldn't have been allowed, lest every woman in the room be drawn in by the hypnotic motion. His hips had not one but several extra pivot points, and I couldn't pull my eyes away from the fluid motion. I knew he wasn't *trying* to be sexual—he was just dancing—but the heat flared from my ears to my cheeks and spread southward as I imagined what other uses his magic hip thrusts could serve.

"Have you been hiding the fact that you were a back-up dancer in the *Step Up* movies?" I asked, and he laughed.

He took the last swig of his beer and tossed it into a recycling can, all without missing a beat. "Look, I'm not one for generalizations but...*yo soy Boricua*." He imbued the words with extra weight, as if explaining something to a child. "I'm from Williamsburg, and I'm not talking about the part of the neighborhood where you get artisanal coffee. I could meringue before I could walk. I was bacha-ta-ing like an old man while other kids were learning 'I'm a little teapot.' If the right salsa song comes on, I could spin you across the room and back before you knew what happened. And if you think I would only be a backup dancer in one of those movies, then I obviously need to practice." He held out his hand.

Oh shit. I found Edwin attractive when he was doing regular things like talking, hammering stuff and breathing. He'd never been this brazenly cocky before, even when he had reason to, and damn if I didn't like it. Not enough to humiliate myself by dancing with him, though. I tried to back away, only to be met with the wall at my back.

Edwin advanced, eyes flashing with mirth. "Is Little Miss Rock Star afraid of the dance floor?"

No, I'm afraid of you and your piston-fueled hips. I could belt out a song in front of anyone, but dancing made me feel naked. Everyone else on the dance floor looked so free, even if they weren't great dancers. Arms were being flung with abandon, and hips were being shaken. I could feel all the parts of me that were supposed to be loose stiffen at the thought of putting myself out there for everyone, Edwin especially, to see. The heavy dance beat was perfect four-four time, but my limbs wouldn't even respond to my pleas for a simple two-step.

"Why don't you dance with Danielle?" But when I looked to my side, she was gone, probably already foreseeing that I would try to pawn the dance off on her. I grasped at my last straw, even though it wasn't something I was excited about. "One of my floor mates wants to meet you, and she's hot. The girl with the braids under the disco ball. You can ask her."

He looked over at Niesha, who was dancing with her strawberry-blond friend and laughing. She was highlighted by a rain of silver sparkles of light reflecting off the ball above her. Her moves were graceful and confident—everything I wasn't feeling at the moment.

Edwin turned back to me and raised a brow. "I already have a hot girl in front of me. Why should I walk all the way across the dance floor?" His words shocked me enough that I stopped tensing against the wall, and he took advantage of the opportunity to pull me into the crowd.

He nestled us safely at the center of the crowd, where we were shielded from onlookers by a ring of partiers. One hand held mine, and his other rested on my hip. My body went hot at his touch, and I knew he could feel it. He began a simple two-step, although nothing about the way his hips flexed was simple. "Just follow me. If you let me lead, it'll be painless."

Oh my God. Why were we in a room full of people?

"Just relax, Mags. Yeah, like that. You see the way I'm moving?" Was he kidding me with that question? It was taking everything I had to look into his face. "I can only do that because I'm relaxed. Now, just swing your hips side to side...yeah, that's it."

He was trying to be helpful, but his coddling explanation rubbed against the flint of my competitiveness. It wasn't that I didn't know how to dance, and it wasn't that I didn't like it. I just didn't want to be seen while doing it. I moved awkwardly in his embrace, hating myself for not just letting loose. He didn't seem to mind my stiffness, but I was humiliated. The next song that came on was a popular meringue song that had been played at every school dance for as long as I could remember. Enough that I knew the words, or a reasonable facsimile of them.

"*Suavamente, besame,*" I sang along with the song, and with the singing came the release of tension in my body. Edwin sensed it, pulling me closer. Both of his hands slid to my waist and rested there, exerting the slightest pressure to direct me as we moved.

"Just move with me," he said in my ear, the low tone in his voice making me want to do exactly that. We were close enough that our bodies molded to each other, the expanse of his chest and stomach pressing into mine, making me thankful I'd gone with the padded bra that night. He slid a leg between mine, and with that and his hands I was forced to follow the movements of his body; my feet moved in time with his and my hips followed the same path, my pelvis chasing the circles and shifts his made to the best of my ability.

He made a sound of encouragement, but I was barely thinking about the dance anymore. It was hard to be stressed about keeping time when his muscular thigh was nudging against sensitive areas as we danced. The slide of his jeans against mine had the sensitive skin of my inner thighs buzzing with feeling and transmitting that pleasure up the seams of my pants and toward the junction that was growing embarrassingly damp. I wondered if he could feel my heart beating wildly and whether he would care that it wasn't the cardio that was driving up my heart rate, but being pressed up against him.

It didn't matter whether anyone thought I was moving the wrong way, because everything about moving with Edwin felt right. How he laughed and cracked flirty jokes as he spun me and pulled me close again. The way he sometimes threw in a particularly emphatic hip thrust that I knew was simply part of the dance but that elicited a responding pulse in my core every time.

By the end of a three-song set, we were both sweaty and tired but smiling like fools. "I haven't danced like that in a minute," he said as we stepped out of the now-stifling room to get some air.

We made our way out of the Student Center and sat on one of the picnic tables out front, taking a table that wasn't occupied by others also escaping the funk.

"That was fun," I said, feeling happiness bubbling at the back of my words and pushing them up to a higher register. "We used to have dance parties at home, but I don't think I've ever moved like that."

"There were always parties in my neighborhood," he said. "Probably too many." He chuckled in the way people did when remembering their misadventures. "They threw a party for me the last time I was home, over that Christmas break before the Flare. My mom and Claudio." He sat down on the bench and I sat down next to him. I leaned into him just a bit; people often needed that extra bit of support when launching into memories like this. I might have been sheltered, but even I knew that.

"Was it a Christmas party?" I asked.

"New Year's. They rented a hall and invited all our friends, and all my cousins and other family members. There were so many of us." He paused, and not by choice. He cleared his throat after a minute. "Mom was trying to hook me up with some girl who was visiting from PR, but I spent most of the time dancing with her and my brother. There was always a circle around us, and not because of me. Those two had so much life. They were magnetic."

A police car with siren flashing rushed by, momentarily distracting us. It was still a rare sight, like a unicorn galloping across campus, and everyone looked after it silently until the sound faded.

"Maybe they were magnetic because of you," I said when the sound had faded. "Two magnets that have the same polarity can't stick together on their own. Mykhail taught me that. They need something between them to hold them together."

He looked at me. His expression was drawn, but there were no tears in his eyes. "I think they'd be happy I was dancing again," was all he said. But he kept looking at me in the weird way he'd fallen into the habit of doing—right until the girl a table over started puking. None of her friends held her hair, and I felt sorry for her.

"Freaking moonshine," I muttered. I wondered what it

meant that Edwin had chosen me for his first dance partner, but shut that door of my ego quickly. Right now it was good to know that, metaphorically, if I was the one yakking, he would hold my hair, no questions asked. That would have to be enough for now.

15

The last weeks of September and first week of October were...pretty awesome. At the farm job, Devon and I were still in compost hell, but the work got easier and less vom-it-inducing as students and staff alike began to get the hang of composting and not just throwing their garbage away mindlessly. The fact that I would stop mid-conversation to loudly shame people in the dining hall probably helped spread the word. Or perhaps it was the cute and amazingly rendered posters Danielle drew and hung at each trash can station. I held only a middling interest in comic books and that world, but even I was captivated by her work. She had to keep replacing posters as people stole them to hang in their dorm rooms. She took it all in stride, as she did with seemingly everything.

"If I can contribute to every inch of these ugly dorm

walls being covered, it would be my pleasure," she'd said with an exaggerated shudder.

At my maintenance job, the tool belt Edwin had bequeathed to me gave me the confidence to push to do some real work besides reading at my desk, and Joe finally assigned me to a job replacing the floors in a faculty house that had been destroyed by the bursting and thawing of pipes over the last couple of years. I wasn't surprised he'd assigned me to the same team as Edwin and Felix, in addition to three other people I knew in passing, but I was shocked at how fun it was. I was no stranger to the kind of work we were doing, but doing the same things with my parents had been stressful. My dad was chill—as long as you did everything exactly the way he wanted it. I appreciated the results of his perfectionism, but helping him achieve it was another thing entirely. People often thought Gabriel had inherited his exactitude from my mom, but underneath her prodding she was easygoing. It was Dad who lured you in with that twinkle in his eye and then disowned you for not placing nails exactly two inches apart down the entire length of a two-by-four.

Working with Edwin was different. He would tell me how he wanted the floorboards laid out, show me once and then go about his business. He didn't hover, simply trusted me to get the job done. Perhaps more than he should have, since I had to rip up a board or two, but making mistakes without disappointing him meant I could focus on what I did wrong and how not to repeat the mistake instead of fuming over being yelled at. And on the job, with his fellow contractors, he was in his element. He'd never been shy, but my family was hard to outshine, as I knew all too well. Here, he was the lead contractor, and he took his leadership responsibilities seriously, including making sure his team had fun while they worked.

"Larry, you just flashed me more ass than I've seen in a year. While I appreciate it, maybe try a belt tomorrow?" With the project almost wrapped up, everyone was in a playful mood.

I laughed as I hammered away, ignoring the way my ears homed in on his words like satellites picking up transmissions. I stopped myself before I wondered aloud exactly whose ass he'd seen in the last year. It was none of my business.

"Come on, Edwin, don't play like you're some innocent." Dina was a mom of twins who'd worked at the school before the Flare and had come back when the school reopened. Her kids were finishing up a high school program, but they had spots reserved for them, thanks to their mom. "I've seen the way half the women here look at you. I'm sure it's not for want of a willing partner that you've gone so long without. If you're even telling the truth."

She put her hammer down to retie the bandanna she wore to hold her hair back. She rocked a different color every day, depending on her mood. Today's was bright red.

Edwin smiled as the rest of our crew joined in on the ribbing, but there were no telltale crinkles at the corners of his eyes and he kicked over a box of nails in an uncharacteristically ungainly move, sending the little metal divots flying. "Shit." He shook his head and bent to scoop them up, and I headed over to help.

"I got it," he said, not looking up at me.

"Don't tell me you're a virgin, man," Larry said, seeking good-natured revenge for the crack about his crack.

I froze. The thought had never occurred to me. I'd worked him up to be some sex god in my mind, but what if he was in the same boat as me? Maybe he'd just been embarrassed when I'd thrown myself at him.

The husky laugh he let out at Larry's words disabused me of that notion. There was some knowledge amplified by the rough timbre of his voice that couldn't be faked. I remembered how his hips had moved in sync with mine as we'd danced—I'd thought of that way too much lately.

"There's nothing wrong with being a virgin," Edwin said. That let me know for sure that he wasn't one. I felt my cheeks heat up and dropped the nails I'd collected into his hand without saying a word. I knew he was saying those words for my benefit, and a humiliation I hadn't felt in weeks reared its annoying head. "People experience things at different times, when it's right for them."

His words were met by confusion, except by me, the person they were meant for.

"Do you mind if I cut out early?" I managed to choke out. "I have to meet Devon. We're working on a song, and I wanted to catch him before he has his environmental group meeting."

"Who is Devon?" Felix asked, at the same time Edwin said, "But we're celebrating the end of the project tonight. Larry made his special chili and everything."

Larry nodded ruefully. "It's been cooking all day. It'll be at peak spiciness by the time we get to my house."

Shit. I'd forgotten that we were supposed to go to Larry's place. But the longer I stood there, the more foolish I felt, and when I felt foolish I said the first thing that came to mind. "I would love to taste your chili, but speaking of virginity—"

Edwin stood quickly. "Yeah, maybe you should go. I'll walk you out to sign your time sheet."

The conversation picked up as we left the room, and as soon as we were out of earshot Edwin stopped and stepped in front of me. It wasn't a threatening motion, but it showed that he wanted to talk whether I was in the mood to or not. He didn't usually use his size as a factor in our interactions, and it freaked me out a little bit. "So, you and this guy are an item now?"

I didn't understand why he'd be bothered by it if we were. In that moment, I realized how much I'd come to depend on Edwin's solidness. Now that things were just the slightest bit off with him, the reality of how horrible it could be if everything went wrong between us hit home. I didn't want him to be mad at me, but I didn't understand why he was staring at me like I'd done something wrong.

"No. Maybe. I don't know," I said, and it was true. I was still upset about how Devon had lied. I couldn't trust him. Even though we hadn't gone any further than that first kiss, I felt something for him that didn't feel quite like friendship. Something enough that it was weird for me to talk to Edwin about it. "We're just hanging out right now."

Most nights at the dorm, and at work too. And unlike you, he's told me flat-out that he likes me.

Edwin nodded. "Okay. Maggie, I don't want to be that guy—"

My heart gave a huge, heavy thud in my chest. *That guy who changes his mind about the girl crushing on him as soon as she finds a boyfriend?* Part of me was really rooting for Edwin to be a fickle asshole.

"—who interrogates his friend about her love life." Oh. I snapped my gaze up to his and tried not to show my disappointment. "And I know I even told you to give Devon a chance before. It's just, I think something might be up with him. Think about what a dick he was to you before he realized who you were. How mean he was to Danielle."

I raised my hand. "I was way meaner to Danielle than he was."

"He lied to you about the foundation of your previous relationship, the one you're using to justify whatever thing you have going on with him now." He looked like he knew he'd said the wrong thing as soon as the words were out of his mouth.

"Justify? Excuse me, who exactly would I be justifying my relationships to?" My voice went all hoarse and adolescent boy, the way it did when I was really feeling my indig-nation. "In case you were wondering, you're totally being *that guy* right now. Maybe you should worry about your own dating situation if things are getting so bad that Larry's plumber's crack is a distraction for you."

His mouth tightened, and I had my answer to my question from a few weeks back—his dimples were even deeper when he was mad, like some weird evolutionarily designed trap. "You can do whatever you want with whoev-er you want, but you're my friend, and I want you going in with all the available information. Devon is hanging out with a bad crowd."

I didn't understand. "The only people Devon hangs out with besides me are the hippies from his grown-up 4-H club. They talk about using algae as light sources and call that a good time." I was defending Devon, but every time he'd mentioned his friends I'd gotten a weird vibe. I didn't know why I was being contrary when all Edwin was doing was trying to look out for me. Maybe because I wished his interest in my love life wasn't confined to making me feel stupid about my decisions. He never meant to, of course, but that didn't change the humiliation of him thinking I was gullible enough to be duped by Devon twice.

He closed his eyes as if reining in his annoyance—it was a look I'd seen on my family members' faces often over the years. "Hippies used to be considered public ene-mies, you know," he said.

"Thanks for the history lesson. Are you done, or do

you need me to adjust your tinfoil hat for you?"

"Maggie." He sighed. "Just be careful you don't get mixed up in something without realizing it."

"Sheesh, way to have faith in my discernment."

"I have faith in your ability to forgive people. Even those who don't deserve it. I don't want that to bite you in your ass." I'd catalogued all of the ways Edwin looked at me, and right then, I was expecting "my friend's lil sis is annoying me." Instead, he was staring at me with an intensity that didn't make sense and that I couldn't classify. I wished I had some kind of emotional Shazam app, like the one that could identify songs for you with just a few bars of music. "You can be pissed off at me," he said. "Just be careful."

"Maggie!" Devon's perfect voice penetrated the little bubble that had enclosed Edwin and me during our argument, reminding me that we were in public. He loped up to the front door of the building, his cheeks ruddy from jogging in the cool autumn air. "I have great news—we have our first gig!"

Edwin's warning still rang in my ears, but I couldn't help the delight that burst in me. Devon had mentioned trying to book a show, and it looked like he'd managed to set up our first college engagement. "Really?"

"Come on, walk me to my meeting and I'll tell you about it." He spoke to me as if Edwin wasn't there, which reminded me that he was. I turned to Edwin but couldn't meet his eyes after regressing to the brattiness I'd been trying to break myself of. Being able to differentiate between me feeling dumb and someone thinking I was needed to happen sooner rather than later. I gave Edwin a quick hug. "I gotta go. But I heard you. I'll be careful."

He nodded and walked off; it seemed he was in agreement with Devon that they should pretend the other didn't exist. They were never in the same place at once, actually. That accounted for why I'd unconsciously started thinking of my days as split between Devon time and Edwin time. I pushed that troubling thought out of my mind. It was always Maggie time, and it was best I remembered that. Edwin had warned me about Devon, but he didn't know he was dangerous for me too, in a way.

When I walked up to Devon, he threw his arm around my shoulder. It felt cool, but unnatural, like a popped collar. I shifted, trying to get comfortable with his touch and wondering if being comfortable with him should require so much thought.

"Are you ready to become the most famous girl at the university?" he asked. His arm cinched tighter around me. His behavior felt more like territorial pissing than a display of affection.

"I don't know if I'm ready for that," I deadpanned. "Being mobbed by tens of people might be too much for my shy nature."

"You can't stop the inevitable, Maggie." His words felt weighted, like his arm as it pulled me close. "We've got big things ahead."

16

"Stop twitching your eye." Danielle hovered in front of me, wielding her mascara wand.

"I *can't*. I'm not doing it on purpose." I squeezed my eyes shut, but as soon as she got close to my lashes, my body's defense mechanism alerted me to impending danger. My eye twitched again.

"You're going to show up at your first gig with one eye missing if you keep this up." I felt the brush glide across my lashes as she spoke, meaning her reflexes had been faster than mine. She jabbed at the other set of lashes and when I opened my eyes, she was smiling at me. "Perfect."

I doubted I looked as good as she did, her signature panda hat accented by a black dress and knee-high boots, but I jumped in front of the mirror to see what she'd done.

"Dani! Thank you! This looks amazing!" She'd given me a dramatic smoky eye using shimmery black eye shadow. Blue liner at the inner corners and on my lower lash line made the look pop and accented my slouchy blue tee and tight black jeans perfectly. I rubbed gel in my hair and scrubbed my hands through it so my hair spiked out in all directions. After throwing on my heeled booties, I was ready for Devon's and my debut. As a band, although I was worried that he was hoping this led to something more. The performance was at the off-campus house where several members of Devon's club lived, and he was a bit too excited to introduce me to his friends.

There was a knock at the door, and I opened my mouth to say "give me a minute," but Devon was already walking in. He stopped in his tracks when he saw me. "Erk." His eyes went wide and his gaze traveled over my body like he was taking notes for later.

I knew what it meant for a guy to look at you like that, and my libido appreciated it, but I still wasn't sure if I was ready for anything more than a duet with Devon. The whole situation would have been much easier if we'd been total strangers, but life couldn't be that simple.

"You do good work, Danielle," I said, glancing over at her. She often clammed up when Devon came around— not being cold, but not being herself the way she was when we hung out with Edwin. I'd asked her if Devon bothered her in any way, and she said he'd apologized for being a dick that first day. She was too excited on our behalf to rein in her demeanor.

"I'm the daughter of engineers. Precision is in my genes." She turned and began gathering up all the little pots of makeup and brushes she'd scattered over my bed.

"Well, thanks to your parents too, then," I said.

She slid past Devon as he walked over to me, carrying an armload of stuff to the tackle box that served as her makeup storage and kneeling down to return everything to its rightful place, leaving me with Devon and his anxious glances.

He was as handsome as I'd ever seen him. He'd gotten the hair product memo and had done something to his usually shaggy locks that gave them a perfectly mussed style. His tan had faded weeks ago, but the olive shirt he was wearing complemented his eyes and sandy hair, giving him the appearance of a golden glow.

"You clean up well," I said with a grin. I felt just the smallest tremor of something more as he gazed down at me with unvarnished interest in his eyes. He stared into my eyes, but the intensity wasn't attractive, like it was with Edwin. It was insistent, like he was trying to force me to acknowledge the feelings he had been hinting at over the last few weeks. I wished I wasn't so ambivalent, but I wasn't sure whether the guy I'd cared so much about was real, or even if he ever had been. That doubt alone should have meant case closed, but communications between the brain and the heart weren't always that clear-cut.

I know you're just being a tease. A voice from the past that I never wanted to hear again.

"You're always beautiful," Devon said, his voice drowning out the ugly echo of my memory.

I'd read about crooked smiles and wondered what was so endearing about them; the one Devon gave me now illustrated what the big deal was clearly. The way just one side of his mouth tilted up rendered him more vulnerable somehow, as if he didn't dare hope for enough happiness to commit to the full motion.

His hand smoothed down over the spiky hair I'd just worked hard to arrange.

"Knock it off!" I said with a laugh as I ducked from under his hand.

"You're not escaping that easily," he said in a low voice, and then he pulled me into an embrace. I froze. Devon touched me all the time, but not like this. Sometimes he was a bit too familiar for my liking, but there was always room for doubt, to tell myself that we were still friends getting reacquainted. Right now there was no doubt of what he wanted, though.

I should have wanted to sink into his touch—and part of me did—but the bigger part of me was fighting the instinct to shrug him off and break free. I told myself it was because I didn't want to make Danielle uncomfortable, but I wasn't ready for him to touch me with such easy familiarity, especially after the memory that had just shouldered its way past my defenses.

His smile might have been charming, but I couldn't

risk more with him. Not when he knew so much of the truth about me and I still hadn't completely untangled fact from fiction for him. Not when his nearness had brought me back to my most helpless moment.

I held my face away from him, trying to preserve my makeup, and when I looked at him he was already waiting to meet my gaze.

Isn't this what you wanted? my libido demanded, but annoyance trailed that thought like tissue stuck to the bottom of your fuck-me heels, ruining the fantasy. Devon had once said he'd learned to get people to like him in five languages. That took a lot of work. A lot of ego. As the green of his irises receded and his pupils widened, I wondered how much of his desire for me was fueled by the fact that I held him at arm's length. There was a difference between challenging someone and being a challenge for them, and I didn't want to be the latter.

Danielle's hand landed on my shoulder. "Do you have a thicker coat than that, Marge? Unless you plan on letting Devon button you up in his pea coat and carry you there." I didn't know if she could sense my discomfort or if this was her way of turning the hose on us, but I was grateful for the disruption.

"Marge?" I scoffed, pulling away from Devon and heading toward my closet to layer on a thick hoodie and John's blazer, topped with a long wool scarf that could make up for the warmth I'd lost when I cut my hair.

"I think Marge suits you better than Maggie. It's like

one of those tall tales. 'Large Marge Seong with a voice so strong they could hear her in outer space.'" I laughed, and she pulled on her coat and burled out another one. "Large Marge Seong, who could fell trees with her mighty guitar. She crushed undeserving men beneath her heels and used their femurs to stir her morning coffee." She didn't look at Devon, so I wasn't sure if it was a jab at him or just her imagination getting away from her again.

He glanced at his watch. "We should go. Greg doesn't like it when people are late."

I scoffed, feeling the familiar annoyance with the way he acted as if this Greg guy was the boss of anyone, especially me. "Is Greg paying us for this gig? If not, he can wait for Danielle to zip up her coat."

The look of adoration faded from Devon's face and he shook his head. "He's paying with exposure, like how we pay for school by digging through trash. That doesn't mean you can show up for class anytime you want, does it?"

"I'm ready. Let's just go," Danielle said. She plucked at the frayed string hanging from her hat. I wondered how someone so conflict-averse put up with me on a daily basis.

"Alright, let's do this," I said, trying to be civil. There was no reason to argue, anyway. I had no say in who Devon looked up to, and acting like I did would only give him ideas. "We have to walk in the cold or wait for the campus van in the cold. Both require us to freeze our asses off, so we might as well get it over with."

We hurried out of the dorm, and the frigid gust of wind that smacked me in the face almost knocked me over. I couldn't believe we had to walk a mile in this weather and enviously eyed the vintage muscle car parked in front of our building. I needed to befriend some of the rich kids in my dorm.

The jingle of keys grabbed my attention; Devon walked over to the car and opened the door, as if that was normal. "Or we can ride there in style." He was so full of pride that I wondered if he even remembered all of the lies he'd told me.

"This is your car?" I couldn't keep the accusation out of my voice. Devon had said his family didn't have money back when we used to talk, and he'd commiserated with me about having to learn to drive in my parents' old van, as if he had a shitty car too. Even when he'd revealed his parents were diplomats, I hadn't thought otherwise about that. It wasn't as if working for the government meant you were rolling in dough.

Maybe it was a gift. Maybe he found it. Maybe it was a labor of love that had been restored from a cheap piece of crap.

"Old cars are really the only thing available now," he said, immediately going into defensive mode. The smile had dropped from his face and he looked annoyed, as if I was the one who'd done something wrong. "Okay, so my family had more money than I let on before the Flare. That doesn't matter now, does it? I dig through just as much garbage as you do at the farm." His chest heaved and a stream of condensed air huffed from his nose. "It's too cold to stand around fighting. Driving us over was supposed to be a nice surprise."

In my mind, a series of connections were being made, past and present and future, making me feel unstuck in time. I recalled one of our past conversations. I'd complained about how it sucked not being as rich as everyone else, how I hated when classmates came into my parents' store when I was behind the register. He had agreed, telling me how he'd been picked on for being poor. That couldn't have been true. I realized now that he carefully avoided talking about the government-run shelter he'd been taken to because of his dad's status, how when I brought up bad things that had happened after the Flare, he empathized but shared nothing. A relationship with Devon would always be hydroplaning on a thin level of mistrust, and I'd always have to be prepared for the inevitable spinout.

"You getting in or what?" He was mad, but also a little scared, like he knew how close I was to walking away. *Why can't you just be normal?* I wanted to scream at him. I wanted to tell him to fuck off and grow the fuck up and other important things that relied on the f-word. But I also wanted to play. If George could put up with John and Paul, and Zayn could put up with Harry and Co., I could also deal with an unstable asshole of a musical partner for the night. I wasn't about to blow off what might be my only gig because he had a problem with telling the truth. That would be unprofessional.

I looked over at Danielle, who was shivering, despite her warm winter jacket.

"Can't keep our adoring fans waiting," I said. I climbed in and settled my guitar between my legs. Danielle clambered in the back, and when I glanced back she was carefully pulling her hat down on her head.

The car started with a rumble, and we slowly pulled off.

"We're gonna have fun," Devon said, as if he could command it. I hoped he was right.

17

We drove past the section of town that had been cleared for "rejuvenation," which sounded like something out of a sci-fi film, and into the restricted area. Here, the buildings didn't have to live up to even the most basic of health and safety codes. The stretched-thin police force didn't come to this part of town unless there was good reason; it was the one place John had tried to pull big brother rank on me and forbidden me to go.

Something hit me then that had been lost in my excitement to perform and the willful ignorance I'd been participating in when it came to Devon. "Most students aren't going to travel all the way out here."

Devon scoffed. "Their loss, then. We're still in town, just not the part some government organization has deemed safe. This is what the world is like in most places right now, and if students can't deal with that that, they're gonna have a hard time after graduation. Everything isn't as safe and sanitized as government incorporated would have you think."

"Should we go back?" Danielle's voice sounded hollow from the backseat, even though she was only inches away. When I turned to look at her, she was plucking at a frayed area on her hat.

My eagerness to play in spite of Devon's shortcomings as human being was fading by the moment, and I refused to force her to be any place she didn't want to be. "We can go back if you want to," I said.

Devon glanced at her in the rearview. "How are you gonna do that without a car? Call one of your imaginary cartoon creatures to give you a ride? Because we have someplace to be, and I'm not turning around to take you back."

I'd been ignoring the niggling thoughts that told me something wasn't quite right, but his words sent a different kind of feeling through me now—déjà vu. My breathing went wonky and sweat broke out on my scalp. I was in a car with a guy who was being an ass and could quickly become much worse. Again. My hands balled into fists. Danielle picked up on my apprehension, and her scared look matched what I was feeling. She was here because of me, and I couldn't slide into the panic that was threatening to pull me under.

I channeled that fear into anger.

"News flash, Devon. We're going to some shitty house that's probably condemned, not the Rose Bowl. You're being a dick right now, and for no reason."

"I'm being a guy who's pissed off after waiting for you to make the final song selection for tonight's set. For you to get your makeup done. For you to acknowledge me in the cafeteria, or not, or to only remember that I was your first love when it's beneficial to you. I'm tired of waiting for—" He jerked to a stop behind a group of cars that were clustered in front of a house with warped aluminum siding. His voice was strained when he spoke. "I'm tired of waiting for your forgiveness."

"You're gonna do this right here? Really?" Anger gathered under my skin, raising my temperature and making the several layers I was wearing suddenly too much. "Let me remind you of something—you're not the victim here. You're the one who lied to me, several times over. And now you want to act like you're the injured party, even though I've done nothing but treat you like a friend?"

He turned to me and the anger on his face was startling. "We're supposed to be more than friends." His words came out low and dark, so unexpected that I cringed away from them. There was a sudden rustling in the backseat, then a cool breeze and a loud slam as Danielle made her escape. The biting night air she let in cooled my skin and cleared my head a bit. There was too much going on in that moment, and Edwin's warning about Devon echoed in my head.

"If we were really more than friends, you would

know I don't owe you a damn thing," I said. "And even if things did work how you think they should, nothing you've done thus far has earned you enough brownie points for forgiveness. I bet it never even occurred to you to just be a good person and see what happens." I eased my door open and clambered out, pulling my guitar case onto my back as I stood.

Danielle was a few feet away, picking at her cuticles. She bit her lip and then spit out what she was going to say. "Maggie, I know you're excited to play, but I don't think you should go to this party. It's not okay for him to talk to you like that."

I slid my arm through hers. I was freaked out too, but I had to keep cool, for her. "He's just being a jerk."

She shook her head. "I couldn't stay in the car. It was like being back with my uncle, after the Flare. He would get so mad at me for everything."

She pressed her lips together as if trying to prevent emotions, or more words, from escaping, and I wanted to clutch her close and tell her she could confide in me. But not there, with Devon climbing out of the car with a sullen expression on his face. Not with a group of his eco club friends approaching with bottles of beers and goofy smiles on their faces.

"If you want to go, just say the word." I spoke quietly, as if we were being surrounded by jackals instead of people who were supposed to be friends. Maybe that should have been my cue to leave, but she shook her head.

"We need a ride back. Staying here is better than walking through this part of town."

I often thought of her as flighty because of her age and her predilection for all things cute, but she was good at making quick assessments.

"There is an option three, in which I hot-wire a car and we drive ourselves back," I said. "My father taught me how, in case I was ever in a dodgy situation." The wire cutters I kept for replacing guitar strings served a dual purpose.

That got a small laugh out of her. "Of course you can hot-wire a car. Let's just get through the next couple of hours. I'm fine. Are you? I meant what I said—he's usually nice to you, but the way he's acting tonight isn't okay."

I watched Devon from the corner of my eye as she spoke. He plastered a smile on his face as he greeted his friends with fist bumps and handshakes. If I hadn't been in the car, I wouldn't have known that he was pissed off. There was something frightening about the fact that he could hide the emotion that had flared in the car so easily.

"Is your girl ready to go?" The question came from a guy with long, thin black hair. He wore faded black jeans and a stained white T-shirt with the word *Obey* scrawled across it in marker. He had to be in his mid-thirties, not ancient or anything, but years older than everyone else at the party.

I hadn't met him before, but something about him wound a spring inside of me that was ready to snap when he did something to provoke me. *When*, because he had the smarmy look of a guy who was just waiting to push your button. Even an apocalypse couldn't adjust that personality type.

He looked me up and down slowly and gave me a deliberate smirk. "You didn't mention your girl was super hot, Dev." It was like he could sense that I didn't like him and he was poking and prodding for a reaction. Worse, he was speaking of me like Devon and I really were a couple...

My gaze flew to Devon, and he no longer looked like the carefree guy hanging with his bros. He was doing that hunched-shoulder thing, like a puppy did when it expected to be kicked. No wonder he'd been so upset with me. He'd had it all planned out—I'd forgive him, we'd hook up and I wouldn't have to know he'd told these guys we were dating when we weren't, and vice versa. It occurred to me that with just a few words, I could ruin his cred with these people. I wanted to give a shrill whistle and, once I had everyone's attention, point out what a lying creep he was.

I was an inhale away from doing it when I managed to implement some of the impulse control I'd been working on. While humiliating him would be satisfying in the short term, it could also screw me and Danielle over. Like she said, he was our ride back. I had nothing to hold over him if I embarrassed him this early in the night, and he could easily ditch us, or worse. Given his earlier mood swing, I thought it best to save any petty acts of vengeance until we were back within the safety zone of the university.

"'Your girl' is a very pretty name, but mine is Maggie, actually." I squinched my face into a bright smile and held out my hand to Greg. He made a derisive little sound and gave a limp handshake that managed to be both hot and clammy at the same time. He gave my hand a tug in his direction before he let go, so I was already stepping in his wake as he turned toward the house, a petty display of dominance that threw me off-kilter for a second.

Devon is hanging out with a bad crowd. Edwin's words piped up again. I wished I'd listened then, but doing things right the first time around didn't seem to be how I operated.

"It's show time," Greg called as he walked through the metal cellar doors. Dozens of faces stared up at me through the opening.

"The show must go on," I muttered as I followed him down below.

18

We shuffled in behind him into a crowded, low-ceilinged basement and were immediately shoved toward a stage. Well, four palettes tied together with rope. It looked like these people needed my contracting skills more than they needed a singer, but the palettes were only slightly wobbly, so they'd serve their purpose.

I turned down the offer of a beer, and then a shot of moonshine that was thrust at me in its place. Unlike a real rock star, I didn't have an entourage to make sure I got home in one piece and I certainly couldn't rely on Devon for that. I put my guitar down and scanned the crowd milling around the cramped room. Danielle had rooted herself in a corner at the bottom of the stairs. I tried to catch her eye, but one of the girls from the club walked over and started chatting with her. She smiled and launched into conversation, and I gave a sigh of relief. I owed her big-time.

"Thanks," Devon said as I unzipped my guitar case. "I didn't tell them we were dating or anything, by the way. People just assumed…"

"And you didn't correct them." I began tuning, trying to feel the thrum that let me know I was hitting the right note, since dozens of conversations were drowning out sound. I focused on that instead of the anger that built up in my head like a sinus headache.

He looked away, and the anger was replaced by an unexpected sadness. Not for him—for the boy I'd thought he was. For the friends we could have been.

"Look, let's just get this show over with, okay? We have a captive audience." I didn't add that our first gig was going to be our last, although if he had any sense at all he could've guessed that. Maybe I should've left without even playing, but the music was calling to me as I began strumming chords, and I wasn't going to let an entitled jerk who thought he deserved a cookie, *my* cookie, for pretending to be nice take that away from me. Our friendship had turned out to be a farce, but the music was still real.

I'd been dampening the sound of the guitar, but I removed my fingers from the strings and played a loud chord that got everyone's attention. All eyes were on me, and suddenly nothing else mattered but making music and getting these people to feel it as much as I did. I gave Devon a look, counted off and began playing, starting off with an oldie but a goodie that would draw everyone in. "Today is gonna be the day," our voices launched into "Wonderwall" in unison, the notes threading through each other in perfect alignment as they spread out over the crowd like a fisherman's net. As the song progressed, the talk died down and the crowd began to push in toward us. The net was closed—they were ours for the rest of the night.

The next hour passed in a flash. My mouth hurt from opening wide against a smile to push the words out to the farthest edge of the basement. My fingers buzzed from being bashed against the strings as I tried to draw the most sound from my acoustic. My entire body thrummed from the noise and the unseeable but relentless pulse generated by the crowd's enthusiasm. The anger and betrayal I felt were exorcised through my fingers and vocal cords, my endorphins pushing away the hurt. When we finished our last song, a cover of The Doors' "Whiskey Bar" that I'd stolen from Arden's repertoire, I felt as drunk as the song's protagonist.

I let out a loud *whoop* and fought against the urge to slam my guitar to the floor, like I'd seen in old concert footage. I jumped up and down instead, considering playing just one more song, my mind searching its mental jukebox for something that would leave the crowd even more crazed. I stopped myself; it was better to leave them wanting more. The urge to do *something* was strong, though, and I wasn't the only one feeling it—I had just high-fived a girl in the crowd when I felt something snag me from behind. When I turned, Devon's mouth was descending toward mine, his eyes intense with longing. He pulled me into a kiss, right there on the stage.

The audience loved it, urging him on with hoots of encouragement, but his mouth against mine snuffed out the jangly energy left over from our set.

I pushed him away, this time not caring about whether it made him look bad in front of his friends. To drag me into a kiss in front of a bunch of people seemed like yet another manipulation. I stumbled back, immediately turning away to search the room for Danielle. The space at the bottom of the stairs where she'd glued herself earlier was empty. I pushed through the crowd, clutching my guitar to my chest to shield it from the sweaty bodies that might crush it.

"Where's Danielle?" I asked the girl I'd seen her talking to.

She blinked a few times, eyes glazed and smile slow. "She started freaking out in here when the crowd was pushing, so Greg gave her something to help her relax and took her outside for some air."

Relax? Fuck. My stomach churned with worry and I let the recriminations begin. I should have left before the gig, when I first got the weird, sticky feeling in the pit of my belly that signaled something was amiss. At the very least, I should have kept an eye on her throughout the show. My fears for Danielle propelled me through the people blocking the stairwell like twigs in a drainpipe. It was only when the cold night air ripped through my sweat-soaked T-shirt that I realized my jacket and scarf were in my guitar case, still downstairs. It didn't matter. Danielle had come to this party for me, and I had to find her.

I heard a man's laughter and turned to find Greg clutching a barely standing Danielle to his side. The panda hat was twisted pitifully to the side, seeming to give me an imploring look as her head lolled. The way Greg's hand was planted on her hip sickened me, because in that moment I realized it was the first time I'd seen anyone touch Danielle. Earlier that night when I'd linked arms with her was the first time *I'd* touched her for a prolonged period of time.

"Tell us more about these cartoon cats that fight crime. They're fascinating." Greg pulled a face at the guys next to him, and all the muscles in my neck and back tensed in anger. Copping a feel off a passed-out woman was bad enough, but managing to be a condescending prick to her while doing so was a new height of assholery.

His thumb moved over the thin curve of her hip, and all of the grown-up impulse control I'd been working on flew out the window. I didn't think. I barreled forward and pulled her away from him, gathering her weight against me. I thought I would spin and walk off, but her body jolted in a sickening way; Greg had her by the wrist, his mouth was twisted in a smirk. If my hands weren't full of passed-out Danielle and guitar, I could have destroyed him for that ugly curl of his lips alone.

"I believe the phrase is 'thank you,'" he said. His thumb was rubbing again, over the inside of her wrist. I refrained from tugging her because I didn't want to hurt her—I could only hope she hadn't already been.

Fuck. Please let nothing have happened. Please.

"Let go of her. And tell me what you gave her to get her like this. Are roofies considered environmentally friendly?" The words came out at a near shout, propelled by my anger as the full extent of what could have happened to her hit me. The groups of people scattered around the house looked our way with interest, sharks scenting blood in the water.

Greg's gaze narrowed. "I didn't roofie her." His voice was just as loud, making me realize I'd called him out on his own turf in a dangerous part of town. "Maybe next time don't bring someone who starts freaking out just because things get a little tight. That's what happens at a party, so I don't know what she was expecting." I thought about Danielle's frightened cat drawing. "I gave her something to help her chill out, and I guess it made her a little sleepy. Don't worry, it's all natural, grown right on the farm where you work three days a week. When you're not working with the maintenance crew or sleeping in Campbell Hall. Ground-floor dorm rooms must get a little scary sometimes, huh?"

I was suddenly plunged into waters way over my head. Greg was obviously threatening me by dropping this detailed information about me, but why? Just because I was trying to take care of my friend? Even scarier was the likely source of his info.

Devon.

I wanted to shout *fuck you*. I wanted to hurt him, like my mom or Arden would have. But I was just Maggie, and as I'd learned on more than one occasion, trying to be brave or adventurous usually ended up biting me in the ass. I stood there seething, tears of frustration filling my eyes.

Greg scoffed. "Get the fuck out of here. And don't even think about trying to tell people I drugged this bitch. I don't like attention, Margaret Seong, and you don't want to be on the receiving end of mine." I'd thought he was full of shit, his demeanor a parody of the bad boy every girl was supposed to love, but the look on his face frightened me. He was still a joke, but a guy with something to prove was often more dangerous than anyone.

I hobbled away, struggling to maintain my grip on Danielle and my guitar. None of the people standing around offered to help. Greg had made it clear that I was not one of them, and they treated me as such. Danielle shifted against my side, and her eyes fluttered open to thin slits. "Large Marge, you saved me," she whispered before going slack again. I felt the tears well up again. Saved her? I'd gotten her into this mess.

With a pang of regret, I let my guitar drop gently to the ground, then hauled her up into a more manageable position.

I realized that we had no ride—I couldn't trust Devon after what Greg had just threatened me with—and I'd left my wire cutter along with the rest of my stuff. There would be no hot-wiring high jinks to save the day. The thought of dragging Danielle through a dangerous part of town made me want to vomit. I didn't know what else to do, though.

A familiar voice in front of me rang out as I started to walk away from my precious guitar and into what could be the worst night of my life.

"Your first gig, and I had to find out through a third party?" I'd thought Devon had a great voice, but in that moment Edwin's playful tone was the most beautiful thing I'd ever heard. "Not cool, Maggie. I think you're letting your celebrity go to your head."

My heart filled with an emotion that it was too small to accommodate, a burst of happiness that could have passed for angina. I was happy for the pain because it was prompted by Edwin's presence, and that meant Danielle and I were safe now.

He gently gathered Danielle's weight from my side and waited as I walked back and picked up my guitar. I thought he would say something to Greg and his acolytes, who watched with blank expressions, but he didn't look at them at all. Simply turned and started heading in the opposite direction of the group. I followed him.

As we moved away, a beer bottle landed by my foot and smashed against the broken-up concrete that was common in this part of town. I jumped, and hated myself for it, but Edwin kept walking.

"Anything else comes flying this way, and I'll break

your fucking necks one by one." His voice was as calm as when he'd greeted me, which made the threat that much creepier.

Nothing else was thrown in our direction.

"Pikachu sent me a text earlier saying you and Devon were fighting and she was worried about you. The network has been acting up, though, so I didn't get it until a little bit ago."

God. Danielle had been worried about me, and I'd stopped paying attention to her as soon as I got the crowd's attention. She'd certainly scored in the shitty friend department.

Edwin's truck was parked just around the corner. He loaded Danielle into the back and went to slam the door, but I stopped him before he did. With shaking hands, I pushed her jacket aside and gave her clothes a cursory check. Her jeans were buttoned and zipped, and her hat was the only thing askew. I pulled it down and straightened it.

"I don't think anything happened." My voice sounded weird and my hands were shaking as I tucked Danielle's jacket around her. An arm went around my shoulder—Edwin's arm—and there was no wondering whether or not it felt right, no moment of ambivalence like I'd always experienced with Devon. I leaned into him and tried to block out all the horrifying thoughts that had played out in my imagination when I'd seen Danielle out of it and surrounded by a group of strange men. "Anything could have happened to her. Anything. And it would have been my fault."

Edwin's warmth ensconced me from both sides now as he pulled me into his embrace. This wasn't like the fleeting hugs he used to give me when visiting my family; there was a tenderness that was a testament to how close we'd grown over the past few weeks. He sighed and ran his hand down the back of my head and over my neck, sending a riot of confusing sparks colliding with the anger and fear already in my system.

"Give me a second." He turned and grabbed her wrist, looking at his watch and counting off. He pulled back her eyelids and did the various steps of a basic medical check I'd seen Gabriel perform a few times over the years. "Her vitals are fine. I think she needs to just sleep it off."

"Are you sure?" I asked, stepping back and forth to keep the autumn frost from freezing me in place.

"People having adverse reactions to drugs was kind of a big problem when I was a cadet. So yeah, I'm sure."

I let his words anchor me and my shaking subsided. Military experience could come in handy in unexpected ways, even if he didn't like to discuss that part of his life.

He hopped down and shut the door behind him. "We need to get out of here. One, you're freezing, and two, I'm strong, but I actually can't break, like, twelve necks in a row."

I barely registered anything about him helping me into the truck and tucking his sweatshirt around me, except for the moment the tip of his nose brushed against my jawline as he tried to buckle me in. I was still shaken up and just beginning to feel sick to my stomach, but that brief touch, accidental though it was, made me crave more. I wanted to be held and told it would be okay. Not by my mother, not by my brothers or Arden, but by a man who cared for me. In my twenty years, I'd never experienced the physical comfort provided by someone I needed. Edwin had given me a taste of it, and I wanted more.

He got into the driver's seat, but as if he could sense my need, he reached over and held my hand. He didn't caress me or place my hand in his lap, like other guys would have. He simply let me hold on tight. He was just there.

He reached his left hand around to awkwardly turn the key in the ignition, then clutched the wheel. "I understand that you're upset. But that back there? That wasn't your fault. Allocation of guilt is one subject I'm an expert in. It would have been the fault of whoever touched her, and the guys who stood around and let it happen."

His voice from a few weeks back flashed into my mind. *I didn't protect her.*

We drove in silence, but the thoughts whirling in my head needed release. My body felt tight with anger, with the need to tell him that thing I'd never talked about. The thing I'd treated as no big deal because, in this day and age, it wasn't. "It would have been my fault, because I know what men are like. I usually don't think about it, and I don't let it affect me, but someone...a guy...tried to force himself on me. One day when I was coming home from my program."

The truck swerved just the tiniest bit. I only noticed because he was such a careful driver at all other times. I don't know why, but it made me feel better that he was thrown for a loop. I certainly had been.

"Maggie." His grip tightened on mine, as if he was trying to pass something to me through his touch. Comfort. Strength.

I took a deep breath. I wasn't going to cry. "My parents' van broke down. I knew how to fix it, but I didn't have the tools I needed. One of my classmates, a guy who had been friendly to me, Kenny, offered to drop me off close to home since he passed near the cabin to get to his family's house. I was wearing my cutest skirt that day, one with little birds in flight, because I'd felt so good about myself as I got dressed that morning." The words got tangled in my throat then, testing my resolve not to cry. I'd never told anyone about this, except for Devon. The imaginary Devon I'd occasionally still talked to in my mind, not the guy he'd turned out to be in real life.

"Kenny's hand started creeping over to my leg while I was in the middle of talking about our last exam. He was still driving, but his hand went right up to my... you know, and he started moving his fingers." Suddenly the potty mouth I'd been chided over was out of commission. In my memory, the story was much more graphic, but some self-defense mechanism compressed my words to their simplest form as they spilled out. Humiliation scalded me, even though I knew it wasn't my fault. Part of that shame was because Edwin already knew how this story ended.

"Before that, I'd always convinced myself that if a guy tried anything like that with me, I'd kill him. But I was so shocked, I just sat there. Finally, when his fingers moved my underwear aside, something inside me snapped back into place. I grabbed his hand and pushed him away. And you know what he did? He laughed. He laughed and said there was no need to be coy because he knew I wanted it, that Asian girls liked to play hard to get before giving it up. That's how it worked in all the porn he'd seen. And then he shoved his hand back under my skirt."

I didn't tell Edwin about grabbing the wheel and almost driving us off the road in an effort to distract him when I wasn't strong enough to push him away. I didn't tell him how Kenny had called me a cock-teasing bitch. Of course I'd wanted it to happen, he'd said. Why else would I have accepted his ride? I did tell Edwin the last thing he said, shouting at me from a few feet away from where I'd jumped out of the car and tumbled to the ground: "Not every guy is going to be as nice as I was."

Edwin took a deep breath, and even that brief moment of silence felt like an eternity. I didn't know what he was supposed to say, but I was so scared that whatever he said, he'd think less of me.

"Jesus. Maggie, I'm so sorry that happened to you. That feels really fucking inadequate right now, but I'm sorry."

I knew what I said next was going to make him feel

even worse, but he deserved to know. We needed to finally usher out the elephant in the room. "He was right, you know," I said. I began fidgeting, hating that I couldn't control the shake in my voice and the full-body humiliation that almost made me stop talking. I pushed forward, though. "I realized that even then. As I walked down those miles of road home, it was all I could think about. I decided I would get rid of my virginity on my terms, with a guy I wanted. That way, when I inevitably met the next Kenny, I would know I hadn't let him take *that*. I fixated on it to keep my mind off the fear that pushed me to hide from every passing car. And when I got home, the person I wanted was there, alone in Darlene's old bungalow, and—"

The truck swerved to the side of the road, a controlled turn this time, and then he was leaning over the seat and hugging me close, running his palm over my hair, my ear and the wetness on my cheeks.

I gave a shaky laugh. "You shouldn't feel bad. You couldn't have known why I suddenly tried to jump your bones." My attempt to lighten the mood failed, and I gulped back a sob. Even though he hadn't known, his rejection had felt like an abandonment. Like he was sentencing me to something terrible by not giving me something good. All my rude behavior to him from then until the move to Oswego had been fueled by an act of desertion he hadn't even been aware of.

"You came to me, and I turned you away." I felt him shake his head. "If I'd known, I wouldn't have done what you asked, but I would have done this." He gathered me closer into his embrace, as close as the seat belt allowed. "And then we would have figured out what to do about Kenny, like use him for target practice. I'm sorry I didn't help you."

"It was an extreme request. I think I was in shock." I shook my head and snuggled closer into his warmth. Behind us, Danielle snored deeply.

"Is there anything I can do to help now?" His face was close to mine, and his hand rested on my shoulder. His gaze was intense and hot and made my insides go warm, like he'd doused me in liquid accelerant. He wanted me, I realized. All the weird looks he'd been giving me over the last few weeks had been flashes of this suppressed emotion—desire. But his desire wasn't a pressing thing. It lurked behind the anger and the pain that he felt on my behalf, and that made it even better. Edwin Hernandez knew all of my greatest traumas and humiliations, and he still wanted me.

"I still haven't had my first kiss," I said. The fear in me was changing—it was still fear, but a different form, one that nipped at your heels as you stepped forward into a new phase in your life and tried to scare you away from change. But I'd never let my fear bind me. I'd walked down that road after Kenny had left me and wished someone else would try to hurt me, just so I could use all the self-defense moves I'd been too shocked to use on him. I'd demanded that my biggest crush get it on with me and scared him out of his wits. And I was older and wiser now.

I placed my hand on Edwin's shoulder and trailed it

up the muscles that bunched along his neck. He shuddered at that slight touch, a vulnerable motion on such a large guy. My own body was still, finally, but his shiver seemed to pass through me, leaving a lingering buzz in its wake.

His mouth drifted closer to mine. "Not to be a jerk, but I'm gonna have to call you out on that. I saw Devon kiss you a few weeks ago. Remember, that whole weird scene in his room? The douchebaggieness, then the face-sucking?" He didn't seem to be jealous, but he wasn't entirely pleased either.

"Technically you're right. Devon has kissed me twice, actually, but without preliminaries and without asking. I want to kiss someone and know it's about to happen." To need the kiss like I needed to sing and play. Like I needed Edwin.

He looked at me for a long time. "Maggie?"

"What?" My voice was a hoarse whisper caught at the back of my throat.

"It's about to happen." He moved his head toward me slowly, his eyes on mine as if he were ready to stop at the slightest flinch. I wanted this, though, and leaned forward to meet him. When his mouth pressed against mine, I made a sound of surprise—his lips were much softer than I could have possibly imagined—and the pleasure that thrummed through me was something entirely new. When Devon had kissed me, it'd been great, but there had been so much emotional feedback that it was hard to separate what was real from the echoes from our shared past. Now Edwin was pulling me close as his lips brushed and brushed and brushed, and each touch resonated in me clean and pure and true, and so damn deliciously good. It wasn't cool to compare—it wasn't fair to either one of them—but it was the difference between playing a cigar box guitar and a handcrafted Fender. Transcendent.

I leaned into the kiss, wanting more of the exciting new feeling. Waves of heat washed through my body as his tongue met mine and showed it what to do by example. His leadership skills extended beyond the job site, it seemed. I tried to get closer to him, but something was holding me back. Not emotion this time—my seat belt. I groaned in frustration, and he thrust his tongue into my mouth harder. Then I was groaning because the rhythm pulsing between my legs responded to how he was both rough and gentle, to the way his hand settled on my thigh but didn't move further. His fingers pressed into my jeans, as if preventing his hand from traveling of its own accord.

A loud snore sounded from the backseat, and he pulled away and leaned back in his seat, breathing heavily. I looked over my shoulder.

"We need to get her home," I said, guilt edging up under my giddiness. I didn't regret the kiss, but there was a time and place for everything, and whatever was happening between us could wait until Danielle was comfortable.

"Mags—"

I held my hand in front of his face. "You'd better not

apologize for that, or give me some weird bullshit line about protecting my emotions."

His dimples shadowed against his cheeks before he pushed my hand aside. "What? If I'm worried about anyone's emotions right now, it's my own. I'm nice, but shit, I'm not altruistic." He started the car and we were on our way again. "I was gonna ask if you were hungry. Larry saved you some chili the other night, and it's been cluttering up my fridge."

"Oh. Yeah, actually, I am."

"Good. We can put Danielle to bed and keep an eye on her while we have something to eat. I have cards— maybe we can play I Declare War or something?"

Poker was more my thing. I Declare War was boring, and the game took *forever*. That meant he had bad taste in card games, which was a deal breaker, or he wanted to spend some time with me, and not just to build up his credit toward getting what he thought he deserved. A bright wash of happiness drowned out the bad parts of the night at the possibility that it was the latter. I tried to tone down my feelings. One kiss didn't prove anything about a guy's intentions, as Devon had so clearly proven. But the worst Edwin had ever done to me was try to protect me from myself. It might have been naive to believe in him, but that was what college was for.

I knew that unpleasant things awaited me in the morning. My lost guitar case and, more importantly, John's couture jacket. The awkward conversation that would occur when next I saw Devon. Figuring out whether I should be worried about Greg's weird aggression toward me. But for the rest of the night, I was going to give being a normal college student a shot.

"That sounds great," I said. "As long as jokers are wild."

19

After stopping at Edwin's dorm so he could run in and pick up the food, we headed back to my dorm. I wondered what his room looked like. Was he the kind of guy to hang up shitty posters? Were the walls bare, or did he have a lone picture of his family? Did it smell like him—that piney, Edwin-ey scent that was quickly becoming one of my favorite smells? His sheets probably smelled like that... The thought set off a tumult in my belly. I thought of the way his hand felt against my thigh again and wished it had gone higher, explored further. But there was a good reason it hadn't.

I turned in my seat and looked at Danielle, who appeared to be sleeping peacefully.

Edwin came around the truck and opened my door, pulling my gaze in his direction. The smile I gave him was involuntary. Maybe it was the drama of the night, or the relief at finally being able to speak to someone about what'd happened to me, but just seeing him filled me with an appreciation that smoothed away all the rough edges of the earlier events. He paused as he climbed back into the truck with the food, and I wondered if the expression on my face gave everything away. I'd tried to hide my feelings from him behind a don't-give-a-fuck attitude for so long that the thought was scary, but I didn't look away.

"You look really pretty tonight." I barely had time to register the compliment before he shoved a sleeping bag into my lap and dropped the tote bag full of food containers on top. I was sure my makeup looked like some kind of Rorschach test after my crying jag, but if he liked what he saw then that was fine with me.

Danielle managed to wake up enough to stumble to my room with assistance. "He told me it was just tea," she slurred as we tucked her into the bed, then fixed us with a hopeful look. "Are we having a slumber party?"

"Yes," Edwin replied seriously. "Maggie's closet is too messy to play Seven Minutes in Heaven, though."

I rolled my eyes at him, but it got a sleepy laugh out of Danielle, so it was okay by me.

"My parents said I had to wait until junior year to have a sleepover, but junior year never happened." She smiled sadly.

"We can have as many sleepovers as you want,"

I said. When I saw the excitement that lit up her face, I added, "Within reason."

After chugging some water, she said she just wanted to sleep, so we tucked her into my bed. She flew up into a sitting position just before she started to drift off and pulled her panda down tightly around her ears. "Please don't touch my hat." Her eyes were wide with real fear. I knew a thing or two about security blankets, but the terror in her eyes was heartrending.

"We would never do that without asking," I said.

She stared at me suspiciously for a minute, then her eyes slowly drooped shut and she turned over and settled into my pillow.

Edwin left to heat up the chili in the communal kitchen. In the silence, I wondered if Devon was still there and if he knew what had happened. Would he even care? Weariness descended on me then. It had been a long enough night; I wasn't ready to come to terms with the many levels of his betrayal just yet.

When Edwin came back, he held a pot and two spoons.

"Ooo, classy," I said. I placed a towel on the floor under the pot and accepted a spoon from him. I didn't know what to say, now that Danielle was asleep. I spooned the too-hot chili into my mouth instead, immediately squealing and spitting it out into my hand.

Way to reel him in with the sexy, Maggie.

Edwin shook his head and handed me a napkin. "Yeah, it's hot. Hence the steam pouring off of it?" He pointed to just above the pot, and I burst out laughing. When I took my next bite, the few taste buds I hadn't burnt off transmitted the news that Larry's chili was everything I could have imagined and more.

"Mmm. Thank you for making sure I didn't miss out on this," I said.

"Ready to play?" he asked. He clumsily shuffled a deck of cards he'd pulled out of his pocket, making me cringe. I reached out and snatched them from him, showing him how to do it without bending the cards.

"I forgot you were a card sharp," he said. "Remember that game of UNO we played around Christmas last year? The one where Gabriel thought he was gonna win until you hit him with that Skip, Reverse, Draw Four combo? That was the closest I've ever seen that dude come to crying."

I giggled as I remembered the shock on my brother's face when I'd broken his ten-game winning streak, and the thrill of victory as I'd slapped the Draw Four on the pile. An interesting thought came to me as I dealt the cards. One of the reasons I'd clung to Devon was because of our shared history, and the things he knew about me that no one else did. It'd never occurred to me that Edwin and I had our own inside jokes, and Danielle and I did now too. That was how life worked. I hated to think of it, but even if the Flare hadn't happened, I could have drifted away from my high school friends, like Marisa. Sharing a past with someone was important, but sharing a future, whether as lovers or friends, was no small potatoes either.

"I'll try not to make you cry," I said as I dropped the last card in front of him.

"Your mercy is appreciated in advance."

The game was boring, but we talked throughout, joking and flirting and pretending that we weren't both thinking about the kiss in his truck. Each time he took a bite of chili, he licked his lips, leaving them sleek and moist and tempting. I tried to focus on the game, but I couldn't stop sneaking glances at him. We were half an hour in when Edwin first began slapping down his cards one by one, and I followed suit. Our gazes were locked on one another in what could have been mock intensity, but nothing about it felt playful. "I. De. Clare. War!"

Even though losing cards was a big sore spot for me, I didn't care who had come out on top. I was studying the smoothness of his lips and the dark stubble that shaded his jawline. His eyes, a lighter shade of brown than mine, didn't move, but his gaze deepened in intensity. "This is so fucked," he muttered before swiping the cards out of the way and stalking toward me on hands and knees.

"What, that I'm your friend's sister?" I whispered, trying to be annoyed but distracted by the fact that his momentum carried him right over me, guiding me back so I was on the floor beneath him. The solid heft of his body was an intoxicating weight, pushing me into the floor that I wished I'd swept now that I might be getting some action on it.

"No. Well, maybe, but I was talking about the fact that poor impressionable Pikachu is right up there on the bed, but that doesn't stop me from wanting to kiss you." The bulge at his groin twitched, and I jumped in surprise, sliding against him in a way that drew a hiss from him. He gave a rueful chuckle. "Okay, I want to do more than that. I want to know what the skin right here tastes like."

He ran his calloused fingertip over the patch of skin below my ear, trailing it down my neck, and I felt the caress run straight through me. My hips lifted of their own accord, seeking the pressure and release I was used to getting from my own hand. Edwin's jeans-clad thigh was between my legs, and the friction of his corded muscle tensing as it came into contact with the bundle of nerves between my legs was something entirely new. I let out a gasp. I could give myself carpal tunnel syndrome for trying and never achieve the same body-clenching pleasure that came from the shift of his leg. Even though Edwin was holding up most of his body weight on his elbows, his thigh was pressing down hard against my clit, moving back and forth as he circled his hips.

"Think you can be quiet?" he asked in a whisper. I thought I'd catalogued all of Edwin's smiles, but the one he flashed me was new. It was devious and probably the last thing Little Red Riding Hood saw before the wolf ate her up.

"Yes," I lied. I'd say whatever it took to ensure that he wouldn't stop, wouldn't take away the terrifying deliciousness swirling up my spine and making me dizzy with want. Heat screamed through my veins and pressed at my vocal cords, trying to channel the surge of desire outward, like notes through an effects pedal. I pressed my lips together, closed my eyes and focused on the sensation, on my heart pounding in my ears like someone going wild on a drum set.

"Really? I don't know if I should be impressed or insulted," he said. He nipped at my collarbone, and I swallowed a soft sigh. Quiet was going to be harder than I thought.

"Whichever one of those things makes you touch me faster," I said, arching up into him, seeking more than his thigh—wonderful though it was—could give me.

His lips found mine. Enamel scraped over my lower lip, followed by the soothing warmth of his tongue. I ground against his thigh, meeting each press of hard muscle with my clit. His hips moved at a steady rhythm now, and the brush of his cock against my leg was a teasing temptation of what could happen between us.

His hand glided over my stomach, hooking the hem of my T-shirt with his thumb as he pushed up over the swell of my breasts. His fingertips against my bare skin were four little revelations, each one highlighting the fact that I'd been a fool to think he would've been the kind of man to just take an inexperienced girl for the hell of it. I could feel Edwin's desire for me transmitted through touch, revealing all the things he would do to me—in his own sweet time and because he wanted me, not as a favor.

His palm circled over one nipple through the thin material of my bra, and then the other, and I finally understood what all the fuss was about. It was if his touch was changing me, giving life to nerves that had lain dormant, waiting for just this stroke and just that pinch. His hands were magical.

"Fuck. You're like a wizard," I said in a strangled voice, and he choked back a laugh that could have killed the mood, but was tender enough that it only bolstered my pleasure.

"That's a first," he said. "I usually prefer to go by God, Jesus or *Papi* at these moments, but I'll take wizard." He paired the grinding press of his thigh between my legs with the lightest, teasing strokes across my breasts, and I wanted to shout from the staccato sensations of pleasure pummeling my body everywhere, not just the places where he touched me.

I bucked against him in frustration. "I need—"

Before I was even finished, he slid one hand from my chest to replace his thigh, his fingers rubbing in a hard circle over just the right spot below the zipper of my jeans.

"Oh God," I gasped.

"That's more like it," he whispered, eyes glinting. His tongue snaked out and lapped at my nipple right through the material of my bra at the exact moment he switched from circling index finger to strumming thumb. Just like that, the pressure in me burst like one of the pipes frozen solid by the winds off the lake—I was far from cold, though. There was warmth between my thighs and warmth in my heart as my climax splintered through me. His mouth moved toward mine, but I wasn't in control of my body; the arch of my back was so intense that it forced my head to the side, the gritty floor tile pressing into my cheek. His hand slipped over my mouth to cover the animal sounds I was making.

We lay there quietly after, my heavy breaths slipping through his fingers, my body still shuddering as he pulled his hand from between my legs and, eventually, away from my mouth. I pressed a kiss into his palm, and he groaned. He looked at me, his gaze intense, and suddenly burst out into quiet laughter. For a horrifying moment, I thought maybe I'd misjudged him, that he really was what I feared from any man I let touch me. Before I could react, he reached out and plucked something from the side of my face. One of the cards had gotten stuck there.

"Guess which one," he said, gathering me close to him. He unrolled his sleeping bag and settled us onto it, a surface only slightly more comfortable than the floor.

"Joker," I said, aiming for self-deprecation. I loved how he'd made me feel, but this type of exposure seemed alien, the act of allowing yourself to come completely undone for another human. That people did it routinely was even crazier.

He squinched his mouth in disagreement and twisted the card so it faced me. "Queen of Hearts."

That exposed feeling doubled down. Before we'd become friends, I'd assumed that Edwin didn't want my virginity because he'd expected me to fall for him after, to chase him around like some kind of lovesick fool. Wasn't that what guys thought virgins did? I'd vowed I would never be that stupid, but I still hadn't come down from my orgasm and already wanted more.

I plucked the card out of his hands and tossed it across the room, where it wedged in a pile of laundry.

I gave him a saucy smirk and ran my hand over his chest, channeling the same energy I'd had when I'd first strutted down the stairs to be whisked away to school. Better to project cool confidence than to show any fear.

His hand came down over mine. "Maggie."

I didn't know what he was going to say next because a siren, several sirens, sliced through the silence of the night.

One minute Edwin was under me, the next he'd pulled some kind of cross fit–inspired jump that had him on his feet and already slipping into his jacket. He'd gone from relaxed to Jason Bourne in a few seconds.

"Where are you going?" I stood—like a normal human and not an action star—and pulled my shirt down.

"Those sirens mean someone's trying to break in to one of the priority buildings."

"Probably some kids, right? I mean, this *is* a college campus. Maybe a couple is trying to have a romantic night at the lighthouse."

Edwin shook his head. "We've been getting a lot of reports about possible subversive activity from the department." He'd gone into soldier mode, and it was both hot and frightening at the same time. "I don't think these are drunk lovers having a tryst, unfortunately."

"Well, why do *you* have to go? You're not in the military anymore." I sounded petty, but the thought of anything happening to him was terrifying.

"Maggie, you know I'm on assignment here for the Department of Infrastructure Repair. I take classes and work on projects, but ultimately I work for the government. Because most security personnel is over at Falling Leaf, I'm one of the few people on campus right now with training to handle this shit."

"Remember the whole 'I can't break twelve necks in a row' thing? You don't even have a weapon."

"My guns are locked up in my dorm room. I have to stop there first," he said, as if that was supposed to calm me. I looked away from him. "Mags?" He held out his hand for a fist bump, eyebrows lifted as he waited for me to give my blessing. I reached my hand out to give him a reluctant pound, and he grabbed my fist and pulled me in for a kiss. His kiss was teasing and playful, doing a little to ward off the fear the situation had stirred in me. "I'll be back soon."

He went out the door and hopped over something, then took off down the hall at a quick jog. I looked down and my stomach turned. I should have been happy to see my guitar case and John's blazer, to have my cell phone back. But seeing them tossed there left me cold.

Devon.

I pulled the pile into my room, placing it next to a similar heap of clothes, and then locked the door.

"What is that noise?" Danielle was sitting up in bed,

her hands over her ears. Her voice was slightly less stoned. "Are we under attack?"

A shudder ran down my spine. "No," I said. I hoped I was right.

20

Danielle and I eventually wandered out into our floor's common area, where our classmates had gathered to pass information.

Devon was nowhere in sight, and I was relieved. It was mean, but I wished he would be shamed enough by his behavior to become a hermit so I'd never see him again. But then, just thinking of all the ways he'd lied to me, and for no reason at all, made me kind of wish he *was* in front of me. I'd give him the dressing-down he deserved instead of worrying about him like I had when I thought we were friends. The bottom line was simple for me—friends didn't lie to each other and friends didn't manipulate each other, and he'd done both. I'd thought trying to forgive him was the adult thing to do, but learning to expect respect from the people in my life was just as important.

Theories about the sirens were swirling in the common room: "Lydia saw a van speeding down the main street toward the maintenance building." "Kyle was walking home from a party and said he heard people screaming, but he'd dropped acid before that so it could've all been in his imagination." "I felt a rumble that was maybe an explosion."

There was one thing I was glad of—no one tried to go see what was happening. Tragedy had touched everyone just enough to kill the type of curiosity previously seen in horror movies and bad reality TV. Those of us who had internet-ready devices tried to pull up the bare-bones social media networks that were the fastest way of getting news, but we watched our hourglasses spin in vain. The internet was down.

I remembered Edwin saying that the network had been acting up earlier, resulting in the delay in receiving Danielle's message. Apparently, the same thing had happened to me. When I checked my phone, I saw John had sent a text earlier in the evening. Weirdness abounds. Stay indoors and call Hernandez if anything odd pops off. I'll be passing through tomorrow. Make sure to tell your harem they have to vacate the premises before I arrive.

I felt a rush of relief when I read the last sentence. I didn't know what was going on, but suddenly I was just a little girl who wanted her brother to tell her everything would be okay. Including the fact that his buddy had made her combust on the floor of her dorm room only hours earlier. I didn't know how we'd handle that little bombshell, or if there was anything to handle this early in the game, but I'd figure that out in the morning.

The sirens stopped eventually, but still there was no word. Danielle and I went back to her room to avoid the scarier ideas our floor mates were bandying about. As I sat and wondered about Edwin's whereabouts, I appreciated her decorating choice for once. It was hard to feel hopeless with dozens of badass animated heroines thrusting their bosoms at you as they dispatched bad guys with giant swords and ridiculous guns—cutesy didn't have to mean rabbits and kittens. A sketchbook lay open on her bed, and I picked it up to move it before I sat. She went to grab for it, but I turned and kept it just out of her reach, even though my gaze was latched to the page.

"Holy shit. Danielle! This is amazing!" I sat and stared at a drawing of me, or a much cooler version of me. The character was drawn in an anime style, so my eyes and chest were larger, but my short hair and obnoxious smile were the same. My tool belt encircled my waist, with two drills holstered where guns would be. In one hand I gripped the neck of my guitar, an ax-shaped monstrosity that rested on my shoulder. One foot was propped up on a pile of suitors with hearts in their eyes. The work was incredibly detailed, down to the buttons and indentations on the drill, and so full of admiration that it made me wish I could ever be so worthy.

When I looked up at her, her head was turned shyly.

"It's just a hobby," she said.

"Are you kidding me? You're crazy talented!" I'd known she could make cute little doodles, but this... My fingers itched to turn the pages and see what else was there, but that would be the same as going through someone's journal. I looked up at her, eyes imploring.

She sat down on the bed next to me and flipped a page without speaking, as if she was holding her breath.

All of my fears and anxieties about what was happening outside and Edwin's whereabouts faded to the background as I was pulled into Danielle's interior world. Many of the newer portraits were caricatures or comic scenes with people from around campus. My boss Joe with a hunting dog chasing after his two missing fingers, which, blessed with appendages of their own, ran from him. Melba, one of her co-workers at the library, transforming from waifish woman into a muscled shield-maiden as she ate the pages of a giant tome labeled *Viking Warriors*.

As we flipped further back, the images grew darker and more tense. Shadows looming over kittens that spilled out of a sack, abandoned. A balding man tugging at the collar of his shirt, his expression angry and his gaze searing off the page and into the viewer. Although the images were just as arresting, they seemed to be drawn more hurriedly, with less deliberation—except for one. This was a two-page piece. A man and woman sat surrounded by control panels that looked so real I almost ran my fingers over the page to press a button. Their gazes were fixed ahead and down, as if I was seeing them hard at work, but their arms reached across the page to grasp each other's hands. Their fingers, perfectly drawn, threaded through each other's so that their palms pressed together. Even though their features were changed to accommodate Danielle's drawing style, I could see the resemblance.

"Your parents?" *I'm the child of engineers,* she'd said earlier.

She nodded and closed the sketchbook.

"They must have been so proud of your ability," I said. I lay back on the bed, still in awe of the drawing she'd done of me. A rush of emotion surprised me, as did the lump that stealthily roughened my throat. It was silly, but I knew when I wrote a song about someone it was only because I felt very strongly about them, and there had been nothing dismissive or mocking in her work. It was nice to be important to some-one who'd only known this version of me—not the girl with good grades or archery medals, but the woman that girl had become. I didn't need self-validation—I thought I was pretty awesome—but I needed friends and now I had one.

"My parents were very supportive. Other people weren't." She hit the switch on her desk lamp and curled up onto the bed next to me. "I think whatever Greg gave me is kicking in again." Her voice didn't sound sleepy at all; she sounded suddenly tired in a different way, though.

"Do you want me to leave?"

"No. If you're here, I can be sure Devon isn't in your room with you trying to talk you into forgiving him."

I was grateful she'd slept through my encounter with

Edwin, for obvious reasons, but that meant I had a lot of explaining to do. "Oh, let me fill you in before we go to bed."

Talking about what had happened with Edwin was easier than lying awake thinking of the bad situations he could be getting himself into. I didn't remember when I fell asleep. Sometime after Danielle had berated me for hooking up while she was in the room, even though I'd tried to avoid mention of it. "It's a college rite of passage," I'd said in my defense as she hit me with a pillow.

I awoke to sunlight pouring into the room and birds chirping outside the room. No, inside the room. My phone was ringing.

"Answer your phone, harlot." John's voice echoed in the hallway outside the door, and then my message alert beeped. Beside me, Danielle was still sleeping deeply, and I managed to ease out of bed and slip through the door without waking her. There I found John, looking dapper and businesslike in a tailored suit with his long hair pulled into a sleek bun. Mykhail was clad more casually in jeans, a nice wool sweater, and his usual floppy blond hair.

Mykhail was busying himself leaving a note on my message board. "You know texting exists, don't you?" John said as his fingers flew over his phone's keypad. He turned toward the noise of Danielle's door opening and smiled when he saw me. His eyes widened slightly as he took in the scene behind me. "Slumber party or sexual awakening?" he asked as he pulled me in for a kiss.

I turned and scribbled a quick message on her board

so she'd know where I went. "Danielle is very cute, but we're just friends. Have you heard from Edwin? Do you know if he's okay?"

John and Mykhail shared a look, communicating in their weird staring/eyebrow wiggling language I swore was some form of telepathy. Mykhail cleared his throat and pushed his glasses up on his nose. "Funnily enough, that's the first thing he asked us about you. Hernandez is fine. He'll be joining us for breakfast. Unless that would be awkward?"

Ah. John was letting Mykhail do his dirty work.

"Why would that be awkward? We always have breakfast together," I said. *And last night I was humping his thigh like a dog in heat. What of it?* I waited two beats to push past them and unlock my room door so I could change into something less skeevy. "Give me a minute," I tossed over my shoulder. After running to the bathroom for a speed shower and tooth brushing, I scrambled around my room, searching for something clean to wear. When I stepped out of the room in a green wool dress over black tights, hair coiffed and a fresh face of makeup, John gave me a knowing smile.

"What?" I growled.

"You look like an adult," he said and sighed. Mykhail took his hand, as if giving him support.

"I've *been* an adult. Boobs, menstruation, legal voting age—remember those fun milestones?"

"I know. But sometimes it hits home that you're not a little kid who's safely tucked away with Mom and Dad. I'm glad you're getting to live your life. Trust me, it's something I've been worried about for the last few years. It's just, after last night I kind of wish we had listened when you first refused to come here."

I took John's other hand as we exited the building. I was an adult, but adults needed their big brothers too. "What's going on? Is there some kind of danger here? Do we have to leave?"

A sudden dread filled me at the thought of losing meals with Edwin and Danielle and banter with my work friends. I'd even miss Professor Grafton and her colorful hair, which was now lime green. Not seeing Devon ever again would be convenient, but not worth losing the life I'd just started to live.

Mykhail leaned past John so I could see him more clearly. "No. Not yet, at least. But anti-government and anti-progress groups are starting to get way more active. If this isn't checked now, we could have an even worse situation than immediately after the Flare."

"How could anything be worse than that?" I'd been safe, but I'd learned so much about the madness that had taken place in the aftermath of the loss of a functioning society. Mykhail wasn't prone to hyperbole, so his words struck an icy chord of fear in me.

John took over. "An organized collective of disgruntled groups is way more dangerous than random gangs trying to survive. Assholes being assholes because they can is one thing. Assholes waging a campaign against the government could fuck shit up." His voice was laconic and overly flip in a way that meant he was really worried.

I showed my ID at the dining hall and signed in my two guests. Mykhail pretended to be delighted at my mastery of the waffle maker, and John pretended that the coffee didn't taste like swill, but they couldn't hide their interest when a freshly showered Edwin sauntered in and took the seat next to me. There was a sudden tension in the air, that subtle shift in the world that occurred when you became the center of people's attention. I'd felt the same thing the night before on the stage.

"Hey," Edwin said to me. He grinned.

"Hi," I replied around the forkful of waffle I'd shoved in my mouth. I realized my shoulders were hunched, as if I were swinging my long-gone curtain of hair in front of my face. I leaned back and tried to look casual.

John's coffee mug hit the table with a loud ceramic *thud*. "Oh God. You guys totally got it on. Although a Korea-Rican baby would be super adorable, please tell me you used protection."

"John," Mykhail warned.

My brother arched a brow and took a small sip of coffee, looking so much like my mom it was as if she'd temporarily possessed him. "What?" he asked innocently. "We're all family, right? Do you think it would be better for me to talk behind her back?" Yes, he was definitely channeling his inner Mama Seong.

"What we have or haven't done is none of your business, okay?" I looked at Edwin, but he just shrugged and reached over my plate for the pepper.

John shut his eyes in relief and reached for Mykhail's arm. "Oh good. They haven't consummated yet."

"John!" My cheeks were blazing.

Still he pushed on. "Edwin, I have to say when I asked you to take my sister in hand, this was not exactly what I had in mind."

Edwin laughed but had apparently had enough of the focus on our relationship. "Considering I was there for the afterglow of one of your first hookups, you can't say anything that would embarrass me, man. Have you spoken to Dr. Simmons recently, Mykhail?" He bit into a piece of toast with a triumphant smile.

John pulled his hand away from Mykhail frostily and crossed his arms over his chest.

Mykhail threw his hands up toward the heavens. "I was on your side, Hernandez! Now I'm going to get the silent treatment for two days because you brought up you-know-who."

"All's fair in prying older brothers," Edwin said. "Besides, the silent treatment from John isn't a punishment. It's a vacation."

I was seriously annoyed—why was he laughing and joking around? Then I remembered that he no longer had an older brother to harass him about his love life. This was a special treat for him. I glared down into my scrambled eggs and tried not to let my embarrassment push me into doing something stupid, as it often did.

The sound of burbles and squees drifted into the dining hall, distracting me.

"Oh, speaking of cute babies. Bina! Altaf! We're over here." John waved his napkin in the air. Edwin went stiff next to me and when I looked at his face there was a slight panicked edge to his expression, as if he was considering getting up and running away.

I glanced behind me and saw a beautiful dark-skinned woman approaching, clad in jeans and a dark wool coat. A green-eyed man with olive skin held her hand and made silly faces at the baby strapped to her front with a long black cloth. Bina and Altaf, John's co-workers at Burnell whom I'd met briefly during one of my trips. They were responsible for the new telecommunications systems that were being tested across the country.

"Nice to see you again," I said with a cordial nod in their direction. That wasn't entirely true—if they were here with John, it meant something major was happening.

Even before meeting them, I'd heard all about them, and not just from John's "can you believe my co-workers" stories. Bina had become legend in my family as the woman who'd saved Mykhail. She was also a telecommunications genius. And judging from the way Edwin looked at her, there was one more thing she was: the woman who'd made him so sad. The one he hadn't protected. I didn't need a telepathic language to understand that.

21

They held each other's gazes for a long time. The smile she gave him was reserved but kind, and the way he returned it made me feel like I was eavesdropping on them. Maybe I should have been jealous, but the regret in Edwin's eyes canceled that out. I couldn't imagine what it was like to see someone you had disappointed in such a way. I'd been rude to Edwin for years because he'd made me feel like a silly child. What had happened between him and Bina wasn't even in the same stratosphere. I wanted to hold his hand, not to stake my claim but because he looked like he could use the comfort. I didn't, though.

He stood, and she kissed him on both cheeks. Even her greetings were leagues classier than anything I could pull off. She gave me a friendly smile. "Nice to meet you again, Maggie. I hardly recognize you now—has so much time passed since we met? John speaks of you so often, and Arden and Gabriel did, as well. How are you adjusting to life at school?"

In my imagination, I leaned my chair back on two legs and told her that everything was awesome. But when I opened my mouth, the truth came out. "It can be hard sometimes, but it's good. I thought I wanted to stay at home, but I'm glad I let John talk me into coming. I feel like I'm living the life I was supposed to. Making up for what the Flare stole away."

Bina smiled and nodded. Now that she was closer, I could see there was something sad about her smile that made it even more beautiful, like she was smiling in spite of instead of just because. Something about her reminded me of Danielle in a weird way. "I remember when I first came to the United States for school. I tried to be very brave and decided I didn't need anyone for anything. I thought I'd already experienced all there was to know of life, and that no silly American could teach me anything. But the very first day, I couldn't get the key card on my door to work." She laughed. "It wasn't because this technology doesn't exist in my country, but because for some reason I can never remove the card fast enough. So I tried for a full hour. Finally, another student came over to help me and I let her. And so on my first day here I learned that I could be outsmarted by a piece of plastic and that I should choose my allies wisely."

A rumble of laughter passed through our group, and even the baby burbled, as if she agreed with her mother's assessment.

I glanced at Edwin. "I think that's the game plan I'm working with, minus the superior plastic."

"Is this Joanna?" Edwin's rough voice cut into the conversation. He had been sneaking glances at the baby while we spoke. He stuck a finger of his large hand out toward the little bundle, and a tiny tan hand reached up and clutched his finger. His eyes widened and he looked from Bina to me with a goofy grin on his face. "She's strong!"

Bina chuckled and gave the baby's dark curls a caress. "Yes, this is my miracle baby. She has to be strong."

"Did you have a rough delivery?" I asked and then wondered if the question was improper.

"No. But this world is designed to crush her. Us." She looked at me in a way that let me know I was included in her statement. "I didn't want to bring a baby, especially a daughter, into this world. But then I realized that the work I do every day, that all of us do, is to ensure there's a future. She's my second chance at life in a way, even though that sounds selfish. But we all deserve second chances. Our pasts cannot haunt us forever." This time her look was directed at Edwin.

He chewed the inside of his cheek and nodded, as if slowly absorbing her words. He turned his attentions to Joanna again, making silly faces to entertain her. She was cute, but I knew part of her current appeal to him was that she couldn't talk and thus he wouldn't have to either.

"Hopefully our work won't be in vain," Altaf said.

"These neo-Luddites have been a huge pain in the ass. The crazy thing is that they use technology themselves to stop technology! Social media websites for organizing and re-cruiting, signal jammers and the like. A pack of hypocrites, pretending to be saviors and using their influence for no good. That's one thing that hasn't changed about the world." His gaze narrowed when it landed on Edwin. Bina might have been willing to let go of the past, but Edwin was still one of the soldiers who'd detained them, who'd let unspeak-able things be done to them.

I didn't protect her.

How did you move forward from that?

Perhaps Bina knew Edwin punished himself. It could never be enough, but we had to start somewhere with our second chances. Then again, sometimes you gave someone a second chance, and they turned out like Devon.

As if my thoughts summoned him, he straggled through the dining hall behind a few of the guys from the eco club, one of whom might have thrown a bottle at me the night before. His eyes were focused on his tray, and I deviously hoped someone had dropped a dollop of the slippery okra I'd had to search through in the compost room last week in his path. Where had he been the night before when Greg had threatened me? It occurred to me then, like a punch to the gut, that I'd never thought Devon might help me yesterday. I'd never thought of going back to the base-ment to search for him, or expected him to give me any assistance if he came outside.

John followed the path of my gaze. "Who's he?"

Mykhail answered for me. "Probably the ex she emailed Arden about."

"Arden told you guys?" I would throttle her.

"No," Mykhail corrected. "She told Gabriel because she can't keep anything from him. Then he got all worked up and called us. She threatened us all with a thrashing if we bothered you about it." He shrugged. "But he seems to be out of the picture, so that's water under the bridge."

It was true. When I looked at Devon, I didn't feel any lingering desire. But the part of me that considered him a friend, that part of me felt like it had just been put into a trash compactor. We'd had fun over the past few weeks. And now there would be no more, because his desires had overridden our friendship. Because his lies had been more important than me—and they always had been.

He sat at a table with his back to me, and it felt like a rebuke. An unfair one.

"All of these fuckers and their assbackward ideas," Bina said with a curl of her mouth. I thought she was talking about Devon, but she was responding to Altaf. "I'm tired of idiots who try to drag people down because they'd rather everyone remain in the gutter. The frightening thing about this is that so many people, men especially, are attracted to the kind of power a reign of stupidity brings." She glared at everyone at the table, excluding me from her perusal.

Altaf sighed. "I wish I could say you were wrong. But

if I had to bet on who tried to take down the telecommunication servers in the area last night..."

"We should probably get to work checking that out. It's a long ride back to Burnell." John downed the last of his coffee and grimaced. "I'll send you some better coffee in my next care package."

"You're leaving?" I felt a sudden sharp tingling in my sinuses. Getting caught in the familiar ebb and flow of conversation had been comforting, like the waves of the lake lapping at the shore. I was suddenly a kid again, dreading the end of John's and Gabriel's visits from college and med school. After lavishing me with attention, they'd go back to their busy lives, where there wasn't time for humoring little sisters. My bottom lip poked out in a pout, and I dragged it back in with a press of my teeth.

John came around the table and pulled me into a hug. "I was hoping we'd get to stay too, but this is kind of serious stuff."

"Now I really don't want you to go," I said, squeezing him more tightly.

He gave a dry chuckle. "I'll be fine. If I survived your teenage reign of terror, I can laugh in the face of anti-government militias. But seriously, we have guards and hopefully this is all just a bluff."

"Do you think I should be prepared for something to happen here?" I asked.

He disengaged and made room for Mykhail to

step in for his hug. "The school itself isn't a target, but they'll be beefing up security anyway. I'd tell you to be vigilant, but you're a Seong so that's standard operating procedure."

That got a laugh out of me.

I said my goodbyes to Bina, Altaf and Joanna, who was sweet even though she puked when I waved at her. I had that effect on people sometimes.

As everyone turned to shuffle out, Edwin and I fell into step together. Our hands brushed awkwardly, once, twice, until finally I grabbed his just to stop the way the surprise of his touch made my stomach flip. I didn't know whether it was the right thing to do, despite the fact that being in undefined relationships with guys seemed to be my forte. I was kind of disappointed in myself—here I'd thought I was going to school to become an independent woman. But when I glanced at Edwin from the corner of my eye, I didn't regret anything.

"Do you maybe want to go finish that card game?" I asked. I wondered if he could feel my pulse begin to race through my palm as I thought of his lips and tongue and the way they'd left me senseless.

"I do," he said, but not in an enthusias-tic-to-jump-my-bones kind of way. More in the wise-sage-who-knows-more-than-you tone that I didn't particularly want to hear at that moment. "If you need some time to think things through, that's cool too." His gaze skipped across the dining hall in Devon's general direction.

"Like what?" I asked, not following. The naughty fantasy that had begun to play out in my head skidded to an abrupt stop.

"Like whether you want to be with me for real or you're just mad with dude about what happened last night. We're friends, so if we do this we should give it some thought. I'm fine with whatever you want, but I think it would be good for everyone, especially you, if you were sure—"

"Are you kidding me?" I dropped his hand. My voice came out in a harsh whisper, trying to avoid a situation that pulled John into the mix. "After everything I told you last night, you think I was acting on a whim?"

"Maggie. I don't want you to feel like just because something happened last night—"

"I thought we were past this whole 'wise older man' portion of our relationship. I'm not a stupid kid anymore. I made a decision, and you're second-guessing me, and that's shitty."

"What decision? Since when is hooking up with someone a decision?" His brow furrowed in confusion. "Need I remind you that you've made out with Devon before too? Should he assume that everything is good to go between you guys because of that?"

My self-righteousness was whacked right out of me with that. It was a low blow, but no less true for that. I'd been mad at Devon for assuming anything about our relationship, and now I was mad at Edwin for just the opposite.

The longer he looked at me, the stupider I felt, and I gave in to habit—I got mad and I ran.

"You're right. Maybe I should think things over. Wouldn't want to rely too much on my own feelings, now, would I?" Just because I was wrong didn't mean I could admit to it.

"Do what you have to do, Mags, but I'm getting kind of tired of being cast as the bad guy every time I don't jump to get in your pants. Maybe you should think about what it is you really want because, honestly? I'm not sure it's me." He shoved his hands into his pockets and jogged up to walk next to Mykhail. I followed behind, the literal ass of the group, my position matching my behavior.

As I shuffled past the plate-glass window of the dining hall, a motion caught my eye. Devon, standing with his friends to leave. The look he gave me could best be described as unkind, and more accurately as a glower. He pulled on his book bag and turned his back on me. Although my brief run as Oswego U's resident player had been fun, I was now down two friends and my world was spiraling out of control again.

I crunched through a pile of fallen leaves. *Why do these things happen to me? What's next?* Funny thing. When you ask those kinds of questions, the universe has a way of answering, and not in the way you want.

22

When I showed up for my shift at the maintenance building later that morning, I was almost sick with nervousness and tongue-tied from rehearsing my apology. *I overreacted. I was being shortsighted. Please tell me this isn't over yet, because I can't stop thinking about your mouth and hands on my body.*

But when I showed up, Joe assigned me to the equipment room where I'd spent my first weeks. "Sorry, Maggie. But things are tense right now."

"Where is everyone?" The anxiety that had been a lead ball in my stomach grew instead of abating.

"I sent some people over to the plant." He meant the building on campus where water, electricity and other maintenance-related stuff was housed. "Among other things, they're prepping for the incoming storm—first snow of the season, and it's supposed to be a screamer right off the lake. They're also making sure no one has futzed around with anything in there. Nothing seems out of the ordinary, but we found one of the fuse boxes pried open and some of the wires pulled out. Not the right ones, but you never know what else they got into."

"Some people tried to break into the telecommunications building too," I said, realizing he had to be aware of that already, given his position. He nodded, and then patted a passing co-worker on the arm and signaled for him to hold up before giving me an apologetic glance. "I have to check some things out around here. Why don't you head on downstairs?"

And then he was off down the hallway.

My shift was only a few hours long, but it felt like approximately a Jurassic Age. Every time someone walked by the closed door, I expected it to swing open and Edwin to walk in and perch on my desk. But each time the footsteps passed me by. I knew what it was to miss someone so much it hurt, and I never wanted to feel that way again. That didn't stop the need for Edwin's presence, or the lack of it, from crawling over my skin like poison oak. I fidgeted around the room, rearranging shelves, dusting off cabinets and finally sitting down with a pen and pulling out a notebook to jot down the song that had started forming as I'd separated screws and rewound extension cords.

I huddled over that piece of paper for the rest of my

shift, and when it was over I had more scribbles and scratch-es than viable words. This was something new to me, being unable to write. Usually I could take all my unruly feelings, extract the necessary parts for my music and then move on. But there was a disconnect between my words and what was churning in my belly. My control of simile and metaphor alike had abandoned me. Each word landed like a lump of coal instead of soaring and pulling me up out of my morass with it.

I ripped out the paper, taking what small satisfaction I could, crumpled it like the garbage it was and shoved it into the pocket of my sweater. I decided to make my way to the library, where I had to pick up a book for my Disaster Lit class. I had to check on Danielle too. If I got over my ego, I could admit I wasn't eager to go back to the dorm, where my chances of running into Devon were pretty much 100 percent. He'd decided to save me the trouble of avoiding him, though.

He was standing in front of my job, impervious to the blustery wind that cut through my tights. I thought it was the cold that made my eyes tear up, but I couldn't be sure. The past few weeks of hanging out hadn't made me love him the way I used to, with a tenderness I could feel in my bones, but I still cared. If we'd actually dated, it would be easier. There was a protocol for breaking up with a guy who was a lying jerk. But what were you supposed to do when the person who had betrayed your trust was a friend?

"Hey," I said. Just because the sight of him made me want to run far away didn't mean I had to show it. "Did you enjoy the rest of the party?"

He grimaced. "Not so much. It was no fun without my best friend."

I tilted my head. "Oh, who's that? I don't think you've introduced us."

He stamped his foot a couple of times, not out of anger but because the thin material of his shoes wasn't made for the dropping temps, and he stared at me impatiently. I didn't cave.

"I know you're not talking about me, Devon. If you lie to, force yourself on and abandon your best friend, I pity everyone else you come in contact with." His outburst the night before had been shocking in the moment, but had gotten lost in the memory of the show and everything that had come after. Devon had a temper, and I should probably be more afraid that he'd shown up at my job. Instead, the pain in my chest outweighed everything else. I sighed and made the decision I thought was best for me. "We probably shouldn't talk anymore. Maybe...maybe if I feel like I can trust you again. But honestly? I don't know if that's even possible. I think you could be a great guy, but it would be more useful if you were a great friend. That's what I deserve."

A shadow of anger crossed his face where he should have registered regret. "Is this because of Danielle getting herself into trouble last night?"

I held up my hand. "Danielle didn't 'get herself into trouble.' Greg gave her something that made her pass out, and the blame is totally on him. That has nothing to do with this, but the fact that you're framing the situation in such a gross way proves my point."

I hated the way he was looking at me, like I was a bad smell and he was trying to figure out the source. "Why don't you just say it? This is because of that guy who's always sniffing around you. Did he tell you to stay away from me?"

I scrunched my brow in confusion. "Edwin? He doesn't have any say in who I'm friends with."

"Now who's the liar? I saw you holding his hand this morning. I get it now. To think, all this time I thought you were into me, but you were just using me to make another guy jealous. So typical." He shook his head in disgust.

"Even if I was dating Edwin, he would have no say in who I'm friends with. He's the one who told me to give you a chance to explain yourself." He didn't like that bit of info, but he needed to know that not every guy was like him. "And typical? Typical of what?"

"When I first told the guys about you, they said you seemed like the kind of girl who got off on attention from guys. Those tight pants you wear, the red lipstick, the crazy hair and fuck-me heels. I told them they were wrong. Shows what I know."

It was a sweet superpower, being able to twist reality so you always turned out to be the victim even as you left a trail of carnage behind you.

"Un-fucking-believable." My teeth pressed against

each other hard from the angry clench of my jaw. Indignation spurred me past him and onto the path toward the library. I'd done nothing but try to be a friend—yes, there had been the hope that there could be something to salvage from our teenage romance, but that had always been a long shot. He'd run several plays out of the douchebag playbook, but *I* was the bad guy. I could have explained everything wrong with his logic, but in his mind I would always be the one who'd mistreated him. "Good luck getting laid with that attitude."

"I had no problem with that last night," he called after me. Okay, that stung a little, but only because it reminded me of what had happened with Edwin the night before and his anger when I'd blown up at him earlier.

I rewarded Devon's revelation with a loud laugh. I didn't think he'd try anything, but I let my hand rest on the hammer that hung from my tool belt as I walked away, just in case. I channeled the rock star swagger that had run through my veins on the stage and bopped confidently away from him, just to show I didn't care. At least not in the way he wanted me to.

"Fuck you," he yelled after me, his angry voice echoing as if it bounced back from the dull gray sky overhead. I'd once thought he had the most beautiful voice in the world. I'd felt privileged to match my own voice to it. But sometimes even discordant notes can briefly produce a beautiful sound.

23

The cold whipped at me as I walked toward the library, the battering breeze a refreshing distraction from my anger. Despite my reluctance earlier that morning, I wished I had driven off with the Burnell crew. I remembered that they had their own program opening next year if everything went on track. If I could just tough it out for a semester and a half, maybe I could transfer. Or maybe when I went back home for Christmas break, I'd call it quits then. It was the cowardly thing to do, but I'd never claimed to be brave. There were enough other Seongs filling that role.

When I walked into Penfield Library, which looked more like a fortress from the outside than an institution of learning, I headed over to the information desk. "I'm looking for *Nuclear Courage,* the book about the Falling Leaf Five? I need it for my Disaster Lit class."

The girl behind the desk didn't look up from the book she was reading. "We're out of copies. If you have credits, you can buy it at the bookstore."

I sighed. I should have finished it before Arden took it to California with her. "But everything at the bookstore is way overpriced. My teacher said it would be in the library."

She held up the book she was reading and wiggled it in my face just enough that I could see the title in simple font. "This is the last one, and I'm not done yet. Maybe next time don't wait until two days before the assignment is due?"

My anger nearly boiled over right then. Edwin, Devon, Greg, neo-Luddites, and now this—the irrational part of my brain was sure the world was conspiring against me.

Then the girl looked over my shoulder and pointed. "Or you can ask her. Her uncle wrote it, so she might have a copy. The weird chick with the hat."

I turned and saw Danielle pushing a cart laden with books. She gave me a bright smile and a wave. I left the girl at the desk to her reading and strolled over to her. My mood lightened just a bit as I took in her T-shirt, which featured a smiling kitten shooting a glitter cannon. The words *Fuck Off* exploded in a sparkly streak across her bosom.

"How are you?" I asked. "I got your message that said you were feeling better. Sorry about not waking you for breakfast, but I thought you'd want to sleep in."

"I'm fine. Are you okay, though? And what was up with your brother coming? Was it related to the sirens last night?"

I filled her in on what John and Mykhail had relayed, and she scowled and gave the cart an annoyed kick. It was strange seeing real anger on her face. "I hate these neo-Luddites. They don't care what people have given up for us to get to this point."

"Yeah, they suck," I said. "That reminds me. Your co-worker told me you might have a copy of that *Nuclear Courage* book. I didn't know your uncle wrote it. That's cool."

Her eyes went wide, and then her gaze slid away from me. "Sorry, I don't have any copies. I have to go put these away now." She pushed the cart away without a good-bye.

I almost sniffed my armpits; something about me was repellent. Or maybe I should have asked Mykhail whether Mercury was retrograde. He didn't like being teased about astrology, but the world seemed off-kilter.

As I was leaving, Sassy Rudebritches at the information desk waved me over. Her eyes were red and puffy and her face splotchy. "Sorry I was a jerk earlier. I was at a rough part of the book when you interrupted me, and I took my feelings out on you."

"Yeah, I think we've all suffered from book-induced psychosis before. No worries."

She sniffled and smiled at me. "Someone just returned a copy if you still want to check it out." After scanning it, she handed it over. "It's so good. There's even a love story!"

I trudged back to my room under a sky that was one

solid gray cloud. I wondered if they had been able to prep at the facilities building and if Edwin was okay. I wished I'd been able to help; it sucked to think of my team doing hard work while I'd sat around in the equipment room. Then a thought struck me, one that contributed to the general shittiness of the day—maybe Edwin had specifically asked Joe not to send me to the plant. Maybe he'd said he didn't want to work with me again. No more Larry and his cheerful smile. No more Rosie and her colorful moods. Felix's protective curiosity would be a thing of the past. I couldn't bear to think of work without Edwin. Or work *with* Devon. Oh fuck, I hadn't thought of that.

When I reached the sanctuary of my room, I dug into my emergency supply and pulled out the venison jerky my parents had sent in a care package. I also grabbed a chocolate bar. Salty and sweet would be my pals, even if no one else was up to the task.

I glanced at the author photo. The smarmy-looking dude seemed familiar for some reason, but I figured it was because he was related to Danielle. The book hadn't gripped me the first time around, so I expected it to be boring, but I was immediately pulled in. Even though it was nonfiction, it was storytelling in the best possible way—each chapter was an overview of the day preceding the Flare for each engineer, interspersed with smaller mini-chapters describing the way the nuclear plant worked. On their own, each chapter was well-written but innocuous. Together, they built an enormous tension, clearly exhibiting how each engineer depended on one another and how each system was interdependent. All of these twined together to create a fierce sense of dread as the Flare, and the inevitable breakdown of the system, approached. Morbid curiosity made you keep flipping the pages.

When I got to chapter seven, I realized it was about two engineers and not one, a married couple. The chapter started with Leanna Donninger sitting at the breakfast table before her shift as her daughter served her pancakes in the shape of teddy bears.

Danielle's work study form flashed into my head again. Danielle Donninger. The last name couldn't be a coincidence, and the picture of the couple with their much younger daughter—hatless and happy—proved it without a shadow of a doubt. I, and most of my classmates, had been assigned to read about Danielle's parents' death. Now I understood why she'd been excused from Disaster Lit. All of my concerns about my love life wilted into insignificance.

My food sat uneaten as I powered my way through the following chapters. Leanna and David Donninger had succumbed to their radiation poisoning years ago, a slow and painful death that I would get to experience with them in the last chapter. But first I would read about that last morning at home with their daughter, Danielle. How David had helped her with her homework that night and worried when the electricity was out the next morning and his wife hadn't returned from the plant. By the next evening he couldn't take not knowing whether his wife, and his co-workers, needed him. He dropped Danielle off with his brother and headed to the nuclear plant.

I remembered distinctly what it'd felt like when my parents had left and not come back right after the Flare. A horrible, numbing dread that followed me like a shadow. Nightmares, horrific thoughts and, worst of all, having to get up every day and pretend everything was okay. They too had gone to help others at expense to themselves, but my parents had come back. I'd been spared from that agony of loss so many of my friends and peers had experienced.

When death happened on such a wide scale, you had to cut yourself off from it or you'd go insane. I had become a pro at predicting when someone was going to reveal something painful, and I could throw up defensive walls to protect myself. But this book had caught me unawares. Danielle's uncle was a master at pointing out the little, humanizing details, like the matching panda hats David and his daughter had bought on a trip to Niagara Falls. How, toward the end, their daughter had kept her rapidly deteriorating parents entertained with outlandish stories.

When I was done, I curled against my pillow and sobbed until my eyes ached. I'd often worried about one or the other of my family members being killed, and with good reason. To imagine my whole world taken from me was unbearable. Yet so many people carried this weight every day. Danielle. Edwin. Mykhail. How did they go on? How did they put one foot in front of the other?

I wiped my face off and dragged myself out of bed. When Danielle opened her door, I was holding a chocolate bar and trying to be normal, but she wasn't fooled.

"I don't want to talk about it," she said. "You can only come in if you don't talk about it."

I nodded and entered. "I just wanted to see if you wanted some of this sea-salt chocolate bar. I don't think I should eat the whole thing."

She sat on the floor in the middle of a semicircle of sheets of papers that radiated out from her. Her pencils sat at her side and her fingers were stained with ink. Each paper had a variant of the same drawing. A lone wolf girl howling up at a full moon that encircled the silhouette of two large wolves loping away.

I sat stiffly on her bed. I felt as if I'd violated her trust somehow, even though all I'd done was my required reading. I broke off a piece of chocolate and handed it to her.

"My uncle is a fantastic writer but a horrible man. Do you know he made me read drafts of the book as he was writing? I had to spend the better part of a year down in the bomb shelter with him because he was so paranoid the power plant was going to blow." She took a small bite. "He belittled my art and said my parents had coddled me. He said my interests were a disgrace to them and their intellect." Her eyes were blank when she looked at me, like an unfinished drawing that was a few strokes of graphite away from that spark of life. "Lots of people have started to figure out who I am and why I got to come here. It sucks. I hate having to answer questions and for people to think they know everything about me when they know nothing."

"I'm sorry. I—" I didn't know what to do.

While I was dawdling, she came to a decision. Her hand went up to her hat and before I could stop her, she pulled it off. The back of her hair was thick and lustrous, but her hairline went back almost as far as the crown of her head. She ran her fingers over the raw, flaky skin. "I twist my hair off in my sleep. Nerves. I wish I sucked my thumb instead." She shrugged and pulled the hat back on. "I wanted you to know. The hat is cute, but I don't wear it because I'm some airhead stuck in fantasyland."

"Thank you for sharing that with me." I was scrambling. My first friend in forever had confided something enormous in me, and I had nothing to give her in return. Maybe not nothing. "Was 'Sweet Child of Mine' really your mom's favorite song, like it says in the book? I know it...I can sing it if you want."

She had reached a hand out for her pencil and it hovered there now. I wondered if I'd said the wrong thing, but then she gave a single nod. "I'd like that," she said. She picked up her pencil and began her sketch anew on a fresh sheet of paper. She stretched her arms as she worked so the paper was out of reach of the tears that dripped from her chin. She worked quickly, and a moment after I warbled the last note she put down her pencil and examined the final product. "I think this is the one." With that, she stood and tacked it over one of the posters beside her bed. "Thanks, Maggie."

I left the chocolate on her bed when I made my exit, then went and washed my face in the bathroom. This time, I did examine myself in the mirror. What was reflected was maybe the luckiest person at the whole damn school, yet I was working myself up over boy troubles.

"Perspective," I whispered. My phone rang, the chirping echoing off the bathroom tiles. An unfamiliar number flashed on the screen.

"Maggie? This is Felix. We were wondering if Edwin talked to you after he left here?"

I was already through the bathroom door, jogging back to my room. Felix wouldn't call just to say hello. "No. Why?"

"He kiiiinda got electrocuted and—"

"What?" I shouted. The student in the room I was running past slammed his door shut.

"I don't think it was, like, getting-struck-by-lightning electrocuted, but he wouldn't go to the hospital and now he isn't answering his phone."

I knew Edwin was probably fine. I knew I shouldn't blow things out of proportion. But I'd just read a book that was a personal meditation on loss. By the end, a certain refrain had been made clear. *If I'd known that was the last time I would talk to him, I would have...*

"I'm going to his place now," I said and hung up.

I couldn't help but think of the way I had left things with Edwin. I needed to make things right—if I still had time.

24

I was out of breath by the time I got to his dorm across campus, partially from running and partially from the thought of anything happening to him. When I'd thought I lost Devon, the pain had been very real, but it had been for the idea of a person and not who he really was. With Edwin, it would be so much worse. I knew his particular smell. I knew the texture of his skin and of his tongue. I knew the way he tilted his head to the side and lowered his eyelids at me when I did something to annoy him, and that intense look I now knew meant that he wanted me. I couldn't lose that, either via freak electrocution or my own stupidity.

I followed one of his dorm mates in and hurried through the unfamiliar hallways searching for room 4J. Four flights and one unintentional man ass viewing later, I was outside his door. I knocked hard, ignoring the several notes from women asking him when he was free scrawled across his message board. I knocked again, harder, and then heard the sound of something crashing to the floor, followed by a muffled *"Carajo!"*

I tried the doorknob and pushed hard, expecting resistance where there was none so I stumbled in over the threshold into darkness. I ran my hand over the wall until I hit the light switch and squeaked at what I saw.

"Oh my God!" Edwin stood groggily next to his bed clad in nothing but the smooth expanse of brown skin, the aforementioned deity had blessed him with. His body was muscular, not like a bodybuilder's but like someone who went to the gym regularly and had a job in manual labor. Dark hair curled tightly over his chest, losing its kink as it traveled down over the ridges of his abdomen and into the thatch that surrounded... I slid my eyes away from his groin, focusing on the girth of his thighs instead, which seemed less pervalicious.

"Mags?" He blinked at me, and the appendage at his groin nodded a greeting at me, as well. He turned to put on a pair of shorts, but not before his erection raised to half-mast before my eyes. I was intrigued at how his penis seemed to have an agenda of its own, straining outward, while Edward tried to make himself decent. It felt silly to be surprised, but it wasn't as if I'd had much experience. I wanted to know more, though. My instinct was to walk over and grip him in my fist, to explore every part of him until nothing could surprise me anymore. At that thought, I felt a clenching need low in my body; it seemed Edwin wasn't the only one with autonomous genitalia.

"What are you doing here?" he asked, his voice hoarse. He sat on his bed, and I took a few steps closer.

"Felix called me and told me you got electrocuted. I came over expecting to find, well, not this." I motioned to his now partially clothed glory, and he laughed.

"Disappointed?" The raise of his brows indicated he already knew the answer to that.

"Why did Felix lie to me?" I asked instead of responding. I hoped he would say it was part of his clever ruse to get me to his room, but he shrugged.

"You know he can be a little overprotective. I opened a door at the plant that had been wired to a car battery."

My breath left me in a rush. "What? Why would anyone do that?" I knew why, obviously. They wanted to hurt someone, and that someone had almost been Edwin.

"There was a lot of mischief done at the plant. Whoever it was wanted to take the electricity out, and when they couldn't do that they went apeshit everywhere else. Lucky for me, they had no idea what they were doing. I only got a bit of a shock, but I think it really freaked Felix out."

"I know Felix is careful, but he's not one to freak out over nothing. Tell me the truth."

"Okay, maybe I got thrown back a few feet, but seriously, I'm fine!" His last few words were said on a laugh as I stomped over and made like I was going to push him for lying to me. He held me by the wrists and lay down, pulling me onto the bed beside him in one quick motion. He released my wrists and lay on his back, closing his eyes.

"I'm trying to recuperate," he said quietly. "You're supposed to be bringing me ice cream and stuff, not wailing on me."

"You could have been hurt, Edwin," I said. I shifted a bit closer to him, wanting to feel the warmth of him along my side.

"Nah." He motioned upward with his head. "You forget that I've got some people up there looking out for me. If I've made it this far, I'll be okay."

My throat went tight at his words, and I placed my hand on his shoulder. "I hope they're not looking now," I said before I leaned in and kissed him. I surprised him, although I didn't understand why, as he'd just pulled me into bed with him while in a state of undress. This was the next reasonable course of action.

I took advantage of my momentary upper hand and licked over his bottom lip, testing the plumpness of it between my teeth. He groaned, a deep and satisfied sound that already had me plotting how to draw it out of him again. His tongue snaked out to meet mine and I felt their joining in my entire body, a decadent ripple of pleasure that spread down my neck and back. The same frenzy that had descended on us in the car returned as his soft lips pressed bruising kisses into mine, as his hands cradled my neck gently and then roughly grabbed the edge of my hoodie instead, as if he wouldn't exert that kind of strength on me, only my inanimate clothing.

I pushed him for real then, rolling him onto his back as I straddled him. He brought his hands between us to unzip my hoodie without removing his mouth from mine, without stopping the ridiculously sexy thrust of his tongue that matched the rocking of his hips up from the bed. My hips were moving in kind, chasing his without any effort of my own, the same as when we'd danced. Once I picked up on the basic rhythm, I inserted my own variations that made what we were doing our own unique dance. His hands slid up my thighs, under my shirt, to grip the bare skin of my waist and settle me lower down on his body. When the thickness of his cock bumped against my behind, my rhythm went off completely and I gasped into his mouth.

He stopped moving, except for kissing my lips, my cheeks, the smooth skin beneath my eyes. "We should stop," he said.

"Why would you say something crazy like that?" I asked. I tilted my head so I could catch my lips with his, and the low groan he made when I licked into his mouth drove my need even further. I clasped his face with my hands as I kissed him, but he gently pulled his head back and looked at me with the "wise old man" look that always showed up just when we were having a good time.

"Your first time should be special," he said.

I moved my ass against him a little, and he thrust up involuntarily. "Did you rent a room at the Ritz for your first time?"

He laughed and his body shook beneath me. "*Pssh*, no. It was in the bathroom at my friend's grand-mother's house."

"Classy," I said. "If that's the case, then this is the equivalent of a date with caviar and champagne."

He smoothed his palm over the back of my head and down my neck. The warm weight of it pushed pleas-antly against my spine as he moved down to cup my ass. "Maggie." He sighed. "You've barely even had time to date anyone. I don't want you to regret this."

Disappointment and humiliation slowed the movement of my hips, made it awkward and jerky instead of sinuous and sexy. "If you don't want to have sex with me, that's fine." My voice shook embarrassingly, but I continued. "But in case that shock earlier scrambled your memory, I've wanted this for a long time now. I'm pretty sure there's no way I'm going to regret this unless the top three men from my list of hot Brit-ish actors bust down the door in the afterglow and state that they'd been traveling for months to pop my cherry."

He didn't laugh. "You came to me before because you had a specific goal. I don't want to just be the guy who helped you meet that goal. I have feelings for you, and I have for a little while now."

It was my turn to be shocked. I sat up, and he fol-lowed so that I was settled comfortably on his lap, with my legs wrapped around him. His biceps looked like convenient armrests, so I placed my hands there. "How long is 'a little while'? Have you secretly liked me this whole time and I've been suffering for nothing?"

A furrow formed between his eyebrows. "No. Why would I wait for years to tell you I liked you if I knew the feeling was mutual?"

I let out the breath I'd been holding. "I'm confused."

"I mean, I always thought you were cool, but for a long time you were my friend's weird little sister who tried to bang me out of nowhere. I know because I have a penis, I'm supposed to think that's great, but...no." I cringed, shame dousing the heat that our kissing had built up within me. "Then you were my friend's weird little sister who hated me because I hadn't banged her."

"I didn't hate you." He stared at me and raised his brows. "Okay, maybe a little bit," I admitted, looking away from him.

His hand cupped my face and gently turned my head to his. His other hand brushed against my stomach and squeezed into the bit of space where the apex of my thighs wasn't flush against his body. The slow circle he worked there was enough to make me forget what we were even talking about. "But when I came to visit a couple of months before you went to school, I drove up and heard this amazing voice belting out a song. It was a woman's voice, not a girl's, and it grabbed me by the dick and dragged me around the side of the house and led me to you. You were snapping peas or some other Betty Crocker shit, but your voice was ethereal. And then John came outside and when the singing stopped, you started joking with him and you were hilarious."

"I've always been able to sing, and I've always been funny," I said, letting my immodest flag fly. And why not? I was practically humping the guy's hand at the same time, so he had to know I wasn't some meek little thing. "Why then?"

"You always held something back around me after that day in Darlene's place," he said. "And I was okay with that because you were just my friend's sister. The day I caught you singing I got to see the real you, who you were when I wasn't there making you feel awkward."

"Why didn't you— Fuck." I paused as his fingers hit a spot that made my whole body go tight. I leaned my forehead against his and rode out the trembling pleasure that momentarily stole my ability to speak. "Why didn't you say anything?" I was learning it was hard to have a conversation when a guy was trying to get you off at the same time.

"Things were already weird, given our history, and then when you got here, Internet Dude was on the scene." He looked regretful, even though he was the one making me hot with the friction of both his hand and syncopated thrusts from his still-hard cock.

I let my head fall back as sensation raced up my spine.

"I don't want to hold anything back from you tonight," I said. "I don't want to be with you because of some stupid goal. I want you because you make me laugh, and you make me crazy and you're always on my mind."

"Are you—" he began, and I hopped out of his arms

and off the bed, quickly pulling off my jeans, tee and undergarments and placing my hands on my hips.

"Am I sure? Yes. Let's do this already."

His gaze ran appreciatively over my body, followed by his hands. His palms dragged down over my collarbone, then the slope of my breasts, brushing roughly over my nipples again and again. Each pass of his hand over the sensitive skin drew a little gasp from me, higher in pitch after each go-around, like a windup toy reaching the end of its spring.

He flashed me a devilish smile. "I was going to ask if you were thirsty, but this is good too." He laid me back on the bed and his mouth followed the trail of sensation his hands had already made on my skin. He breathed over my clavicle, sucked at my nipples, dragged his teeth over the undersides of my breasts. I dug my fingers into his sheets and tried to process the variety of sensations. His tongue forged a path to undiscovered lands as he licked his way down. The slick slide of it across my belly was magnetic, pulling feathery brushes of tingling heat in its wake.

"Edwin?" I wasn't afraid of him, but I still pressed my knees together instinctively. He parted them gently, settling my legs over his shoulders. His muscles flexed beneath my thighs as he adjusted his position, and then the only muscle I was aware of was his tongue. He licked into me roughly, sliding across every nerve along my clit and propelling waves of pleasure through my body. I couldn't stop trembling and I wondered if the way my body was reacting without my control was normal. Was my abdomen supposed to keep tightening like this? Were my legs supposed to shake with strain, even though he was supporting my weight?

Something nudged at my opening and slowly slid in, and all my anxious thoughts faded into so much white noise. His tongue licked and pressed and his fingers, first one and then, just when I had gotten acclimated, another, stretched me. My hips rocked up to bring my clit to his mouth and down to meet the thrust of his fingers, each motion building to bring me closer and closer to falling apart—or to coming together.

He licked a little slower and curved his fingers on the withdrawal; I scooched down the bed after them as if they beckoned me. I didn't know where the condom came from; I was distracted by the way he pumped himself with the hand he'd just used to pleasure me, the way my wetness was slick on his cock before he rolled the condom over himself. Then he kneeled between my legs again, shoving a pillow under my butt to give me some comfort before the inevitable pain.

He lowered himself over me and our lips met as he slid just his head in and stopped. He pulled his mouth away from mine and dropped his forehead to my shoulder.

"What?" I asked, pushing my hips forward.

He clamped a hand on my waist to prevent me from moving. The muscles of his back rippled under my hand. His eyes were serious and his voice strained when he spoke. "I don't mean to sound like a sleazy cliché, but you're so fucking tight. I don't want this to hurt too much."

"That's so sweet," I said, and it was. I felt every ounce of his care for me in those words, and I knew for sure that I hadn't been wrong to place my trust in him. That didn't stop me from knocking his hand away from my waist and thrusting up. One of us had to be brave, and the longer we waited the more it would hurt.

I cried out—I'd underestimated how painful that sharp pinch would be. I'd started to believe it had to be a myth. Why should something so popular cause such pain? I'd been wrong.

Edwin cried out too, but in pleasure, and thank goodness, then he took over. I lay in shock for a moment as he moved in me, wondering why I'd wanted this, why I'd ever thought it could be good. Then Edwin twisted his hips up and to the left, and his cock rubbed against a spot that sent a burst of undiluted "fuck, yes" through me instead of the shredding disappointment of only moments before.

His gaze caught mine and held it as he repeated the motion, and another ribbon of pain was replaced with something hot and pulsing and fantastic. I nodded, and he kept up the motion. Sweat beaded on his brow and his hands were busy touching and teasing me, as if trying to compensate for the discomfort he'd caused me. His thrusts and the strokes of his fingers between my legs felt amazing, but I knew he was holding back from the way his teeth were gritted and the muscles bunched at his neck. I could feel how close he was from the way he grew even harder and hotter inside of me. He was holding his orgasm off until I'd had mine. Sweet, but unrealistic. It was my first time and, unfortunately, I didn't think life worked like that.

I wrapped my legs around his waist, joining my feet behind his back for leverage while I increased the pace of our joining. His cock pushed even deeper, and I cried out, grabbing him by the back of the neck with one hand and the bed with the other. "Come for me," I managed on a pant. It was creepy, but something I'd seen guys tell their women in books I read, and it was supposed to work like a charm.

Edwin was immune to the command, apparently. "Maggie." My name was dragged out of him, a desperate plea. I couldn't give him what he wanted, though—or I thought I couldn't. Then his thumb pressed into my clit, hard, and the orgasm pulled me under without warning. The sheets bunched between my grasping fingers and my entire body lifted from the bed as I screamed my release.

Edwin followed, grunting and groaning and making strange un-Edwin-like sounds as he thrust hard into me one last time.

He rolled us over onto our sides, running his fingers through my hair, kissing me and telling me how special I was.

I smiled against his forearm, turned my head and dropped a kiss there. "Are you always this wonderful, or is this the post-devirginization special? A girl could get used to this." I winced as he pulled out, even though he was trying to be careful.

"I'm sorry," he whispered, kissing my eyelids.

"Do you need anything?"

"An ice pack," I murmured, and he laughed.

"You're going to give me a big head," he said, and I shook my head.

"We wouldn't want that. If that thing gets any bigger, there's no way we can do that again."

He ran his knuckles along my jawline. "So you're already planning round two then?" he asked, lying down beside me.

"And more," I said as I drifted to sleep. "And more."

25

I'd never thought about what would happen after I was no longer a virgin. I'd looked at it as a one-off thing I'd cross off of my to-do list, secure in the fact that something important to me was no longer up for grabs.

But I hadn't known that one night wouldn't be enough. I'd hoped our night together wouldn't be the last time, but I hungered for Edwin in ways I hadn't thought possible. Without discussion, we began spending nearly all of our free time together, and during that quality time I learned that there was a lot more to sex than the one-and-done mindset I'd had for years. After just two weeks, spending the night away from him left me tossing and turning. I would zone out in class, distracted by the taste of him and how he'd groaned the first time I'd taken him into my mouth, like I was a sex goddess instead of a newbie. Mostly, I thought of how he made me feel in those quiet moments when we weren't all over each other, when we laughed and talked.

Edwin was taking business management track classes, with the exception of the World Mythology course he shared with Danielle. Of course, that was what he loved the most. I hadn't read many of the myths since junior high, so he shared his favorites with me, analyzing the text and how they fit into our modern world.

"Which characters from Greek mythology do you think we'd be?" I asked as we drove back from work in his truck. It was snowing in earnest. The only difference between late autumn and winter in this area was whether we got a ton of snow or a shit ton of snow.

Edwin shook his head. "You really did grow up in the age of the internet quiz, didn't you?" I rolled my eyes, and he tugged my earlobe. "I don't want to be any of those characters. They don't exactly get happy endings."

"And you think we will?" I asked without thinking.

He pulled up to a stop sign and took the opportunity to lean over and kiss me. "Of course we will. Remember, there's a whole Hernandez squad watching out for us. You get covered under my guardian angel plan, like insurance."

It was a small thing, but I felt a sudden tightness in my chest that he would include me in something as intimate as his family's imaginary protection plan. Was that his way of saying that he thought they would have approved of me? I pretended the answer to that question was yes.

He dropped me off in front of my dorm, pulling me in for a kiss that made me deeply regret that I couldn't invite him in. "Are you sure that paper is due tomorrow morning? Can't you ask for an extension?" he asked. His fingers tugged at the button of my woolen jacket.

"You wouldn't be encouraging me to fall behind in my studies, would you?" I asked. "You're supposed to guide me on the path to glory, O wise elder."

I knew he was joking, since he was much more serious about getting his work done than I was, but I was tempted to help him along with the buttons.

"I'll show you glory, all right." He coiled, as if he was going to pounce on me, but I opened the door, letting in the brisk breeze in.

"I'll see you tomorrow night. Remember we're gonna have a snowmageddon movie night? I'm not sitting through four feet of snow by myself." I gave him a last peck on the mouth before sliding out of the car and jogging through the cold to the lobby of the dorm. Once he saw me safely inside, he pulled away. It hurt seeing him drive off. The logical part of me knew that having time to myself was essential, but my desire to be with Edwin bordered on obsessive.

It's normal, Arden had emailed when I'd gone to her with my concerns. Once you learn all his annoying habits you'll get over it. I'd stared at the message doubtfully. I already knew lots of his annoying habits and I was still way too into him for my own good. Arden sent a follow-up message before I could respond. I still get excited like a puppy whenever Gabe comes home from a shift, so take that advice with several grains of salt.

The truth was, I was disquieted by how wrapped I was in him. Edwin had always had a kind of power over me; now it was just acknowledged by both of us. And now he had the ability to take it away. But I wouldn't give up the way he smiled at me because of a few fears. I told myself it was okay as long as I maintained a balance. No fucking up my schoolwork and no ignoring my friends.

I knocked on Danielle's door before heading to my room. When she opened it, I looked shiftily about and pulled open one flap of my coat. "Can I interest you in some fine, high-quality product? Fell off the back of a truck." I shimmied so the two packets of hot cocoa I'd stuffed in my inner pocket earlier showed.

She smiled, but I didn't get the giggly laughter I was used to her from her. Maybe she was mad at me because I hadn't been able to do breakfast as much over the last couple of weeks. I'd worked hard not to make her feel like I was choosing a guy over our friendship, but sometimes a morning booty call meant that waffles had to wait.

"Oh, sorry, it's just...I have someone over. We got assigned to work on a project together. That's it." It was the way her brow creased anxiously and the words ran together as she talked that tipped me off to who was behind the door. She pulled it open a bit to reveal Devon reclining on her bed. Relaxed. Natural. As if it wasn't the first time.

He gave me a brief lift of his chin.

It was all so ridiculous. The sixteen-year-old still latent in my brain screamed at the betrayal, and if Devon had been the man I thought he was, the twenty-year-old me would have too. But I knew Danielle had been scared of him before, and that she had reason to fear men who lost their temper; any possible jealousy was overridden by worry for my friend. I motioned for her to step outside.

She turned to Devon. "Can you excuse me a moment?" And then she stepped out with me into the hall.

"Danielle, is everything okay? I know you never got along with him, so I'm a little confused right now." I was trying not to sound like a jealous ex, but this was all too surreal for me. I knew a lot could happen in a couple of weeks, but she'd never even seemed too keen on being in the same room with him, never mind alone with him stretched out on her bed.

She put a hand to her forehead, and that was when I realized the bear hat was gone. She wore a stylish slouchy beret instead, the kind with silver sparkles laced through the knit work. "Nothing has happened, but I think maybe I was wrong about him. We got assigned to do a project for chemistry, and I'm terrible at it, so he's been meeting me for breakfast to explain stuff to me, which is nice of him." She paused and said almost miserably, "He thinks I'm smart. And he said my art is genius and he can help me get a gallery show in the Student Center this spring."

Anger and unease twisted in my stomach like a nest

of snakes. I knew the charming, seductive side of Devon all too well. It was what had pulled me to my laptop screen every night years earlier, and what allowed me to overlook his huge lie and try to forge a relationship with him all these years later. The ragey side of me wondered just how coincidental it was that he'd suddenly taken an interest in my closest friend. My bullshit detector beeped loudly at the possibility of a gallery show ever happening. Danielle wasn't stupid, but she was young, impressionable and lonely. I knew I wasn't responsible for her choices, but I couldn't help but feel like I'd brought someone into her life who could do her harm.

I felt trapped in a cage made of my own missteps. I hadn't shared with Danielle the more fucked-up things Devon had done to me, partially because I was ashamed I'd been strung along so easily and because she disliked him already, so it hadn't seemed necessary. But now, if I busted out with everything, I would seem like a jealous ex trying to protect her territory. You couldn't tell someone a sheep was really a wolf; they had to find that out when it was time to do the shearing. Still…I couldn't let her walk blindly into even just a friendship with him. I tried to figure out the right way to politely phrase "He might be a psychopath."

"Are you mad at me?" Danielle squeaked, fingers inching up under her hat.

Well, yeah. Kind of. But not enough to hope she suffered. I thought about what her last week must have been like, feeling like she was betraying me while I was off having great sex and cuddle time.

"No. No, of course not. I don't have any lingering feelings for him." Beyond anger and, now, disgust, that was. I took a deep breath and tried to figure out how to say the next thing without being condescending. "I want you to be careful, okay? Devon comes in a pretty package, but he's not all he pretends to be. I won't tell you what to do, but gut instincts are often right, and yours was to tell me to stay away from him."

She looked down, her mouth crumpling from the tentative smile that had appeared when I'd said I wasn't mad at her. "We're just friends."

Even though I was doing what was right, I hated upsetting her. Everything Danielle had told me about her life after the Flare and before Oswego was sad, if not downright horrifying. She'd had less experience with love and more experience with pain than me. I wanted to protect her, but it ultimately wasn't up to me. I thought again of the romance novels we'd all swapped back at the cabin—even the most reviled villain could be redeemed by a little love and understanding. Maybe Devon needed someone like her to help him get his act together. Maybe she could do for him—or they could do for each other—what I couldn't. Even if I thought he could use a quick trip down a long flight of stairs, at this point all I could do was try to watch out for her.

"I get it. Just keep in mind that he can be manipulative. I'll be your friend no matter what, but if anything feels weird to you, you shouldn't brush it aside." I reached into my pocket and handed her the two packets of cocoa. "Here. I need caffeine more than sweets anyway to get this paper done. A sugar crash at two in the morning won't do me any favors."

She gave me a quick hug and a kiss on the cheek before slipping back into her room. I caught Devon looking our way as the door opened.

Before it closed, I shot him a glare, pointing to my two eyes and then jabbing my fingers in his direction. *I'm watching you.* I didn't stop glaring until the door closed, and then I stepped into my messy lair and paced back and forth, trying to tamp down the suspicion that this was the beginning of something bad. It was out of my control, whatever the ultimate outcome was. I'd warned her, and if necessary I would confront Devon. For now, I would do my work and mind my own business. Part of being a good friend was being there to catch someone when they fell—I just hoped Danielle wouldn't need that particular feature anytime soon.

26

The next night, I tried to pay attention to the movie playing on the small screen of Edwin's laptop, despite his constant interruptions. "Just watch the movie!" I snapped with an incredulous laugh after he asked me why a character was doing what they were doing for the tenth time. This particular annoying habit was still endearing…for now. Outside, wind howled past the window, and thick clumps of snow fell and accumulated fast.

I smacked Edwin's hand away as it crept up under my shirt, but only in jest. The movie we were watching was a superhero flick I'd already seen several times over. It was fun, but cuddling under the covers with Edwin beat out the triumphant defeat of aliens. I reached over and closed the laptop screen, and then crawled on top of him. My underwear was hanging from his desk chair after the greeting he'd given me a few hours earlier, and his teasing over the last half hour meant I was already slick and ready for him.

His cock was hard, but it still swelled in my palm as I grasped and pumped. I moved so I was hovering just above him, slowly started lowering myself down—and then stopped before I made contact. "You're not the only one who can tease," I said.

He smirked. "That may be true, but I'm much more patient. Military training, remember?" His body went stiff as he pulled his hand to his forehead and drew himself up into a horizontal version of standing at attention.

"We'll see about that," I said. He was right, though—I was too impatient for this kind of game. I grabbed a condom from his bedside table and rolled it onto him before lowering myself onto his hardness. I gasped at the sensation of his head pushing into me, spreading me. Edwin swallowed a hiss but didn't move from his position, a silent goad. He was well aware that I couldn't resist a challenge.

I splayed my hands on his chest and held his gaze as I began moving. His lips were pressed into a thin line and his gaze was hard and hot as I fucked him. I sank and rose, circling my hips on the downswing to take him deeper into me. I closed my eyes and dug my fingers into his chest, not even caring whether he came along with me because he felt so good. I'd gotten into my own rhythm, an unbearably good friction as I rose on his shaft and my clit pleasantly smacked his groin when I bottomed out, when he thrust up to meet me. His sudden motion caught me by surprise and in the best possible way. Just that one movement brought me close to the edge, the unexpected friction detonating through me.

"Holy fuck." I placed a hand on his chest to steady myself.

"You were having a little too much fun without my participation," he said. His hands came to my hips and now he met me thrust for thrust, pulsing up into me in a barrage so intense that my entire body shook from the force of him. It had been great doing all the work myself, but with him helping it was even better. Like everything was.

I'd thought I'd take him for a long, languorous ride, but I came apart before I knew what hit me. He bucked beneath me and was still shuddering from his own orgasmic bliss when I collapsed on top of him.

"Do you hear that, or is that a side effect of having your brains fucked out?" I asked as my breath came back to me.

He cursed, and not in the "shit, that feels good" kind of way. The sirens were blaring again, after a relatively peaceful week. Each flare-up of neo-Luddite activity had been put down, but they hadn't decreased. The biggest saving grace had been the DIY-ness of the efforts thus far, mostly carried out by people who'd read outdated manuals.

Edwin turned his face into his pillow and growled loudly, then rolled to face me. "You know what this means."

"You have to go investigate," I said. The first couple of times it'd happened, I'd mock-pouted, but as time went on,

I realized how serious this really was. After the trashing of the plant, there hadn't been any attacks in Oswego proper, but a group of armed men had been intercepted on their way to Burnell only the week before. They'd been hell-bent on taking out the telecommunications group, and it chilled me to the bone that John, Mykhail and other people I knew were in danger for simply trying to help.

A transformer refurbishing center in Pennsylvania had nearly burned to the ground in a suspicious fire that would set production in the Northeast back for months and affect projected electrical output increases for the next couple of years. Places that had looked forward to finally being done with rolling blackouts now had to hold off on moving forward with plans for electricity intensive rebuilding projects.

So whereas before the thought of Edwin going to look into these incidents had kind of freaked me out, now it scared the shit out of me. He quickly pulled on his clothes, and I tried to act like a supportive girlfriend, which I supposed I was even though we hadn't made anything official.

He grinned up at me while he finished tying his boots. "You can watch the end of the movie in peace now," he joked, but the words triggered the fear I'd been trying to suppress. A strangled sound escaped my throat and suddenly tears were flowing down my face. "Aw, don't worry—"

Everything went silent just as he pulled me into his arms. The sirens cut off abruptly, and the lights went out right after. Judging from the commotion in the hall, it wasn't a blown fuse in the room. I stumbled over to the window, and he followed, still holding my hand. Outside was complete darkness except for the halos from flashlights and cell phones beginning to pop up across campus.

I, probably like everyone else, was already thinking back to those first minutes after the Flare. I was already thinking of an escape plan and what I would need to survive the next few days, but I forced myself to take a deep breath. Not every blackout was permanent, even if some people wanted it that way.

"Shouldn't the generators be kicking in right now?" I asked, already knowing the answer.

Edwin squeezed my hand and then moved away from me, only to be illuminated by his cell phone a moment later. "Nothing," he muttered.

I ran to check mine and my breath caught. He gave me a quizzical look, and I handed him the phone, the message from Danielle still showing.

```
greg falling leaf pow
```

"Shit. Danielle sent me a text and I know this isn't good." I'd mostly forgotten about my interactions with Greg, focusing instead on what had happened with Danielle and everything that had occurred between Edwin and me afterward. But now I remembered the weird way Greg had let me know that he knew where I lived. Before, it seemed like he was just being a jerk.

"Her parents were two of the Falling Leaf Five, right? Maybe the message has something to do with that?" he asked.

"But then what does Greg have to do with any of it?" I shot back. I started pulling on my clothes too, trying to remain calm but knowing in my bones that Danielle was in trouble and Devon had something to do with it.

"Hey." Edwin stood. "It was after everyone had that assignment when Devon decided Danielle didn't annoy him anymore, right? Aw, fuck." Now Edwin was pacing too, running a hand over his freshly cut hair. "So remember I told you I had a bad feeling about Devon's little club? This week they popped up in one of the debriefing memos. Listed as having possible neo-Luddite sympathies. I don't want to freak you out, but one of the latest plans they've discussed on social media is taking high-profile hostages."

I should have been outraged, but numbness stole through my body, buffering me from the way what Edwin was suggesting matched up with reality. I'd warned Danielle away, but I should have been more insistent. I should have made a kitten-themed slideshow or whatever it took to get the point across that Devon was bad news. But I'd let that last little scrap of hope I had in his humanity distract me.

"Devon is a little shit, but he wouldn't be mixed up in that. Would he?"

There was a pounding at the door, and Edwin went

into that alert military stance I'd seen a few times before. He put a finger to his mouth to signal I should be quiet. I nodded and pulled on my leggings. He tiptoed to the door and peered through the hole, and his shoulders dropped in relief. I released the breath I'd been holding. It was a friend.

Edwin swung open the door and slapped hands with someone. "Felix, man. I'm glad you're here. Can you stay with Maggie? I have a bad feeling about those sirens."

Felix frowned. "You're right, man. Unfortunately you're right." That was when I noticed the gun in his hand, the gun he pointed at Edwin's torso. "Maggie is going to have to come with me."

Edwin's guns were still locked away in his closet. I already saw what was going to happen next: Edwin lunging for the gun, Felix shooting, Edwin gone forever. I yelled as Edwin was readjusting his footing to a fighting stance. "Okay! I'll come. Just don't hurt him."

"No way. No *fucking* way." Edwin glared at me, but Felix reached into his coat pocket and pulled out a set of handcuffs.

"Put these on him and attach him to that pipe. Try anything funny, and I'll shoot him." He sounded remorseful about it, but not enough that I would test his loyalties.

My lungs felt like two blown speakers, unable to function. A few minutes ago, I'd been in post-coital bliss, and now I couldn't even process what was going on. My hands shook as I took the cuffs, like I was already outside in the cold. A memory of being tackled into the hard-packed snow resurfaced. I dropped the handcuffs and then picked them back up.

"I'm sorry." My voice was almost gone from the strain of not crying as I loosely cuffed him. It hurt to see his face twisted in disbelief, to know that the only thing holding him back from attacking Felix was me. I didn't want to become just another woman he hadn't been able to protect, but I wouldn't let him get hurt when the end result would be the same.

Felix pushed past me and tightened the cuffs, and Edwin lunged at him, only to be yoked back by the handcuffs catching against the pipe with a metallic scrape. He turned his tortured gaze to Felix. "How can you calmly do this shit? Like we're not friends?"

Felix looked sad. "I didn't want to do this part, but if someone else came to get her they probably would have ended up killing you."

Edwin's nostrils flared and his eyes were wide with rage. "Why are you doing this? Money?"

Felix shook his head. "Money isn't worth anything right now, and it should stay that way. Keeping the peace has a cost. You should know that." He pulled a second set of handcuffs from his pocket. "Now you." Once my hands were cuffed in front of me, he grabbed my arm and pulled me toward the dark hallway outside the door. "Your brother is a bigwig, and we need good hostages for maximum exposure." He pressed the gun into my side, and every self-defense move I'd ever learned evaporated from my mind. I was sixteen and being attacked by a crazed man in the woods. I was eighteen, and a guy was shoving his hand up my skirt. I was a victim, again, and there was nothing I could do about it.

"Edwin. I— Thank you. Don't worry, everything will be all right." I hadn't taken statistics this semester, but it seemed that my third time being held against my will substantially lowered my chances of getting off scot-free. I hoped this was one of those math things I was wrong about.

"Maggie!" Edwin's voice reverberated down the hall. The hot tears that had been pressing against my eyelids spilled out as I was buffeted by Edwin's anguish. Felix tried not to be rough as he pulled me after him and into the stairwell, but as shock set in, it became harder for me to keep coordinated. He pushed me out the front door and into the cold, where a car sat idling. A familiar, much-too-fancy muscle car.

Felix opened the back door and pushed me in beside Danielle, then climbed in next to me.

"Aw, Margaret. You don't look happy to see me," Greg said from behind the wheel.

I ignored him and glared at Devon, who sat ramrod-straight in the passenger seat and refused to look back. Danielle shivered beside me, unspeaking, and I snuggled close to her.

"Let's get this show on the road," Greg said. He

slapped Devon on the thigh like they were two buds heading out on a road trip, and then turned the ignition. "Next stop, Falling Leaf!"

27

I hated sitting in the middle seat during car rides, but that was the least of my worries.

"Devon, what's going on?" My voice sounded like someone else's, a woman who was angry and not one who was shaking so violently she had to hold her knees together to still them. I could trust him as far as I could throw him, but he was the only one who had even the slightest reason to be honest with me.

"A revolution is what's going on," Greg answered, and he smacked the wheel a couple of times like he was pumping himself up for a night at the club instead of an act of terrorism.

"Led by you? And what exactly is the point of this revolution? You don't want to pay taxes?"

"I can't expect someone like you to understand, since you've already proven yourself a sheep, but think about it for a minute. Over the last few years, people learned to do for themselves. They survived without government intervention. They *thrived*, even."

"You are aware that millions of people died, right?" I asked, but he was already speaking over me.

"You know how half of the casualties died? Police shootings when people scavenged for food. There's your government intervention. And now the sheeple are happy to sit back and let the restructuring begin. Notice I didn't say rebuilding. They want to take away everything that was good about this country and turn it into a haven for the rich." He was working himself into a froth, his voice loud like he was projecting to the back of a theater and not a car. "Now it's a return to destroying the environment with fracking and pipelines and offshore drilling. Constitutional amendments. Martial law. And for what? Plenty of people have lived off the grid for years. We don't need anyone telling us what to do to survive."

I looked at Felix, who was nodding along like he was at church. He believed in Greg and what he was saying. I leaned toward the front of the car. "Before the revolution begins, can you give some citations for where you're getting this information from? Because if I'm going to give credence to anything you're saying, which all sounds like conspiracy theory bullshit, I'm gonna need to see the receipts."

"I don't need you to support what I'm doing. You're a

hostage, so all you have to do is look pretty and be absorbent enough to take a bullet or ten."

His words pierced the thin armor that had been my protection from panic. Breathing became something I had to think about to do correctly, and the front seat of the car looked far away as tunnel vision messed with my perception. I wanted to slump back in my seat, give up and let fate unfurl as it saw fit. But then I thought of all the people who would be affected by their actions, and by non-action, and I had to keep pressing, even if the only thing I achieved was annoying them to death.

"So, you're fighting against something that the majority of society wants because you don't think it's the right choice," I said.

"That's right," he said proudly. He pulled a little bottle of liquor out of his pocket and took a swig. That was the thing that pushed me over the edge. He had kidnapped us and was driving us to the nuclear plant for reasons that obviously weren't good, and he couldn't even take his actions seriously enough to be sober. It was like this was a game for him, and my life and Danielle's life were pawns in it.

"You think it's okay for you to make decisions for an entire country's worth of people," I said. "Why is it not tyranny when *you* decide what happens? Or are you just so up your own ass that it never occurred to you what a hypocrite you are?"

"Maggie, be quiet, okay?" Devon said. He wasn't angry, like the last few times I'd spoken to him. His voice was hoarse with fatigue and tinged with sadness. "You think you know everything because of your brother's job, but I grew up around government people. I know they're nothing but liars."

The disconnect between the situation and the words coming out of his mouth were enough to send me into a rage that blotted out any common sense. I smacked the back of his headrest, my hand grazing the top of his head. "You selfish, useless, pathetic asshole! You're the biggest liar I know, and you dare try to lecture me about my own brother?" Felix grabbed my arms and pulled me down into my seat, but I was still railing. "The people I know working on the reconstruction bust their asses every day because they want to make the world a better place. For us. They give zero fucks about corporations or governments. Meanwhile, you're willing to follow some guy who has to hang out with people ten years younger than him and plans a revolution while drinking shitty home brew and drugging women."

Greg was unfazed. "I told you this chick was a bitch. She's lucky we need her. Until we get inside, that is. Unless there's some other reason to keep her around." And there it was. Of course he'd try to threaten me with *that*.

I laughed, mostly to hide the way I was shaking. My heart was beating too fast and my breath came in shallow little pants. "How do you think you're going to get past the soldiers blocking the place, dickhead?"

"Tell her, Devon," Greg said.

"Why don't we all shut up until we get there?" Devon muttered.

"I said tell her."

Devon sighed, as if he'd been chastised by a professor instead of a pathetic turd half his size. "There are a lot of useful things in trash, which is why I asked to be transferred to the farm. Working in the compost room gave me access to materials for making improvised explosive devices, paired with the stuff Felix could snag from maintenance."

A bomb. A bomb heading for the nuclear power plant.

Beside me, Danielle began to breathe in great, noisy gulps of air. "Let me out! I need to get out of here right now!" She began kicking at Devon's seat, clawing her way over him to try to release the lock on his door. Her behavior didn't make sense, given the speed of the car, but she was in the middle of a full-fledged panic attack.

"God damn it, Devon, was I wrong to bring you? You've gotten your ass kicked by two chicks already."

I was trying to calm Danielle down, but Devon whirled, leaned over his seat and landed three blows to Danielle's head in quick succession. She immediately went slack. He shrugged her back behind him, and she slumped in her seat.

"You're disgusting!" I shouted. I struggled against Felix, but there wasn't much I could do even if my hands were free. Tears slid down my face as I slumped back in my seat, defeated. "I wish you really had died after the Flare so I would never have known what an awful person you are."

He said nothing.

Greg laughed. "Can't live with 'em," he said nonsensically. His banality made me hate Devon even more. If he was following someone charismatic, it would be understandable. But this guy?

It didn't matter what I thought, though. The lights of Falling Leaf illuminated the road a few miles ahead. If they succeeded in their ridiculously narcissistic mission, they would fuck up all the progress of the last three years, in addition to killing thousands and creating a nuclear wasteland.

I tried to think of anything I could do to stall them, to prevent this from happening. As usual, only one skill set came to mind, but it played right into the "annoyance as distraction" plan.

"I hope you guys like show tunes," I said. Then I took a deep breath and started belting. Thank goodness for the Sondheim songbook John had gotten me as a gift. At that moment, "Send in the Clowns" was the only thing between a car full of eco-terrorists and nuclear fallout.

28

My brilliant plan of annoying them to death with the power of my pipes earned me a balled-up cloth shoved in my mouth. It was gently shoved, since Felix had retained his respect for women, but it tasted like burnt hair smelled. I had to wrestle my body for control over my gag reflex; I wouldn't give Greg the satisfaction of making me choke to death on my own puke.

As we pulled up to the power plant, Felix looked at me apologetically. "If you do anything stupid, I'll have to kill you."

It was then that it sank in. I was going to die. I remembered a sick game my friend and I had played back in high school. We'd discussed international disasters and decided how we would have done things differently. "I wouldn't sit there and let them cut my head off." "I would have kara-te-chopped that dude when I saw him trying to enter the cockpit."

I cringed to think of our lack of empathy and our overconfidence. We'd talked a big game, like asshole teen-agers tended to do, but Marisa was dead so I was the only one who'd have to pony up. I wasn't braver than any of the people whose memories we'd disrespected with the stupid shock-value games teens played. Given my track record, I was positive about that. When things upset me, I ran. When I was frightened, I did the same. But there was no running now. I'd either die in this car, or in that power plant if I remained silent and we got through, or when the explosion happened—I doubted they were going to take Danielle and me with them once they achieved their objective. I wasn't even sure they had an exit plan. Fa-natics weren't always partial to that key part of a well-laid caper.

As the floodlights surrounding the plant grew brighter, a sudden melancholy descended on me. My life didn't flash before my eyes. Maybe that was because I hadn't gotten to live it yet. Instead, I briefly revisited a memory of my family playing poker. My parents cheating like mad by signaling each other; Arden and Gabriel dead-set on beating each other even though others were playing; John and Mykhail playing one hand between the two of them because it was always them against the world. I'd won that game, even though I'd been alone.

Not such a bad life, if this was it for me. I'd even

gotten to experience falling for someone. I thought of Edwin, chained in his room and frantic because he had to have figured out what Danielle's message meant by now. I wished there was some way to tell him that it was okay that he didn't protect me. He'd let me make my own decisions leading up to that moment, and I'd chosen to protect him.

We were approaching the gate. I could see the forms of the guards and their big guns, and the way they were all turning to face the car that approached without slowing down. An incongruous muscle car screaming toward them in the middle of the night.

I made a decision. If I was going to die, it wouldn't be in some tool's blaze of glory. I wouldn't let Greg think he'd gone out a martyr. The handcuffs keeping me from moving too much were metal, linked by eight chain links. I stared at them for a long time, then inhaled deeply. I'd sat relaxed for so long, and Felix was so enthralled with the scene approaching through the windshield, that I moved before he could act. I leaned forward with both hands straight out, and when I pulled back and down, Greg's neck was beneath the chain links. I planted my feet against the back of his seat to provide added pressure as I pulled down, then clasped my hands together and twisted at the wrists so they couldn't be pried apart. I garroted him like my dad had taught me once he'd been satisfied with my skills at eye gouging and palms to the nose. "When someone is much, much bigger, or maybe just depending on your mood, you'll need to know how to choke the hell out of them."

The car careened off the slippery road, away from the gate. Devon grabbed the wheel, trying to course-correct, but Greg was pressing down on the gas hard as he tried to bend away from the pressure cutting off his air supply. Felix was hitting me, raining punches down on me, but I only relaxed my grip when the car wobbled and left the ground and my feet could no longer keep me planted back in my seat.

We rolled and rolled for what seemed like an hour instead of a few seconds. I felt the briefest moment of victory, but then the car jerked and there was a sharp pain in one of the arms that were still stretched out in front of me, trapped in that position by the handcuffs. Glass rained around us, the little pebble-like bits pinging against my face and landing my mouth. No one had worn their seat belts, so we were tossed like rag dolls.

The cuffs wrapped around Greg's neck pulled me in the opposite direction my body was flying just as Felix slammed into me. There was a sickening *pop* followed by a searing pain, and I didn't need Gabriel to tell me that my shoulder was dislocated. My head hit the top of the car and then the seat, and then finally we stopped moving.

I closed my eyes for what I thought was a minute, but when I opened them the car was surrounded by men who hadn't been there before. Felix lay beside me unmoving, but breathing. Having his neck cinched hadn't done Greg any favors, though, and he slumped to the side in his seat. Danielle had slid to the floor and was clutching her hatless head;

blood gushed from a cut across her scalp, but I knew head wounds bled heavily.

I couldn't see where Devon was.

My arms were still stuck around the front seat. I lifted my left arm to see if it was working. It was, so I disengaged myself, letting out a wail as my limp right arm dropped to my side. My arm, back and chest were ablaze with a pain that went from bad to excruciating with the slightest jostling.

"We've got movement," a voice said outside, followed by the crackling of dozens of walkie-talkies.

"Please help," I shouted. "They took us as hostages and were planning to bomb the Falling Leaf."

More walkie-talkie feedback crackled in the cold air. I started crawling over Felix and toward the window when a megaphone-enhanced voice shouted, "Don't move!"

Danielle began to come around then. Her eyes were wide with panic, more white than blue, and she suddenly hauled herself onto the seat. "Have to get out of here." She tried to move again, but her leg was trapped.

"I said, don't move!" The voice sounded anxious, and I knew at least a dozen machine guns were pointed at us.

"The woman attempting to exit the car is Danielle Donninger," I screamed, but my voice wasn't as loud as usual and my lungs felt like they'd been used as a pincushion. Each word was like a sharp needle being pushed deeper, but if I shut up, Danielle would pay for my silence—again.

"Her parents died to secure this plant, and she's having a panic attack. That's why she's not listening to you. We were kidnapped by these men. Please don't shoot."

I collapsed into a shaking mess after pushing those last words out. Tears fell from my eyes from the combination of pain and fear.

There was no response. I figured they were consulting with each other, trying to figure out protocol. That was what I hoped, at least. Otherwise, they had just ignored me. Finally, the voice addressed me again. "Is the car rigged with explosives?"

"We rolled like a hundred times, so I'm gonna guess no." I coughed, and a warm, salty taste filled my mouth. "I think I might be bleeding internally, please..."

"We can't approach the car until the bomb-sniffing dogs have given the all clear."

"I always wanted a dog." Why did my words sound slurred? Why was I revealing my unrealized pet dreams?

"Stand back, sir. Stand back!"

I couldn't see his face, but I'd recognize those thighs anywhere. "Edwin."

He was shouting something at them, but I couldn't hear. All I cared about was the fact that his feet were heading in my direction.

"Maggie!" His voice was so warm, like maple syrup. His hand touched mine and then an awful, grinding noise filled the air. The car was hot, and Edwin wasn't next to me anymore. Or maybe he was—I didn't know where I was anymore at that point. I could see orange and red, but that was swallowed by the darkness like everything else.

23

When I opened my eyes, the first thing I saw was my mother hunched over my bed, eating a brownie from a plate of bland-looking food that had been placed in front of me.

"Kit, stop it."

"She's not going to eat it," she said. "And you know I'm an emotional eater. I've eaten half a year's supply of peanut brittle in a week." She stuffed the brownie in her mouth vindictively, then turned and saw me watching her. "Oh!" Her wrinkled brow smoothed in surprise and tears filled her eyes. She jumped up and down and massaged her cheeks as she chewed, trying to get the food down faster. "She's awake! See, I knew if I took her food she would wake up just to have something to hold over me."

There was a scuffle of shoes, and my dad's face filled

my vision. His mustache tickled my eyes as he kissed my brow again and again. "Thank God you're finally up. I'll get John and Mykhail."

"What's going on?" The words didn't come out, and that was when I first realized that something was shoved down my throat, choking me. For a moment I thought it was some kind of karmic payback for Greg, and the horrible memories of the crash started filtering in. I raised my hands to my throat, but only the left one listened; the other arm was completely encased in a cast that encircled my chest, as well.

"You have a tube there," my mom said. She ran a cool cloth over my brow, like she used to do when I was sick. "You got airlifted to Burnell Medical Center after the explosion. Don't worry, we checked with Gabriel and he said the doctors aren't incompetent. Your friend is here too."

"Edwin? Danielle?" Much like talking to a deaf person, screaming didn't make me better understood. Instead it made me feel like I was choking again, which increased my panic. I thrashed the parts of me that weren't constrained by casts, tubes or wires, and tears of frustration and pain spilled down my cheeks. I couldn't remember anything, except now I knew there had been an explosion. I hadn't prevented anything. I had failed, and Edwin... I sobbed miserably and, because she didn't know how to help me, my mom cried too, grabbing at my hand.

"Do something!" she commanded as John strode in. His hair was a tangled mess and scraggly bits of beard had claimed small plots of his face. He ran the last steps, took up my good hand and kissed it. "I should have listened to Gabriel. You're grounded forever. Don't even think about ever going outside again."

I tried staring and waggling my eyebrows at him, hoping I could communicate with him the same way Mykhail did, but when he started to look worried, I stopped.

"The power plant is fine. Danielle told us what she remembered, and it sounds like you screwed up their plans royally when you decided to choke a motherfucker out. They were planning two waves of attacks, with the second wave following on the tail of the first. Your car was supposed to get through the gate, either with hostages or by ramming their way through, and the second would have sped through the aftermath and into a building housing a reactor. They were stopped early because of what you did and blew the car before they reached their goal. Fucking morons." His hands shook as he ran them over my head. "I'm so glad you're in one piece. Recovery is going to be a bitch, but you're alive." He opened his mouth and then closed it, and I knew he had something bad to say. I gripped his hand, and he shook his head.

Mykhail came in, trailed by a doctor. Mykhail's face was red and he kept wiping tears that rolled out from under his glasses, even though he was trying to be stoic. The doctor began examining me and then suddenly I was sleepy again.

"They're giving you morphine," my mother explained.

I tried to fight it. Why hadn't they mentioned Edwin? He couldn't be dead. He just couldn't...

When I came to again, it was dark in the room. I could tell I wasn't alone, though.

"Mom? Dad?" My voice sounded like I'd been screaming Norwegian death metal songs for hours, and it hurt to talk. They'd removed the tubes from my throat.

"I told you I prefer God, Jesus or *Papi* if you're going to call me something besides my name. Remember?" Relief flooded my system, overwhelming me much as the morphine had but with the opposite effect. I wanted to jump out of my bed and run to him, but that wasn't possible. He shuffled toward me in the darkness, and there was a thumping sound punctuating his steps as he walked. The bedside table lamp switched on, and I'd never seen anything so beautiful in my life. Well, half his face was a scabbed-over mess, but it was complete. He was complete.

"Kiss me. Please. I'd get up but—" I glanced at my cast and my IVs. There was also the stuff he couldn't see, like how I was so, so tired and how my body felt like it had been pummeled by angry giants.

He leaned a support crutch, the kind that always reminded me of pictures of people with polio from my history books, against the side of my bed. His hands cupped my face and he gave me the most chaste kiss we'd ever shared, but it thrilled me from head to toe, sending endorphins rushing through my body to counteract my pain and misery. We were both still here, able to touch one another even in this demure way.

"What happened to you?" I croaked.

"The explosion threw me face-first into the ground. Nothing a little cocoa butter won't clear up. My leg bent the wrong way, so it's jacked up too. Your parents already hooked me up with some Tiger Balm, though. That stuff is magic."

"That means they like you," I said. I wasn't joking. I'd tell him that later when each word didn't feel like striking a match against the lining of my throat.

"I hope so. Although I care slightly more about what you think." How could he doubt what I felt for him? My eyes welled with tears, and he wiped them away. "I was so pissed when you left with Felix. Mostly because I was scared I'd never get to see you again, but also because you didn't give me time to respond."

"What?"

"You thanked me. I wanted to thank you too. And I wanted to say I think I'm falling in love with you, but I should probably save that for when we're not all souped up over the fact that we survived a terrorist attack."

"Why? Think you'll change your mind?" I croaked.

He shook his head. "Not a chance. When I say something like that, I want you to be sure that it's not because I feel bad for you or because of some misplaced sense of guilt. I know you can hold a grudge, so I'll make sure I do it right the first time." He kissed my nose, and I bit back a yelp.

I wanted to tell him there was no way he could do it wrong, but my throat hurt too much for all that.

The sense of harmony that spread through me as he sat and talked and made me laugh when there wasn't anything to laugh about proved my point. Edwin was showing me how much he cared for me, even if he never said it again. Finally, when I'd had my fill of reveling in the fact that he was alive, I asked what I needed to.

"What happened to...?" *What happened to Devon?*

He took a deep breath, a bracing breath, but he didn't have to say it. My tears came more readily than I expected. Edwin held me even though he knew I cried for someone who'd done nothing but harm, even though he could never understand how different the Devon I'd originally known all those years ago was. Devon had taken everything good about himself and presented that to me, and while it wasn't entirely truthful, it had been real, to me at least. It had gotten me through lonely nights and rough patches and days when I'd wanted to give up. So I mourned the loss of the boy who'd been most real to me through the glow of a computer monitor.

"Greg...died during the crash," Edwin said when I'd composed myself. "Felix was severely injured and was arrested. Devon tried to escape..." He shook his head. My tears dried then. They weren't for the Devon who'd aided and abetted terrorists and never even given me a reason why he chose lies over me.

We sat in silence for a long time after that. A nurse came in with honey-laced tea, which soothed my throat.

"Does this mean I'm excused from finals?" I asked eventually, trying to get a smile out of him. It worked.

"The program is shut down during the investigation, so we'll have some time on our hands."

"Good." I sighed. "I have no idea what to do with myself. I didn't even at school, to be honest. Everyone else has it together."

"Honey, you saved the world from a nuclear disaster. You can chill on the couch for the rest of your life and you will have accomplished more than most people."

I preened, as much as I could without causing myself pain. "Well, when you put it that way…"

"We've got time," he said. If anyone else had said it, I would have told them they couldn't promise me that. But this was Edwin. I nodded and slipped into the sleep I'd been fighting for most of his visit, confident that he'd be there when I awoke.

EPILOGUE

Six months later

It was spring again, which meant flowers were blooming and rain showers were frequent. The latter was needed for the former, but I was coming off months of physical therapy and I hated the way the parts of my bones that had knit themselves back together were now more reliable than the weather reports.

"I need to trade in this superpower for another one," I said as I placed down my gardening tools, pulled off my gloves and massaged my shoulder.

With no school to distract me, no ability to play guitar and nightmares in which Greg or Devon choked the life out of me occurring regularly, the dull ache in my joint was the least annoying thing about my recovery process. It still angered me, though, a reminder that the pain of the past never truly left. It was always just waiting for the right opportunity to flare up.

Edwin sat hunkered over the small plot of land we'd cultivated behind Darlene's old bungalow, which I'd turned into my own space. Our space, really, since Edwin was with me more often than not. He was the one who'd built my garden boxes months before, so I could have something to look forward to once I was done with physical therapy. He walked over to me and rubbed my shoulder. "Yeah, rain detection is fine, but see if you can trade up for something good, like the ability to blow up chipmunks using only your mind," he said.

I glanced up at him with brows raised.

"They keep stealing the onion bulbs." He smiled at me, and I reached up and ran a hand over the smooth skin of his cheek and the bristliness of the short beard he now sported. Most of his scarring had faded, except for a strip along his jawline, and he'd grown out his beard over the winter to cover it. I'd thought he couldn't be more handsome before, but he had proved me wrong, as usual.

His hand came down over mine. "What is it?"

I should've known he would guess something was up with me. I thought I'd at least have a day to think things over, though.

"I spoke to Danielle this morning," I said. She had

survived the accident, but the months immediately after had been rough. Her uncle had offered her a place at his new home, but she'd had a different plan for herself. She'd checked herself into a program one of her doctors had recommended for people dealing with post-Flare PTSD and other mental health issues that had been exacerbated on a large scale. Her treatment had recently ended, but she still volunteered because it made her feel better when she helped others.

"Everything okay with her?" he asked. He sometimes joined in on our calls, but this time he'd been on a job. He had great contacts in the area, so he was never short on work. We had settled into a pattern of domesticity that had been fun for a while, but was now making me stir-crazy. I was about to disrupt it, and I had no idea what the outcome would be.

"She's doing really well. Actually, she's been offered a job. As an art therapist. There's a push to bring more creatives into the fold and provide them with training, because many patients respond well to different approaches on top of regular therapy. Drawing. Painting. Music."

My stomach was squeezed tight with nerves. We'd been together since after my accident, and I loved seeing my parents every day, and John and Mykhail when they could make it down, but there was nothing for me at home. They'd been right when they'd first pushed me out into the world; I needed to go out on my own and figure out what I wanted from life besides love, laughter and delicious bacon.

"So you're saying this was a recruitment call this morning?" He scratched at his beard, but that wasn't indicator of whether he was angry or nervous or curious.

I tapped my fingers on my knees to ease my anxious energy. "Yes. They're looking for musicians who want to work toward getting their license. In exchange for a spot in the training program, you have to commit to working there for two years."

"And *there* is in Vermont," he stated. I'd never given much thought to where I'd end up after college, but once our program had shut down, I realized it wasn't my parents' backyard.

I nodded.

"This sucks!" Edwin said. He turned and glared in the direction of our blossoming garden.

"It's okay if you don't want to go. I know you have a life here." I said the words because they seemed like what one should say in this situation, but on the inside I was slowly crumpling.

He looked at me and shook his head in annoyance. "The chipmunks are going to think they've won the battle once we leave. Hopefully your dad will preserve my honor and keep the rodents away, at least until the onions have been harvested."

My heart lurched. Even though he'd stood by me for so long, I'd expected him to say no. It'd been too much to hope for, but maybe hoping for too much was what worked best for me. I stood. "Wait. So you want to come with me?"

Edwin looped his arms around my waist and pulled me close, and a relieved breath slipped from between my lips. I let myself feel him, the steady weight that moved tenderly against me in our darkened bedroom and cushioned me when the blows of my nightmares became too much. I'd thought I'd have to choose between Edwin and fulfillment, but maybe my luck hadn't run out yet.

"Maggie, I know how much you enjoy maple syrup and lumberjacks. I'm not leaving you to your own devices in the place that invented maple syrup and lumberjacks. I have designs on you, and I really don't want to have to battle some flannel-wearing giant for your affections."

Bit by bit, my anxiety was replaced with relief. Muscles that had unconsciously tensed began to relax, and I leaned into him. "But what will you do for work?"

"I have connections. And even if I didn't, a government-licensed contractor can find work easily right now. Unless you're trying to get rid of me to go live a life of debauchery. If you are, you should probably go someplace warmer than Vermont."

"You're so sure about this," I said with a kind of awe. He didn't even think twice about coming with me, didn't question whether I was capable of the job or needed to consider other options.

"I'm only sure about one thing—no, two. I love you and I want to be where you are. That makes life choices easy for me."

I hugged him tighter. "I love you too, Edwin."

He kissed me slowly then, his lips and tongue backing up the confession he'd just made. It wasn't erotic, but it was perhaps the best kiss of my life. Rather, it would have been if it hadn't ended up with us soaking wet. My shoulder still ached as the frigid water hit, and we jumped apart, but it was way too direct a stream to be rain.

"Get a room, you two!" my mom yelled as she placed the hose in its rightful place and returned to the house. She poked her head back out the back door. "And make it quick, Edwin! Tonight is game night. John and Mykhail will be here soon, and Gabriel and Arden figured out how to set up an online session of Texas Hold 'Em."

"A change of location would be great, actually," Edwin said as he wiped water out of his eyes. "I don't need any additional commentary from your mom."

I pulled open the bungalow door and was already halfway naked by the time he stepped through and locked it behind him. "Now I get to warm you up," I said. "How's your schedule looking for this afternoon?"

He pulled his shirt off, stepping close until his skin grazed mine. "We have all the time in the world."

Acknowledgments

I'd like to thank the Carina Press crew—Angela, Heather, Carrie, Stephanie, Jenny, Kerri and many others—for all of the hard work that went into this series, and for all of the support they've provided.

I'd also like to think Ana for providing helpful feedback and answering my random questions.

Thanks to Alisha, Bree, Courtney, Mala, Sasha and the countless others who have been super supportive and made me feel like a real author type. Your kindness has meant the world to me.

Thanks to Colleen, Julia and Maya for talking me down from my nervous breakdowns. I owe you both whatever fancy Scotch you'd like. Wait—except for the Macallan.

Lastly, a special thanks to my awesome editor Rhonda. A (bad) poem, for you. :)

Bespectacled vixen—that is to say, foxy—
Rhonda.
Slayer of beloved Oxford comma,
Soother of authorial angst.
Charging bravely into the maw of
a seething manuscript,
slashing,
shaping,
supporting,
until a kickass story
is all that remains.

About the Author

Alyssa Cole is a science editor, pop culture nerd, and romance junkie who lives in the Caribbean and occasionally returns to her fast-paced NYC life. When she's not busy writing, traveling, and learning French, she can be found watching anime with her real-life romance hero or tending to her herd of animals.

Find Alyssa at her website, http://alyssacole.com/, on Twitter @AlyssaColeLit and on Facebook at Facebook.com/Alyssa-ColeLit.

Made in the USA
Charleston, SC
03 November 2016